I0623156

SHE'S THE ONE

WHO CAN'T KEEP QUIET

S. R. CRONIN

Copyright 2022 by Sherrie Cronin
All rights reserved
by Cinnabar Press, Black Mountain North Carolina 28711

ISBN-13: 978-1-941283-90-5

No part of this book may be reproduced in any form by any electronic or mechanical means, including information storage and retrieval systems, without permission in writing from the publisher, except for review.

This book is a work of fiction and, except for historical figures and information, the events and characters in it are imaginary.

To my four great grandmothers. Each one grew up in Russia and made an improbable journey as a young woman, crossing the Atlantic Ocean in the late 1880s to live on the plains of western Kansas. There they fed the chickens, milked the cows, hauled the water, and cooked the meals. Together they bore over 50 children.

I have no idea what they wanted in life, or if they even considered the question. I hope each of them found more than their share of those moments of happiness that snuck in anyway.

Warning: You Are About to Enter Ilari

Welcome to the thirteenth century in a universe almost identical to your own. The one major difference here is the existence of *Ilari.*

Ilari (el ARE ee) is a small hidden coalition of principalities in far eastern Europe. It has never been conquered thanks to its natural protection and the magic of its people. The lack of outside influence means that much will be new to you. But fear not, you have tools to help.

A map of *Ilari* is located at the front and back of this book. The back also has a description of the twelve nichnas (tiny principalities) that comprise *Ilari*.

Ilarians do not use any variation of the Roman calendar, as Rome never invaded their realm. Each chapter starts with a picture of the Ilarian calendar and the darkened area shows when that chapter takes place. Details about the Ilarian calendar are at the back of the book along with definitions for unique Ilarian words. On the last page, you will find a list of the characters you will meet.

All of this information can be downloaded and printed at https://troublesome7sisters.xyz/.

Ilarians of the 1200s have some contact with the outside even though legend says interaction with others used to be rarer. Ilarian scholars know facts about world history and the current events beyond their borders. What they know matches what you know, of course, because the world outside of Ilari is like the one in which we live.

However, the world inside is filled with surprises.

Enjoy your visit!

The Map of Ilari

The Year of Immense Concern

~ 1 ~

Musicians at Your Service

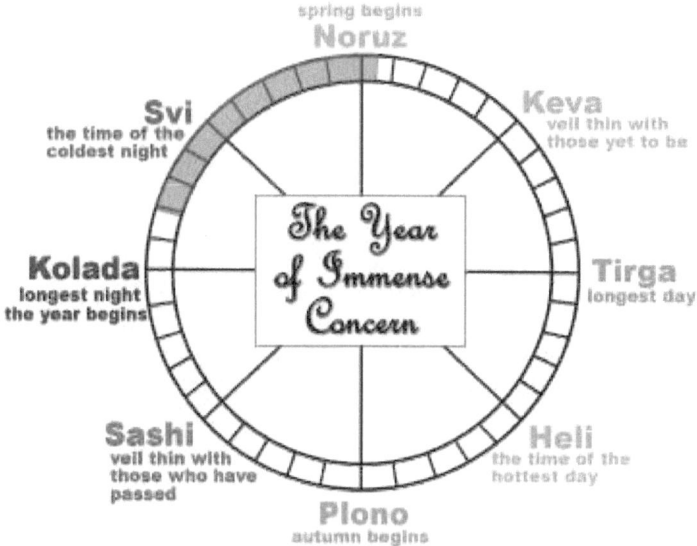

The Year of Immense Concern

- **Noruz** — spring begins
- **Keva** — veil thin with those yet to be
- **Svi** — the time of the coldest night
- **Tirga** — longest day
- **Kolada** — longest night the year begins
- **Heli** — the time of the hottest day
- **Sashi** — veil thin with those who have passed
- **Plono** — autumn begins

"What's your name?"

We stood outside as large snowflakes drifted around us, adding sparkle to the stone pathways and fences as they coated a simple chance meeting with the feel of magic.

My father had paused our winter walk to greet a colleague. He didn't wish to be rude but he grew impatient as she lingered and kept talking. Her unexpected attention warmed me, however. Others who worked with my father hardly noticed me, and even my dad seemed surprised by her question.

"Her name is Celestine," he answered for me, in a voice more curt than usual. He rubbed his hands together and stomped his feet

1

to warm them. "Believe me, you have no interest in her, Firuza. She studies almost nothing besides her music."

"Of course I have an interest in her, Yasen," the woman replied. "I'm sure you named her for the beautiful blue mineral you study, but seriously, how could a teacher of astronomy not be fascinated to meet a pupil named Celestine?"

Her accent had already told me that she came from somewhere outside the realm, and her features and skin tone confirmed it. She had an unusual but pleasant smell about her, a scent of spices I didn't recognize, and she laughed as she spoke. The warmth in her laughter warmed me, too.

"I must get to know you better," she said. She looked into my eyes, and I looked back.

My father had traveled to Pilk in the harshness of winter to teach one of his short seminars, this one on rare minerals, one of his favorite subjects. I knew he liked to use such jaunts to check in on his four daughters in school as we pursued the higher learning most young Ilarians undertook before they settled into jobs and marriages.

I also knew my father disapproved of the narrow scope of my studies. He thought everyone, both women and men, should be well-schooled in the sciences he loved.

"If you can talk her into taking even one of your classes, I'll be forever grateful," he conceded.

"I'm teaching an overview class next session," she told me. "One meant for those with no background in my subject. Perhaps you'd find inspiration for your music nestled in between the stars?"

I thought I might.

"Astronomy? Why are you wasting your time on that?" Zamarran demanded to know.

Only anks ago he and I had decided to start a performing group that would continue past our study time in Pilk. Neither of us had found the requisite mate while in school and in three eights of a year we'd be done. Then I would probably go wait tables in a tavern somewhere, under the pretense of looking for a husband while I sang and played the psaltery on the side. Fate had dealt Zamarran a more difficult hand. Everyone would expect him to have a respectable profession while he sought a wife. Playing in an ensemble barely qualified, but it was better than being a lone performer.

No attraction existed between us, and we both knew it with such certainty that we barely needed to speak of it. It made us ideal business partners. But two people did not constitute an ensemble, especially not when one of them was primarily a drummer, albeit an unusually talented one. We had to have a third and better yet a fourth performer to get the respect we needed. I understood Zamarran's urgency.

However, the mysterious young teacher Firuza fascinated me. I'd find time to take her class.

"We need new sorts of friends," I told Zamarran. "Other musicians do nothing but promote themselves. Maybe I can get some of our realm's future scientists to demand local taverns hire us. Huh?"

He grunted his agreement, his large frame turned away from me as he made adjustments to one of his many drums. He'd already figured out I'd do what I wanted to anyway, as would he. Part of our pact was that neither of us was in charge.

The next day, Zamarran had three musicians for me to meet. I admired the man's determination. The first girl also neared the end of her advanced education but I hadn't seen her before. I'd have remembered those unusually large eyes, beguiling in a way that would benefit a performer. I wished she played an instrument or at least didn't sing with a squeak. I shook my head before she'd finished half a song.

A young man I'd seen around presented himself as the next contender. He had a gorgeous voice, but I already knew everyone found him impossible to work with. We didn't need to add his tantrums to our troubles. I shook my head before he began, and Zamarran threw his hands into the air in frustration.

The third didn't look promising either. A wisp of a girl, she only played the flute. When she picked it up, then hesitated, I started humming a song and motioned to Zamarran to join me. He came in with a low drumbeat. She nodded her understanding and added a jig-like melody that complimented mine and matched Zamarran's cadence. It sounded pretty good. I switched to singing a slow ballad and Zamarran segued to a little metal hoop he liked to play. She moved with us, now weaving a sorrowful melody

3

around my crooning and his clinking. The longer we went the better it got.

I gave Zamarran a nod.

"Really? Her? You do know that's *all* she can do, right?"

The young woman, who'd introduced herself as Mirva, looked confused.

"I know," I said. "And it's more than enough. Most vocal groups don't have a piper. One this good will set us apart."

I turned to Mirva. She looked rather plain for a performer, but then neither her clothes nor her hair flattered her. I could work wonders here. My own face suffered from wide lips, narrow eyes, and thick eyebrows, but I made the most of what I had and others called me beautiful.

"You're in on one condition," I told her. "You let me fix you up so you look like you belong on a stage."

She kept her eyes on the ground as she answered "of course," but her smile told me she looked forward to it.

After a few days of practice, we persuaded a local innkeeper to let us perform for tips. Before our first show, I redid Mirva's hair, braiding her soft brown tresses into an intricate pattern that mirrored the detail in her piping. Then I lent her one of my dresses. The pale pink frock didn't suit me, but it flattered her softer features and paler face. Even oblivious Zamarran gave a low whistle when he saw her.

I'd placed my bet on the quality of Mirva's music, but before long I intended to have our fans praising Mirva's beauty as well.

Nearly a fourth of Ilari's people lived in the nichna of Pilk, and most of them clustered into an area called Pilk Central where our institutes of higher learning set alongside the best markets in the realm. Our army, the Svadlu, headquartered in Pilk Central as did those who worked for our rulers. The beautiful Pilk castle, home to the most influential of our royal families, towered over it all.

Most of these disparate groups socialized with their own kind, so performers tended to face a roomful of merchants, or students, or government workers. The night of our first show, the tavern filled up with soldiers. The Svadlu were prone to drunkenness and tended to brawl, so I wouldn't have picked this audience for our first performance. However, this crowd barely made a sound.

Music goes down better with the audience on your side. If they don't start that way, a good singer has to get them there.

"Hey!" I yelled after a few numbers. The last one had a been a popular jig, yet hardly a finger or toe had tapped while we played. Most unusual.

"I've never seen soldiers so quiet. Did you all party so much last night that you're still worn out?"

I got a few laughs, but not as many as I expected.

"Come on. Somebody tell us poor troubadours what's going on. Is one of your commanding officers coming in to check on you?" I looked to my left, then to my right, then gave the crowd an exaggerated look of alarm. "Is he here now?"

Even fewer laughs. Maybe I'd lost my touch.

One young man spoke up. "You seem like a nice lady, so I'll tell you. Stop trying to make us laugh. We got horrible news today and nothing's going to make us feel better."

"I'm sorry to hear that. Did someone tell you we'd run out of ale in our realm? No more until Kolada?"

I got more chuckles this time.

"No, Miss. The commander of the Mozdols told us that our lands are in the path of a huge marauding horde of thieves. They've been burning and pillaging their way towards us for years and now travelers say we ought to expect them this year or next. We're to begin training tomorrow for this onslaught."

For several heartbeats, I stood speechless. I'd never done that on a stage before. But how does one respond to such news? I thought it couldn't be so dire or so certain. Yet, I sensed arguing with the soldier would hardly win over my audience. What would?

"Then, sir, you should know that the musicians of the realm are at your service."

I stood tall, as if I were a soldier myself, awaiting a command. This earned me a few derisive laughs.

"No offense meant, but musicians can't do much in a war."

"What? Of course we can." I knew where I was going now. "We can inspire you as you assemble to fight." I began to tap a slow beat against my leg with my hand. Zamarran figured it out. He added his strong drumbeat and then I thanked the Goddess I hadn't misjudged Mirva. Her flute began to sound out a war march to match and I added my voice, choosing random phrases about honor and patriotism and weaving in bits of melodies from well-known songs about the beauty of Ilari. It was a mess, but it conveyed the general idea.

"And as you fight, if some do fall, as some may, *we* will be there to mourn with you," I said as the other two moved into the saddest of melodies. I knew enough to only do this for a few breaths. No soldier wanted to dwell on the need for funeral music.

"And, when you're victorious, and you *will* be victorious, we'll be there with you, with a rousing song to celebrate your bravery and our freedom." At that all three of us found an appropriate joyful noise to make and the room broke into applause. We bowed, we collected some tips, and we got ourselves the Heli off the stage and out of there before anyone had time to think too much about my logic.

As we walked back to campus, Zamarran looked at me in wonder.

"*That* was one of the best varmin improvisations I have ever seen, and I've seen some good ones."

I shrugged. I'd been doing this sort of thing since I was in basic school. Not with soldiers, of course, but with classmates, teachers, and the parents of my friends, who'd all found themselves standing up and applauding for me and one of my causes over the years.

Zamarran stopped walking and he looked directly at me. Hard.

"This isn't easy for me to say, but it's better said now. This *will* be your trio, not ours."

"No, we both agreed ...."

"It doesn't matter what we agreed. You've become our voice, and the whole realm will consider it yours no matter what we decide." He smiled. "I might as well learn to live with it."

The next day a tall skinny young man stopped me on the way to class.

"I was in the back of the tavern last night," he said, hurrying to catch up with me.

"I doubt it. I only saw soldiers."

"Of course you did. That's who you needed to reach. Listen. I write music too. I play the rebec and the chittarone – it's like a huge lute."

"I know what a chittarone is," I said.

He looked down embarrassed. "Sorry. And I play the cittern as well."

I softened. "But I don't know what a cittern is."

"Oh it's this great new instrument, stringed like a lute but bigger and with a flat back so you can hold it close to your body and …"

He looked down again, embarrassed.

"What I'm trying to say is, I like your sound. I like your style. I want to be part of your ensemble."

We could use a fourth, especially one as versatile as he claimed to be.

"Let me hear you sing."

He broke into an almost perfect rendition of the war song I'd improvised last night.

"I made that song up."

"I figured you did."

"And you remembered the melody and the words?" *We could use someone with his kind of smarts, too.* "Congratulations. You've made us a quartet, uh … what's your name?"

"It's Feene. Don't you have to ask the others?"

"Apparently not. Last night they decided it was my group."

Despite Zamarran's anointing me as the leader, I'd have backed off immediately if either he or Mirva didn't like Feene, but it turned out they both thought he was great. Soon the four of us practiced our evenings away, amassing a repertoire of popular songs and original ones. We still performed for tips but we did so well I thought we'd be able to start charging before we finished our studies.

When we performed for soldiers, none of them mentioned this potential invasion again. I wondered if they'd been ordered to keep quiet so as not to alarm everyone. Was it my imagination that the Svadlu all seemed to drink more and laugh less?

After the Svi holiday, I looked forward to my new classes, especially the astronomy class with my father's friend Firuza. I hadn't seen her since we met, but I remembered the faint smell that surrounded her and I hoped for the chance to know her better as I became inspired by the heavens, as she'd suggested.

But first, I rode back to my parents' farm to celebrate Noruz. Both spring holidays prompted more sexual activity among my fellow tidzys, even though promiscuity was permitted around all the holidays for the young and unmarried. I'd discovered I had less interest than most young women. Going home helped me avoid the pressure to participate.

I shivered under my best wool cloak as I rode most of the day through an uncomfortable drizzle. I arrived wanting no more than a hot cider in front of the fire, but I found my family in turmoil. Two eighths ago my three oldest sisters had attended the realm's most fabulous ball of the year, the Kolada celebration at the Pilk castle. My troubled parents had sent the three because several eligible royals, and numerous other well-bred young men, had been there seeking mates and my sisters all had yet to find husbands.

Ryalgar, our oldest, outdid herself. She'd caught the eye of no less than a prince of Pilk. As the second son, he wouldn't rule one day, but he had to be the prime catch of her age group. My mother couldn't contain her delight. Her letters continued to assure me their courtship went well.

Yet, when I arrived Ryalgar had barricaded herself in her room where she could be heard crying, wailing, and cursing. An occasional thud followed as one item or another was thrown against a wall. My dad said little. My mother told us Ryalgar felt poorly. We all knew better.

I'd never had the sort of love Ryalgar felt and now I rather hoped I never would. What good was love if it caused so much pain? I'd take the love of my audiences any day over the fickle love of a single human.

~ 2 ~

Crocus Blossoms

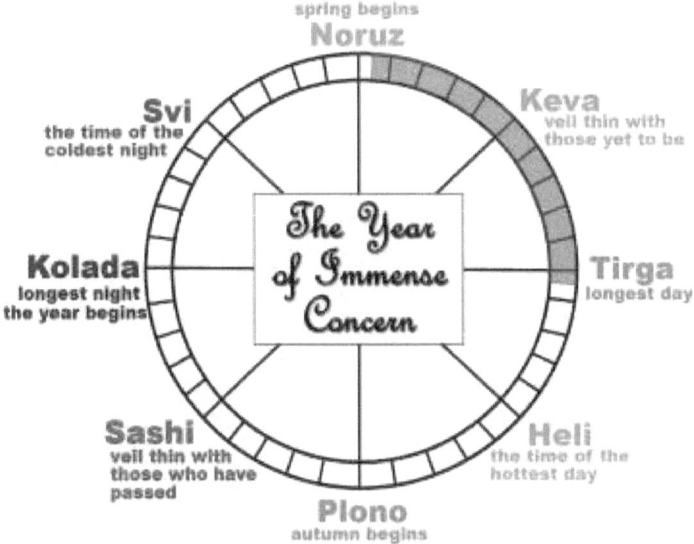

Pilk changed with the coming of spring. Yes, of course, the birds sang more, the sun shone longer, and the crocus leaves peeked through the snow, but that's not what I noticed. Those things happened every year. I saw a new sense of urgency in people's behavior. In every crowd, I sensed something important on their minds as I performed. Something no one would speak of.

I altered my opening dialogs to give less banter and more comfort. Sometimes I added in a short ditty about staying strong and having hope. People responded well to my new approach.

The number of Svadlu in Pilk grew, and the taverns saw less of them. In subtle ways, people showed the soldiers more respect, the way people do when they expect danger.

My own life faced changes, too. I loved living in Pilk, with its crowds and noise and wonderful shopping, but I neared the end of my studies. In two eighths my quartet had to be something my parents would consider a real job, or I was doomed to the drudgery of a wheat farm where I'd help with the world's most boring chores while I sought a husband I did not want.

There was another reason I mourned the end of my studies, one I hadn't counted on. My only foray into science, an introduction to the heavens, had become my favorite class.

I'd never guessed the pictures humans saw in the stars reflected so many passionate stories. I'd had no idea how those pictures moved throughout the night, revolving around a mysteriously important point in the sky. What about this single dot allowed it to command the entire heavens? Except for the moon, of course, which much to my delight was commanded by no one.

I learned that those with exceptional vision could see many tiny stars making up what appeared to others to be a single point of light. Ancients elsewhere called the most famous of these "the seven sisters." The instructor smiled at me when she said this, and I blushed.

And that was the real problem.

The instructor, the beautiful and entertaining Firuza, held much of the class spellbound with her gifted teaching, but none was as smitten as me. By the time the first of the crocus began to bloom, I recognized that my fascination went beyond admiration for her knowledge and her style. I felt a physical desire I'd never experienced, not for any man or woman.

Yes, I knew girls sometimes wanted other girls, and some acted upon this. If they were unwed tidzys then no one cared. A girl needed to learn about her body. But everyone expected girls to outgrow such inclinations and marry a boy. Most did marry, but whether they outgrew the inclinations or not I did not know.

Me, I'd rarely been attracted to anyone, though now I wondered if I'd tried so hard to like boys that I'd ignored my real interest. Whatever the cause, I'd barely acted upon any desires, turning my rather astonishing lack of experience into my greatest secret.

That spring, Firuza made me feel the heat of real desire. No wonder it occupied so much of people's attention. As the last of the crocus bloomed, I decided she found me interesting as well. She gave me little signs, the kind people do. Eye contact. Smiles. Even an occasional careful touch on the arm or shoulder that made me tremble inside. I could have sworn every time she touched me, she trembled too.

But we kept our distance. Firuza seemed cautious by nature, and even if we weren't two women, a romantic dalliance with the child of a fellow instructor would garner rebuke. So although we saw each other often, it was always in public and always above reproach.

We never spoke of our attraction although at times I wanted her so badly my insides quivered. I poured my newfound longing into the songs I wrote. At least my music took a turn for the better.

My twin sister Olivine and I saw more of each other as spring grew warmer. She and I differed outwardly, as her shiny bronze hair made clear from a distance. She avoided people, being utterly absorbed by her art. Me, I couldn't imagine spending every day alone, working to make some small piece of canvas look exactly as I wished.

We differed on the inside too. Sex with boys thrilled her, giving her an easy route to the intimacy she otherwise lacked.

"How long do you think either of us will last living at the farm?" she said as we sipped a lovely pink lunch wine and enjoyed a dish of eggs and chives, the mid-day specialty at one of my favorite taverns.

"How long do you think we'll last without a place to have lunch," I answered. "Neither of us is cut out for the farm, are we?"

"No, but what can we do about it?" She looked as sad as I felt.

"This musical ensemble I told you about? I'm trying to turn it into a paying proposition so Mom and Dad won't object if I spend my time here in Pilk performing."

She stared into her goblet of wine, thinking.

"That could work. Mom would hope you'd find a husband in Pilk. She's already complained to me that you rejected every boy in Vinx."

"Oh, but not just *any* boy will do," I said.

"Of course not," she answered. "It's just as easy to fall in love with a prince!"

I repeated the words with her and we laughed. Mom had passed *that* piece of wisdom along since we were toddlers.

"I'm probably not going to marry royalty," Olivine confided.

"Yeah. Me neither." I thought about saying more, about telling her about Firuza and all the passions she'd awakened within me. Olivine wouldn't criticize, but would she understand? I hesitated for a heartbeat, the waitress interrupted us, and then Olivine stood to leave.

The time for confidences had passed. Maybe next time.

Shortly after, I received word that I needed to be home for Keva. Our oldest sister Ryalgar had responded unexpectedly to her rejection by the perfect prince Nevik. She'd decided to shun men and go live in the woods with the Velka. This seemed like an overreaction, but perhaps I didn't understand the full depths of Ryalgar's sorrow.

Because the Velka lived without male companions, I suppose I should have been more curious about them. Many probably shared my sexual preferences, even though Ryalgar didn't. But while a life surrounded by only women would solve some of my problems, I wasn't interested. The Velka had always seemed so, I don't know, unglamorous as they lived in huts in the woods like hermits, growing herbs and making potions. I imagined their existence lacked art or music or pretty clothes or any of the refinements of life.

No, I'd prefer to take my chances in a less understanding world that held more charm.

One's entry into the Velka, however, required a bit of pageantry sometimes referred to as "a woman's marriage to the forest." The woman's family accompanied her to the edge of the woods dressed for a wedding but with the odd requirement of emphasizing natural greenery on their clothing. No one expected my mom to participate. She disliked the Velka and Ryalgar's loss had left her heartbroken. However, Dad agreed to play along and join us.

Ryalgar wore a beautiful wine-colored gown made for the occasion. Mom showed her support by weaving claret-colored clover blossoms throughout Ryalgar's chestnut brown hair, and my sister Coral made her bracelets and a necklace of the same elegant blooms.

Coral wisely passed on the garish pink frock she'd worn to the Kolada ball where Ryalgar and Prince Nevik had fallen in love. Tenderhearted Coral would never want to remind Ryalgar of Nevik in any way. The soft brown dress she opted for instead toned down her orange hair and complimented the pink mallow blossoms she'd woven into a crown on her head.

Sulphur, a strong woman who kept her golden hair cut short, had one fancy dress as far as I knew and it was the yellow frock she'd worn to the same infamous ball. She wore it, oblivious to any association with Nevik. Someone pinned bright yellow celandines in her hair to compliment it. It was a lot of yellow, but I understood this was as pretty as Sulphur cared to look.

Olivine often wore green to accent her eyes and I tended to wear blue for the same reason. We opted for paler shades in a similar style and then we both adorned ourselves with little tufts of delicate white spignel and added wreaths of spignel on our heads. It gave us a matched set look I think Ryalgar liked.

Gypsum's affection for Ryalgar overcame her inherent dislike of being told how to dress. She picked a simple silvery-grey frock that complimented her tall, thin build and pale blond hair. Then she decorated herself with an enormous amount of green wood spurge blossoms, making her look more like a moving plant than a girl. I wondered if she meant to create that illusion, or if she intended the exuberant amount of wood spurge as satire. Who knew with Gypsum.

Iolite, the sister challenged by a disease that left her shorter than most, rode the small grey horse my father purchased for her. Iolite's condition made her eyes a vivid purple, but because many considered such eyes frightening, she avoided the color. Not today. For whatever reason, she donned an exquisitely-made rich purple dress I'd never seen and covered her silver hair with purple liverwort blossoms, as though she dared anyone to object. None of us did. She looked beautiful.

So off we rode, seven young women embodying the vitality of spring, as we prepared to turn our sister over to the forest.

After that, the days between Keva and Tirga passed faster than days do. Our quartet booked paying performances and our shows improved. Feene turned out to be a brilliant addition, with both his sound and his songwriting talents complimenting my own.

In between performances, I finished my studies and took every opportunity to spend time with my astronomy class. Few courses would be offered in the heat of summer, so when Firuza mentioned she'd teach a short seminar during Heli, my heart raced. She looked right at me.

"It will focus on the moon and its movements and will be a perfect follow-up to this course, for anyone who wants to learn more."

Yes, I wanted to learn more.

"Former students who are done with their education will be welcome to attend," she added.

I smiled at her. She smiled back.

Then, quite suddenly, it ended. The classes were done. My projects finished. I'd completed the two years of advanced education given to most Ilarians.

As I packed up my things for the carriage ride home, a familiar-looking young woman knocked on my door.

"Your ensemble is catching on," she said.

I studied her face. She had a small mole in the middle of her chin but otherwise unmemorable features. Except for her eyes. Those large beguiling eyes looked familiar. Wasn't she the one we'd auditioned on the day we found Mirva? The one with a squeaky voice and no musical talent?

"I'm Ura," she clarified. "You didn't have a spot for me earlier, but I thought you might want to reconsider."

Did I? Five was a good number for a group.

"I'm helpful, dependable, and eager to learn. I'd make a fine addition." She twirled her hair between her fingers as she spoke.

Those were good qualities. Perhaps I'd been too hasty in rejecting her. Maybe she could be taught ...

No! What was I thinking? This girl had no feel for music at all.

"I'm sorry. We have all the people we need right now."

She seemed surprised by my rejection.

"Perhaps you haven't fully considered the advantages of adding me?"

Well, maybe I hadn't ... Maybe I should ask her more questions....

"Celestine!" Zamarran's voice came from outside my window. "We're all out here waiting for you. What's taking so long?"

"Sorry," I yelled back. "On my way." I turned to Ura. "I have to go. The answer is no, we don't need you but I hope you can find another group."

"I hope so too," she said. "Or I'll be back."

It sounded oddly like a threat.

Zamarran, Mirva, Feene, and I said our temporary good-byes. Zamarran had booked us at The Thirsty Owl, one of the biggest venues in Pilk, in two anks.

"Everybody be here, ready to perform," I said. "I still can't believe you got us booked there."

Zamarran shrugged. "It's a work night. Crowds will be smaller than you think. Not such a big deal."

"I'll be here the day before," Mirva offered.

"Me too," Feene said.

I gave Zamarran a questioning look.

"Sure," he said. "I'll come in a day early and we can have a little rehearsal."

"Thanks. I think this performance could be more important than you think."

He grinned. "I hope you're right."

~ 3 ~

Not a Good Wedding Toast

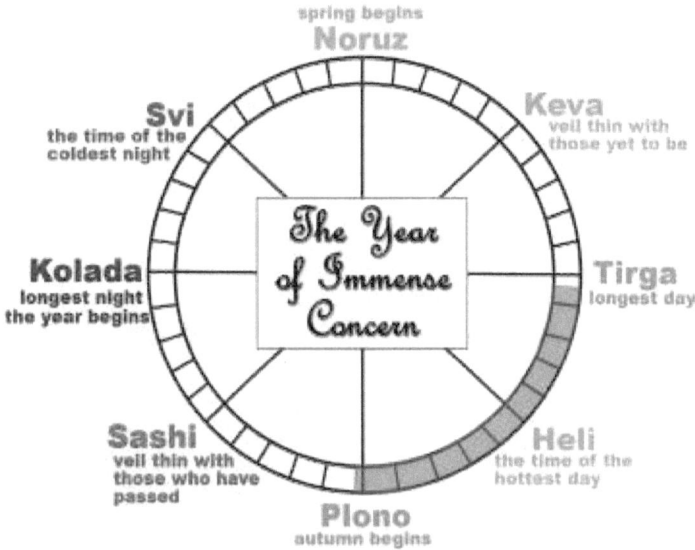

When Zamarran didn't show up on time for practice two anks later, I worried. When he arrived at our inn well after the late Tirga sunset, I met him with harsh words about being dependable. Then I looked closer.

His dusty, tired face showed signs of riding for days. That made no sense. Zamarran lived in Faroo, an easy quarter of a day's ride away.

"Where've you been?" I asked. He reached for a mug of ale on the table and downed it in one swallow. It was Feene's but Feene didn't say a word.

"K'ba," Zamarran said. "Heli, it's a long hot ride out to those settlements and back."

"What were you doing in K'ba?" Mirva asked.

"Trying to turn our music into a full-time job. But, much to my surprise, the K'basta needed little persuasion to pay to hear us." He gave me a funny look. "They've heard about the amazing Celestine all the way out there."

"They have?" This was wonderful news. Over the past decades, K'ba had turned its barren settlements into a haven for entertainers of all sorts and now their performances enticed Ilarians out to the otherwise desolate Canyon River. A quartet that could split its time between exotic K'ba and the taverns of Pilk would be well-off indeed.

"What do they say about me?" I asked.

"Mostly that *your* superb music is only surpassed by *your* beauty and charm."

Those flattering words filled my head that night, leaving no room for worry about how the others felt.

We managed a short practice the next morning but something felt off. Our music didn't meld. I suggested we get some rest instead.

As evening neared, we set our instruments up on the spacious stage of the well-known Thirsty Owl and the crowd grew. I noticed the staff encouraging patrons to finish their food and move on. Did management want the tables for more important guests?

Soon after, I heard the heralds outside announcing the presence of the Royals of Pilk.

That's who wanted the tables? Why hadn't the proprietor warned us? Why hadn't the Royals summoned us to the palace instead? Well, I had heard they enjoyed going out at times, to the surprise of all.

I seldom experienced stage fright, but for a few heartbeats the blood inside me felt replaced by water from a cold mountain stream.

This is what you wanted. Yearned for. Now do it.

I looked to the rest of the quartet. Mirva and Feene looked terrified. Zamarran's normally ruddy face had gone pale. This wasn't good.

"His Majesty the Ruling Prince of Pilk ..." The heralds entered the room and began their recitation again, as the other spectators began bobbing up and down in response. We joined in on stage with whatever bows and curtsies we could manage around our instruments.

Then in came the Ruling Prince and his wife, followed by their oldest son, a grown man destined to rule as soon as he produced a healthy two-year-old boy. His wife, a woman assumed to be desperately trying to get pregnant, followed him.

Behind him walked Nevik, the prince I'd never met, the one who'd charmed my sister and then left her devastated. On his arm was a highly-ornamented young woman with long black hair. He helped her settle into her chair, and they held hands as they waited for the performance to begin.

I had the presence of mind to listen to her introduction. She was a princess! A visiting one, from a larger realm to the west, across the Wide River. Poor Ryalgar. Should I tell her of this? Why? What good could it possibly do her now?

I look up to see the entire royal party, indeed the entire room, staring at me as the herald finished his duties by introducing me, and me alone, with a flourish of praise.

Okay. I have to do something besides stare back at them.

I felt the frightened little girl inside me step aside and turn my voice over to the performer I'd become.

"Honorable Ruling Prince and esteemed Royals," I began. "I and my humble fellow musicians are unbelievably honored at your presence. You have perhaps heard tell of my music?"

Many of them nodded.

"I am grateful but honesty compels me to confess. I am not as good as you have heard."

They looked among themselves. This wasn't an auspicious start for a performance.

"Not by myself that is. So indulge me, gentle rulers, and allow me to acquaint you with my fellow musicians. Without them, I cannot create that of which you have heard. Behind me ...."

I started with Zamarran and introduced each one as all three looked suitably embarrassed. In truth, I'm not sure why I opened our performance that way, only that I knew we needed to work together and everything up until then had conspired to make that not so. My band would either hate or love my unseemly behavior.

Once we began, I knew I'd chosen well. As our music blended as it should, I looked closer into the audience. My gaze found the Elder Prince of Vinx, my home nichna, and his wife, Lady Patela, sitting with the other Royals. The Elder Prince whispered to his nine-year-old son as I sang, but Lady Patela never took her eyes off of me as she tilted her head back and forth and drummed her fingers to the music. I'd made a new fan.

The following ank I returned to the farm, in part to warn my parents that I'd be gone more than they realized because my musical group had met with unexpected success. My presence, and my announcement, hardly caused a ripple. While I'd been gone, Coral had informed the family that she was with child and planned to marry the father. All eyes were on her.

Fine. I could use the time to compose a new song or two.

Then a few nights later, the man who'd gotten Coral pregnant came to call. Older yet attractive, he was the sort who expected women to acknowledge his good looks. The nature of his smile said he found me appealing, though obviously, he wouldn't do anything about it. He waited for my signal in return.

I knew what he wanted. It was the look that said *yes, you're handsome ... under other circumstances ....*

I wouldn't give it to him. I didn't fancy his type and felt he ought to show my sister the attention he wasted on me. He practically ignored her the whole evening!

The days grew hotter and time slowed down as I awaited my two-ank-long astronomy class with Firuza.

"I had no idea so many of you would want to learn about the motions of the moon," she said surveying the packed room once the first night of class finally came.

The number of students delighted her, but it disappointed me. I'd envisioned only a few of us, perhaps meeting in pubs, with she and I lingering after the others had left. Instead, I shared her with thirty-four other students. I resigned myself to an experience other than the one I'd imagined.

"I love my new home in Ilari," she told us one evening "but where I was raised, we considered astronomy much more important."

"Why?" someone asked.

"My people, my original people, traveled more. They used the heavens to find their way."

"Not many people leave Ilari," a student agreed. "Why would we? We have everything here anyone could ever want."

"You do," she said. "A visitor notices that right away. Yet how many Ilarians are truly happy?"

"Huh?" Several students said it at once.

She shook her head. "Sorry. That was an inappropriate question for this class. What I meant to say was 'Ilari is a land blessed by incredible good fortune.'"

"Why did you leave the place where you grew up?" one of the bolder students asked. "Was it less fortunate?"

"I … I left for reasons of my own," she said, hesitating in a way I'd never seen her do. "And then when I tried to return, well, my people weren't there."

"They'd left?"

"Some had. Many of them had died."

The room went silent.

"Was it the …" By then we had all heard rumors of the marauding horde.

"Yes," she said. "I come from the southeast, a place many, many days of riding from here. The Mongols attacked my homeland eight years ago when I was roughly your age."

"They destroyed everything?"

She looked at the floor. "They destroyed much. I wasn't there when it happened so I can't answer more questions." Her gaze rose. "And I don't care to."

"Will that happen to us?" a young woman asked.

"I hope not. Now, back to our theories to explain the phases of the moon."

After that, she never brought up personal matters again.

I cherished this new knowledge about her even as it caused me concern. Her story left her older than I'd guessed. Worse yet, she'd faced hardships and carried a sorrow I could only imagine. How could we bridge such a chasm and build a relationship?

Maybe the large class size had been fortunate. I needed to listen to Zamarran and concentrate on my music.

Her words gave me one gift, though. My quartet needed a name. I'd tried out twenty-five ideas but none felt right until I heard Firuza describe Ilari as "a land of good fortune." It was.

The next day I asked Mirva, Feene, and Zamarran what they thought of becoming the "Good Fortunes." Once Feene pointed out it meant we were also "good for tunes," they loved the name.

Our reputation spread as we performed through the rest of Heli, and our audiences grew. I gave our music all my attention but told Zamarran I had had to have the holiday of Plono off.

"Holidays are our biggest times," he complained. "I've three requests to choose from." He stood with his hands on his hips and glared at me. "Could you reconsider?"

He was a tall and bulky man, with the iron-colored eyes of many Faroojers. He could be intimidating even when he didn't know it. I didn't like being intimidated.

"I can't reconsider. My sister is getting married."

"Oh. Sorry. Of course." He rolled his eyes, but his stance softened. "I'll book us for before and after the holiday instead."

I sat with Sulphur and Olivine at the wedding, knowing we shared an apprehension. With Ryalgar now a Velka and Coral about to be respectably married, everyone would expect Sulphur to find a husband. Yet, Sulphur had never seemed like the marrying kind.

She was pretty enough, in her own strong way, and she had a soft heart for anyone who'd been wronged, yet she was also an adept fighter and tough as steel when she had to be. She wore her golden hair cut short and liked clothes she could move well in, and neither enticed the boys. If she sought them out, it was because she wanted a sparring partner.

When she asked Olivine and me about our love interests, I understood. She hoped one of us would produce a suitable fiancé and take the pressure off her. I'd have been happy to help, but I couldn't. I had problems of my own.

Olivine had never confided in us much and over the last couple of eighths, she'd become quieter than usual. Perhaps she'd found someone who warranted such secrecy, making it unlikely she could help Sulphur either.

At Coral's invitation, I performed a suitable song as the guests finished their dinner. The crowd looked pleased, but I knew it hadn't been one of my better performances. The bride looked so unhappy as I sang about the lasting joys of finding one's true love. The groom ignored me entirely, picking at his fingernails until I sat back down. I guessed he remained annoyed I hadn't shown him more attention when we met.

On the way back to my table I grabbed a glass of wine that hadn't been watered down. I needed a stronger drink. Coral's sorrow combined with watching Ryalgar's prince holding hands with another melded with Sulphur's obvious distress and Olivine's need for secrecy and my suppressed pining for Firuza which appeared to be going nowhere.

After I emptied the goblet, I had another. And then one more.

As I wandered among the guests, I wanted to jump up on a table and scream "Pruck love!" In fact, I wanted to scream it several times, even though it hardly seemed an appropriate wedding toast. But bad behavior at my sister's wedding would harm the Good Fortunes' reputation. I needed to find another outlet for the frustration brewing inside me, and I needed to find it fast.

Mom returned from the privies and sat alone as the hired help cleared the tables. She looked exhausted but smiled when she saw my glance. She viewed me as her most successful creation, the one destined to attract the best husband of all. I'd always relished the title, and I wanted to please her, to make her dreams come true. As I'd spurned suitor after suitor, I'd assured her the right man, possibly even the right prince, waited for me around the corner. She'd remained patient and hopeful.

I walked over and joined her, hiking up my skirt to step over the long wooden bench and take a seat. She pushed all the used mugs and dishes out of the way, making room for me in every sense.

"I was thinking of you, Celestine, and how someday soon you'll have a day like this of your own."

I couldn't help myself. I pounded both of my fists on the table, faced her, and made my declaration.

"I don't *want* a day like this."

She sat up straighter and narrowed her eyes.

"Of course you do, dear. Are, are you not feeling well today?"

"I'm feeling fine." Then out it came, not at all in the way I wanted it to. "Mom, I want to stop pretending. I don't think I like men, not in the marriage way. I think I might prefer … women."

Her mouth dropped open.

"Oh, sweetheart. No. Don't say that. Lots of girls go through such a stage. I've never mentioned it, but I did, too, a little. It's not uncommon. You'll outgrow it. I promise."

I started to reply, but she spoke louder and talked over my words.

"These feelings pass once you marry. You learn to enjoy, well, the acceptance that being a wife brings. It gives you a place in this world. I know you want that. So say no more, please, especially not today."

She looked past me, desperate to end our conversation. I turned and saw Gypsum walking towards us, determination in her footsteps. Gypsum and Mom had the most volatile relationship in our family, but for once Mom waved her over, clearing a spot for her on the other side.

I wanted to end our conversation as much as Mom did. I swung both legs back over the bench and stood to leave.

~ 4 ~

Hot Spiced Wine

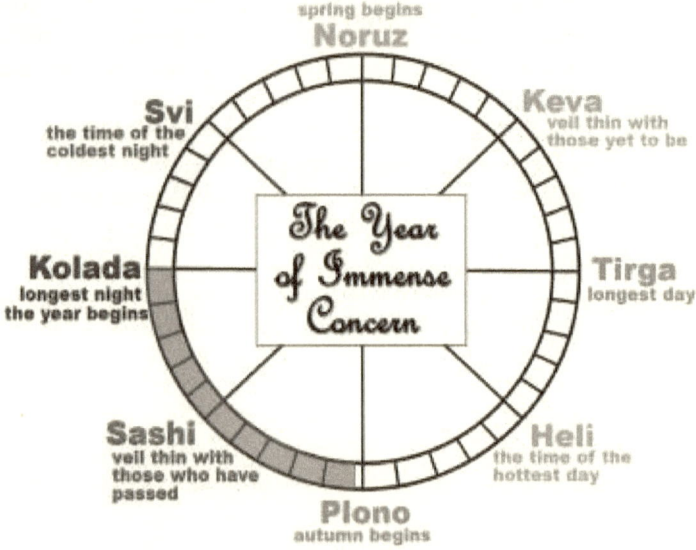

After Coral's wedding, Mom treated me with determined good cheer whenever I came home. We avoided conversation without others present. I wondered if she was embarrassed she'd confessed to having once enjoyed other girls and feared I might ask for details.

I wouldn't have. I dreaded *any* further conversation about the subject.

Meanwhile, the Good Fortunes' popularity grew as Zamarran labored to turn us into a music sensation. It made it easy for me to leave the farm often, although I somehow ended up there the ank before Sashi and made the mistake of mentioning that we had disappointing bookings for the upcoming holiday. The next morning Mom and Dad found me at breakfast, and they both sat down with me.

"Cancel your plans for Sashi," Dad said. "Your mother and I don't know when we'll see you again for a holiday and we'd like to spend this one with you."

"What! I just spent Plono with you."

"Attending a wedding together hardly counts," my mother said. "We haven't spent enough time with you twins since you've finished with your studies. You said you were scheduled to play at an insignificant place, so let your band perform without you for once."

Skunk scump. I needed to stop telling these people anything.

"I'll need to let my ensemble know so they can prepare," I said with icicles dripping from my words. "Pity people will now regard me as someone who doesn't keep her word."

I gave my mother a sharp look. She ignored me.

Nonetheless, I rode to Pilk the next day to give the other three the news.

"Tell them I've taken sick. I know you all can use the money. Play more instrumentals than usual and offer to refund some of our fee."

"This sounds like something my parents would do," Mirva said in sympathy.

"Pacify your folks as best you can," Feene advised.

"And if you do change their minds," Zamarran added. "Just show up. No one's going to complain if you suddenly feel better."

I thought about Zamarran's advice and the morning before Sashi I tried to push my way out of this mess.

"I've decided I can't let my group down like this. I'm leaving," I said at breakfast, defying them to challenge me.

"No. You're not." Dad glared back. My outright defiance hit more of a nerve than I expected. "We've been more than tolerant about the way you girls come and go; I can't imagine other parents putting up with such from two older unwed daughters. But not today. Your mom has done a lot of preparing and this special time means a lot to her. You will stay, or leave and not come back."

He'd never made such an outright threat, not to any of us, and I doubted that he or Mom would stick to it. I considered calling their bluff. It would make a mess of my life, though, while if I simply stayed and tolerated their stupid holiday, this would all go away in days.

I'm not proud of it, but I decided to do what was easiest. I gave up with a sigh.

Mom made a nice meal and poured full glasses of her best dinner wine, but the conversation lagged as they prodded Olivine and me to talk. They wanted to know more about our friends. Our pursuits. Our prospects. It took a while to figure out this was no celebration. It was a well-disguised interrogation.

I simmered inside but noticed Olivine remain spooked. I needed to stay strong. I barely touched my wine. Drink little, say less.

The next day Mom and Dad kept up their relentless attempts to engage us as they insisted we help them with meaningless little tasks. The evening brought more food, more wine, and more questions. Again Olivine and I said little and consumed less. We each made our excuses to go to bed shortly after nightfall.

In the morning I threw my things into my saddlebags and left before breakfast. I had another concert that night and I intended to be there without discussing my whereabouts, or anything else, with anyone.

The holiday had made one thing clear. I had to pay more attention to my coins and find a way to move off the farm. Young women of my social status seldom did such a thing, but I could learn to act like a girl from a less well-off family. I would not *ever* miss another performance for this kind of nonsense.

However, if I planned to become one of those questionable women who lived away from her parents, had no husband, and worked, I had to do some damage control. Nothing could be done about my father's general disdain for my lifestyle and my music, but it would help to be back in my mother's good graces.

When I returned to the farm the following ank, I started in on household chores. Although Mom used hired help, she'd never turned her household over to servants. She oversaw housekeeping, did much of her own cooking, and assigned chores to her many daughters. Some had not minded. I knew Coral liked to cook and Gypsum liked to sew.

I hated chores on principal, thinking she should have paid to have them done. Yet, I now scrubbed down the kitchen cupboards as if I cared. My mother looked suspicious when she saw me, but she gave me an appreciative smile anyway.

Then the next morning my world was scrambled up yet again when three Svadlu arrived at our farm.

Sulphur had returned from keeping Coral company at her cottage so Dad summoned her, Olivine, and me into the front room. I thought of the fabulous Kolada Ball my older sisters had attended last year. It would be held again in a few anks. Perhaps Olivine and I would be treated to the same lavish experience? It would only be fair, right? And maybe they'd send Sulphur again, hoping for a better outcome.

"Did you girls know the Svadlu have recently decided to *double* their numbers before winter comes?" my dad asked us as the three soldiers looked on.

Of course I knew. All of Pilk knew.

One of the soldiers turned to Sulphur. "We're here because we were told there was a daughter with fighting skills. Would you want to come with us?"

Sulphur's eager grin answered for her and I realized she yearned to be a Svadlu. Why else would she spend so much time sparring? I couldn't have been happier for her, but why couldn't we have gotten invited to the Kolada ball, too? I mean, the soldiers *could* have come to announce both.

One event tested my odd combination of truce and ruse with my parents, and they were no happier about it than I was. Coral would give birth while staying with Ryalgar. The Velka were renowned midwives, and Coral's husband wanted her tucked away on the off chance that this feared invasion came as early as this winter. However, my mother wanted Coral to have family with her, and Mom now considered Ryalgar more Velka than daughter. Mom would *never* visit the Velka, and Sulphur had joined the army. No one wanted Gypsum or Iolite to leave school. Olivine must have made adequate excuses before I got the chance, leaving me as the only choice to sit with my sister through this big event. I gathered I was everyone's last choice.

Yet, I remembered Coral with her arm around my young shoulders, patting my head as I cried.

"Stupid boys. Don't let their teasing bother you, they're just showing off for each other in front of a pretty girl. It doesn't mean anything."

Well, this was my chance to thank her. Zamarran had outdone himself for Kolada, getting us our longest and most prestigious booking yet over in K'ba. I would be there. Then, I'd clear my calendar for a couple of anks and be the comforting sister for once.

"Sure. I can do that."

Mom and Dad both raised an eyebrow in surprise.

"Bookings always drop off after Kolada, with the bad weather and all," I explained. "It's good timing. Who knows. Maybe I can sing to her while she's in labor."

Mom smiled at the idea and Dad rolled his eyes, but it was decided.

When I was a little girl, Kolada was my favorite time of the year. There were sweets, and pretty decorations, and gifts to open. The world sparkled and I loved sparkling things.

I still do, but I'm more jaded now. Performing for the public does that to you, as you learn to use sparkle to create an image.

I sat in the center of the stage in a large public room in K'ba, plucking the strings of my psaltery as the little mirrors hung around the many candles on the walls filled the room with glitter. People from the wealthy nichnas of Pilk, Kir, and Lev packed the tavern, hoping to celebrate the holiday in style in this fashionably artistic place.

I seldom bothered to scan the crowds for a familiar face. Those who could afford to travel to listen to the likes of me hadn't spent time in my social circles. It's why I looked right past her, more than once, as I performed. When I finally noticed Firuza, my fingers faltered for a heartbeat, then they resumed.

It had been half a year now since I took her summer class on the nature of the moon, and I hadn't known if I'd ever see her again. If I did, I had no reason to think she'd speak to me. For although the recollection of her scent lingered along with the memory of my longing, what had passed between us eighths ago was surely gone.

Yet, she stood off to the side of the stage waiting to speak with me when I finished. Even in the eclectic mix of people visiting K'ba, Firuza stood out with her wide smile and her dark eyes full of life.

"Celestine. I'm so glad I could get into this show. Your performance was beautiful!" Her voice still carried those traces of her homeland somewhere to the south, and she still smelled of a spice I didn't recognize.

She came to see me. I had to concentrate on my breathing.

When she invited me to share hot spiced wine, I gave my musical group a wave to let them know I was fine and joined her at one of the little tables.

"I love to visit K'ba," she said. "I feel freer here than I do in Pilk. Less observed, if you know what I mean."

Yes, I did. I felt less observed here, too.

She stroked my hand with her fingers, then she looked into my eyes.

"Would you like to take our hot wine back to my chambers? It's quieter there. We could visit and get caught up."

My insides trembled as I answered yes. I knew what was going to happen in her room, and I knew I'd never wanted anything more.

We both set down our wine as we entered. It would still be tasty once it cooled.

After an interlude of intimacy that exceeded anything I'd ever hoped for, we held each other and stroked each other's hair. She called me her nightingale and told me how she'd been attracted to me since the day we met amidst the snowflakes. As I'd guessed, she thought that approaching me, a student and the daughter of a co-worker, would have been inappropriate.

"And our situation is more complicated than that, isn't it?" I said.

She nodded. "I appreciate that many Ilarians are more tolerant than those in other lands, but you and I both know not everyone is. An affair with a woman would hurt your musical career and harm my standing as a teacher, even while others defended us."

"But here, you feel safe."

"I do. As soon as I heard you'd be performing in K'ba, I set up a trip with friends. Can I see you again when you perform here? If you'd like that?"

"I'd like nothing more."

But, I understood the implication. She didn't want to be seen with me in Pilk. At best, our affection would be expressed seldom and in secret.

That saddened me, yet I saw the wisdom in her thinking. A rising celebrity doesn't need detractors, and I owed it to the other Good Fortunes to keep my reputation pristine. The most successful singers appeared both conventional and available, not deeply in love with a former teacher of the same sex.

Firuza ushered me out of her room early the next morning so as not to arouse suspicion. I believed the night meant as much to her as to me, but before I left she didn't ask when I'd be in K'ba again or how she could find out when I would be.

I hoped she thought we'd figure it out somehow.

The Year of
Extreme
Distress

~ 5 ~

Sleeping Donkeys

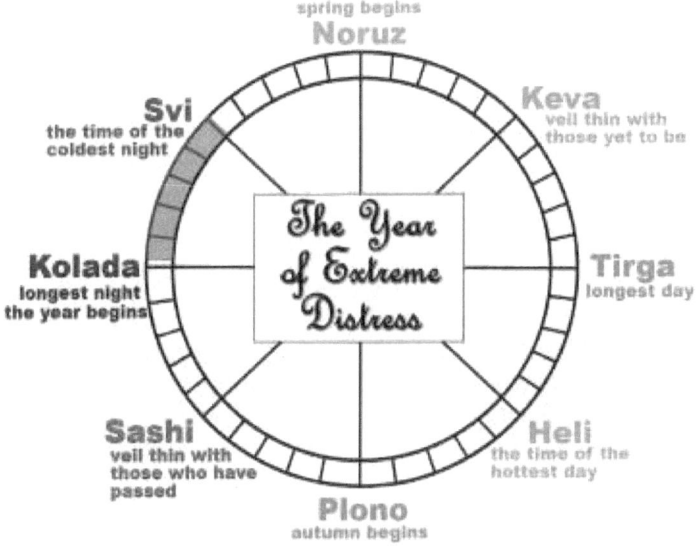

When I returned home, Olivine arrived after spending Kolada in the forest with Ryalgar. With five other sisters and two inquisitive parents, she and I seldom found a way to have a private conversation, yet we understood each other on a basic level. Perhaps those nine months together in the womb counted for something.

I could tell she was in love. I suggested a stroll and as we walked she talked of a man who my family would never consider suitable marriage material and of how she saved coins from the sale of her art, hoping to run away and live with him in K'ba.

So. I wasn't the only daughter plotting to have an independent life.

She had no interest in finding a better match, to please my parents or anyone else. This new fellow, some penniless carpenter from the dirt-poor nichna of Scrud, had been allowed into portions of her heart and mind that no man had before.

Did she recognize the turmoil in my heart as well? Perhaps. She knew of my time with other girls, but did she sense the full satisfaction I'd finally experienced with one?

It began to snow as we walked and the sparkle ignited by the setting sun on the falling flakes reminded me of the day I met Firuza. I didn't wish to hide her identity from my twin, but by the time Olivine finished speaking, dusk began and I struggled with the snow-covered tree roots and stones hidden in the growing twilight. When I stumbled, landing hard on my knees, the fall made me think of how little I knew about the path my heart now walked upon.

Perhaps I'd have told Olivine about Firuza if I'd kept my footing that night, but I didn't. When she asked me why I seemed different as well, I only spoke of my music.

I left soon after to be Coral's companion as she gave birth.

I considered the Velka simple and earthy, so I entered the forest with low expectations. I'd heard about the little donkeys they rode through the dense trees, and the woman who greeted me had one waiting. I hadn't heard about how I'd be forced to duck my head to keep from getting beaned by low branches, however. By the time I reached Ryalgar's home, my neck hurt, my hair was a mat of twigs and leaves, and several creepy small insects had settled in among my curls. Yuck.

Yet, Ryalgar lived in a place nicer than I imagined. Larger than the best inns in K'ba and well made from stone, her lodge featured huge porches and plenty of glass windows. The open front door revealed tapestries and carpets. Perhaps I'd underestimated these Velka.

When I arrived at Coral's small cottage, my pregnant sister moved awkwardly to greet me, uncomfortable in her huge body. Her normally beautiful red tresses were tangled and filthy; I'd never seen hair so much in need of a good washing and a comb.

The first thing I could do for Coral was to make her hair look gorgeous when she brought this baby into the world.

As I heated the water, however, our conversation took a bizarre turn.

She told me how the Velka knew she possessed an unusual and almost magic ability. She could use her voice to make people want to follow her instructions. She couldn't quite make them do things, but she could push them towards an action.

"Wait. Are you telling me you're a luski?"

"Well, yes, but I try not to use that word. It scares children."

I laughed. She was right. Most children feared luskies because parents threatened to use one to coerce obedience. "Do as I say or I'll find a luski who will *make* you do it." That sort of thing.

Because I behaved well as a child, at worst frustrating my father with the time I spent on my appearance, no one used luskies to intimidate me. If they had, though, my response would have surprised them.

Please! Are they real? I want to meet one.

Anyone who could be so powerful with their voice fascinated me. The fact that luskies were almost always women made them even more intriguing. If my sister was one of these fascinating creatures, I wanted to know more.

Coral warmed when she noticed my curiosity and she described her skill by using a word seldom heard outside of musical circles. *Timbre.*

"Timbre is hard to define. It's that part of music that makes a flute sound different than the plucked string of a psaltery even when their pitch and volume are identical," I told her. I asked her to demonstrate.

"Aren't you afraid?"

"No. I'm too curious to be scared."

She told me she'd oblige, but I needed to make her bed first. I didn't think that was part of my job, frankly, but it was a mess and difficult for her to make it in her current state. Why not? A more orderly room would be more pleasant to be in.

She let me finish, all the way to fluffing the pillows and placing them in a pretty arrangement.

"Now dump that bucket of water over your head," she said, pointing to the water I'd heated for washing her hair.

"Don't be ridiculous."

She laughed. "Okay. That's pretty much how this works."

Pruck. That was impressive.

I stared at her, fascinated.

Then my odd conversation with Ura came to mind. Why had I considered adding this woman with no talent to my precious ensemble? Did Ura possess the same skill? She must. Her conversation with me felt exactly like what Coral had done.

Great. A varmin luski wanted a spot in my band!

I worked on Coral's hair and had gotten as far as combing it out when our conversation turned to her future.

"What will you do after you give birth? Go back home?"

"I don't know. I'm scared to death about what will happen to Ilari after my child is born, and I'm trying to find a way to help."

"What are you so worried about?"

"These Mongol invaders, of course. They attack in the winter, and we know they're coming."

Oh not her, too. Now that winter had come, most of Pilk fretted about this.

Then she started in about how Ryalgar had spent nearly an eighth researching this westward-moving horde with alarming results and concluded that somebody had to do something because our army lacked the size or experience to defend us. Coral said Ryalgar believed this threat was a certainty.

I knew that if my intellectual sister had evaluated all her information and decided it was time to panic, it probably was. So, sitting in Coral's little cottage holding a comb in my hand, I began to reconsider.

"Can I help somehow?"

"You should ask Ryalgar."

The next day I went over to the lodge to speak with my oldest sister. The women were all so friendly there, especially the younger ones.

"Do you know where I could find my sister?" I asked the one clearing tables in the common eating area. She blushed and looked at the floor.

"Is something wrong?"

"No, of course not. I just, well, I saw you perform in Pilk and I, well, I've never heard music so beautiful. I mean, here you are,

Celestine, standing in our Velka lodge. Maybe you could do one song for us before you leave?"

"Why thank you. Sure, I'll do one if no one minds. Do you think anyone else here has heard of me?

She giggled.

"Uh, yes. Anyone who's left the forest and been in a tavern over the past year has heard of the famous Celestine."

Famous? I was famous here?

I left messages with several women asking for Ryalgar to come talk to me. She didn't. So the next day I rode a donkey over to the lodge to look for her again and bring back supplies. The women gave me plenty of food and drink, but no one knew where Ryalgar had gone.

The day was overcast and cool, but not cold, and on the way back I saw Coral had come outside for air. As I got closer, I heard her talking to a donkey tethered nearby. *Hmm.*

"Go to sleep, little donkey." She repeated in a soothing singsong voice. Of course. She practiced her luski thing. I hadn't realized it worked on animals, too. Well, maybe it only worked on some, because this particular donkey stayed wide awake.

"Go to sleep, little donkey." I joined in with her, singing along playfully. After a couple of repeats, the donkey gave me a look of understanding, laid down in the dirt, and closed his eyes. It was the weirdest feeling. I started to laugh, then the donkey I rode stopped and also dropped to the ground, spilling food and drink and catching the hem of my skirt tight under his body. As I pulled the edge of the skirt out through the mud, I could hear him snoring.

Coral turned to me in amazement. "You're an animal luski?"

"Certainly not! No animal on our farm ever did what I'd told it to do."

"What made these two respond to you now?" she asked.

I had no idea, but I intended to find out. We needed to gather up all the animals we could find.

As the afternoon wore on, we discovered that cats, dogs, rabbits, and donkeys ignored me whether I spoke, sang, or played an instrument when I gave my orders. I tried giggling, shrieking, whispering, and whistling for good measure but they still didn't care. Coral met with a similar lack of success. They only paid attention if she used her luski voice *and* I sang along.

Ryalgar arrived in the middle of all this and, as was her way, she got right to the usefulness of our discovery.

"We need to know if this works with horses. If we can make the Mongol's horses go to sleep, then we've got the invaders right where we want them. War over."

I couldn't imagine a good horse behaving in such a way. The ones on our farm showed intense loyalty to us. Asking one of them to defy us when we wished to ride was akin to ordering me to dump the bucket of water over my head. It wasn't going to happen.

I pointed this out to Ryalgar and she agreed.

"We need to try this out on horses carrying riders they know and love. And on bigger groups of horses. Noise could be a problem."

Noise was an issue in any tavern. It would be one in battle, too. What did one do with a noisy crowd? One brought in more musicians.

"We should have a lot of singers," I said. "Choirs and choruses of them. Do you think the quality of the voices matters? If not, I can teach half the realm to sing along."

"We need to get out of the forest first and run some tests."

She and I started a plan to amass riders and singers before the weather turned cold again. We were writing out messages to be dispatched when I noticed Coral had gone back inside to lie down.

My father not only complained that I spent too much time on my appearance, he often added that I gossiped and socialized too much, also. He told anyone who'd listen that if I put half that effort into important things, I'd be an impressive young woman. Dad didn't understand. The things he considered frivolity mattered to me. I *was* an impressive young woman as far as I was concerned.

I felt vindicated as I made my list of musicians for the Velka to contact. I had friends around the realm and connections in every nichna. Five in Tolo, twelve in Lev. Eight in Kir and six in Faroo. I could request the presence of forty-seven people and most of them would show up. Who else in the family could do such a thing?

If that wasn't impressive, what was?

We set our experiment up for two days hence, hoping no winter storm would intervene. None did, but nature found another way to mess with us. The next morning, Coral went into labor. First, I had to get the midwives, Ryalgar, and my grandmother. Then I had to send messages all over the realm to cancel what I'd set in motion for the next day.

Over the next many hours, I took breaks outside to get away from the moaning, the smell of all those herbs, and the discussions everyone kept having about the particulars. But when the Velka wandered off to check on other matters, I sat with Coral, holding her hand.

The one thing I remember about the birth is the way she yelled as the baby came. She didn't cry out in fear or pain. No, Coral screamed a song of triumph. I know music when I hear it.

~ 6 ~

Singing Your Fears

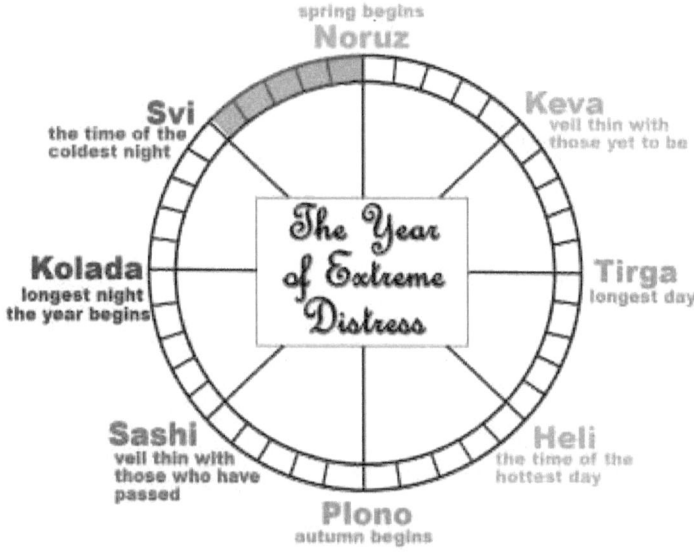

spring begins
Noruz

Svi
the time of the
coldest night

Keva
veil thin with
those yet to be

Kolada
longest night
the year begins

The Year of Extreme Distress

Tirga
longest day

Sashi
veil thin with
those who have
passed

Heli
the time of the
hottest day

Plono
autumn begins

I returned home a few days after Coral had her baby boy, hoping to find a letter from Firuza waiting for me. No letter under any guise had come. The Good Fortunes wouldn't perform in K'ba till spring because of the perils of traveling through the desolation in winter, so I had no excuse to contact her, though my mind kept trying to invent one.

While in the forest I'd backed off the idea of inviting forty-seven singers to our first test with horses. Perhaps I overcomplicated this. Instead, I picked six I knew well, trying to be strategic about whom I asked. I also asked Feene to come, just to help me out. He agreed as long as I understood he wanted no part in the final plans.

We arrived to see five women huddled together, wearing costume-party masks covering the upper half of their faces. These had to be the luskies Coral spoke of. Others glanced sideways at these women in mistrust. Coral stayed near my father who'd brought several of our herdhands and twice as many of our horses. The herdhands kept their distance from the masked women.

I gathered my singers together and pointed to the ladies in masks.

"You know what those women are, right?"

"I don't believe in that sort of nonsense," one young singer said.

"I do," Feene said. "And I'm not going anywhere near them." *Great.*

My singers all nodded. "Real or not, I won't take any chances," one said.

"We can't be that way. Whatever you believe, they *are* our partners in saving this realm. We have to work with them."

I got tentative nods from all. They'd try.

When we began singing our songs of slumber, the luskies spoke to the horses, instructing them to sleep. The animals walked around looking for tufts of grass to nibble on, behaving as though they didn't hear any of us. We sang louder, the luskies spoke louder, but nothing happened

"Maybe luskies aren't so frightening," Feene said when we took a break. "The horses have no trouble ignoring them."

Then someone got the bright idea to get the horses to throw their riders instead. I thought singing about fear could be more effective.

"Come on. Let's give these ladies some help so we can all go home," I told my group. "Let's bellow out our worst nightmares!"

The singers laughed, but as the luskies yelled at the horses to throw their riders, we sang songs about our fear of ghosts and monsters, of thunder and raging fires and wild wolves. Feene even started to howl like one.

It felt good to give voice to our terrors and as we hit a crescendo, the amazing happened. The horses began to buck. All of them. Hard. Several riders hit the dirt and we were lucky none got seriously hurt. We looked at each other. We looked at the luskies.

We'd done it. Together we'd made magic. Magic could save our realm.

Now all we had to do was get good enough at this that we could rely upon it when we had to.

The ank after, the Good Fortunes performed in one of Pilk's taverns. A singer's work usually slowed down in the winter and we hadn't played together for a few anks. After a quick practice, we still felt off when we took the stage.

The crowd eyed us with disappointment as we finished our first song. Was this all we could do? I realized fame had a downside. Once people thought you were great, then you had to be.

Our second number went smoother, and after we finished it I spoke to the audience and got some laughter and cheers. Better. We needed to avoid tough starts like this.

I scanned the audience during our third song. Many nodded their heads and tapped their toes. We'd captivated most of them, but not a young woman at the back who stood to leave. I recognized her before she gave me a satisfied smile.

I'd frustrated Ura with my quick rejection when she tried to join my ensemble and later she'd asked me to rethink my decision. After learning of Coral's talents, I thought Ura possessed them too. Why would she come to see us perform tonight? Her presence bothered me through the rest of the show.

The four of us usually took lodging at a cheap inn in Pilk where many musicians stayed. I suppose it made me easy to find, yet I jumped in surprise when Ura appeared at my door.

"Get out," I said. "I've learned about luskies and I know what you can do. Don't you dare speak."

"How unreasonable. Would you want people to treat your sister this way?"

Of course I wouldn't, but people had no reason to be scared of my sister.

I remembered what Coral told me. No one could make me dump a bucket of water over my head.

"Fine. What do you want?"

"I'm here to ask you to reconsider. Let me join your band."

42

Instinctively I put my hands up over my ears.

"Oh don't bother with that," she said. "I can't use the timbre on you for this. Your mind is made up."

"You're right. No, thank you. We don't need you."

"But that's where you're wrong. I only want to perform a song or two each night, Then, I'll help out as your reputation consultant."

"Our what?"

"You heard me. People are so easily influenced. They can be nudged into thinking performers aren't as good as expected. Perhaps tonight you noticed what a well-spoken comment from the right person can do?"

She'd tried to poison the crowd against us before we began? And she'd done it hoping to get a job? I stared at her in disbelief.

"Yes, you won them over eventually," she said, "But why work so hard to overcome my efforts *every* time you perform? Wouldn't it be easier if I worked on your behalf? People can be nudged the other way too, you know."

I wanted the Good Fortunes to þe successful so badly that I considered her proposal for a heartbeat before I rejected it.

"Get out. Stay out. I wouldn't hire you if you were the last human in Ilari. Do you understand?"

All the conniving drained out of her face, leaving only the hurt. How hard it must be to want a career for which one has no aptitude. Then my sympathy ran out. Nothing excused threatening me.

Hurt left her face as well, as anger replaced it.

"You've made your decision," she said turning to leave. "You can live with the consequences."

Great. Feene already feared luskies, and I suspected Mirva and Zamarran felt the same. How would they react when I warned them about Ura and her obsession with us?

Zamarran surprised me with his practical response.

We sat in an otherwise empty tavern, drinking ale in the middle of the day, which we seldom did, while hoping to practice before our early supper. None of us liked to perform on a full stomach.

"She has a reputation to worry about, too," he said after I'd finished telling the three of them about Ura's late-night threats.

"You want us to make up bad things about her?" Mirva asked him.

Zamarran shook his head. "The truth will work fine. I wouldn't normally publicize how we rejected someone, but in Ura's case if everyone knows she's bitter it will take away her credibility."

"Yeah, but she can still, you know ...." Feene wiggled his hand, implying some sort of magic. "Do we tell everyone about that, too?"

"No," I said. "Coral says luskies value secrecy above all else. We could put Ura in danger by exposing her. I don't want to take this that far."

Mirva surprised me with a different observation.

"It's worse than that. Expose her and she could retaliate by exposing your sister. Or exposing all the luskies working with us. The whole idea of using them to fight the Mongols could fall apart by the time Ura finishes getting even with you."

"Great," Zamarran said. "Ilaria is conquered because our band pissed off one woman."

"That won't happen," I said. "I'll hire people to watch out for her at our performances and to chase her away. She'll tire of this."

"What about the bigger issue of these women and what they can do?" Feene said. "I overheard your sister say she'd bring lots of them the next time we met. They'll ... they'll outnumber the singers. Then what?"

I drained the rest of the ale from my mug and sighed. I had to get Feene past his fear of luskies if he was going to be any help to me at all.

"Would you feel better if there were more of us than them?"

"Yeah. That way we could look out for each other. Make sure no one's been, you know, compromised."

"Okay. I planned to wait before involving additional singers, but if it helps you deal with this, I'll make sure there are always more of us."

I saw the relief in his eyes and realized I'd better get to work contacting people again.

Clouds hung low when we met for our second attempt to make the horses respond, but the rain held off. Good thing, as puddles of mud from melting snow already made walking difficult. I had to put on my boots and hike up my skirts just to move around.

Under a stormy sky, we belted out our songs as the luskies yelled instructions and the Velka played drums and some reczavy who showed up did things with fire. Straw had been strewn everywhere. Good thing. By our third and most successful attempt, nearly one out of three riders landed in the piles of straw. We'd found our plan.

Zamarran outdid himself with bookings for the Noruz holiday, but I was disappointed to learn that all of them were in Pilk.

"What happened to K'ba?" I asked him

"I was going to get us out there for Keva. Why?"

I didn't want to tell Zamarran why. We hadn't performed in K'ba since Kolada, and I still hadn't heard from Firuza. I'd begun to worry that I'd imagined our mutual affection. Could the biggest night of my sexual life have been just an evening's entertainment to her? I didn't think so but even considering the possibility stung.

As soon as the public notices of our upcoming holiday performances went on display, a messenger brought a sealed letter to my hotel room in Pilk. He waited as I read it in silence. It answered all my doubts.

Firuza gently chastised me, in her beautiful script, for not nudging my band into a winter performance in K'ba so we could be together.

"I now see you will perform in Pilk for the Noruz holiday," she wrote. "I miss you. I want you. I'm not willing to wait until you get yourself back to K'ba, so I'll find a way for us to meet safely before Noruz. Respond if you feel the same."

I wrote my answer while the messenger waited and watched me seal the letter. "Please!" was all it said.

Before I left the next morning another messenger delivered Firuza's response. It contained instructions to meet her two nights before Noruz.

Everything inside of me felt lighter.

The famous old inn she sent me to was on the other side of the wall, just inside of Faroo. Firuza had written that the owners of this sprawling old stone establishment understood the need for discretion and would have a picnic supper waiting for us in her room. They'd bring me to her quarters through a back hallway so I wouldn't be seen.

I found sneaking in distasteful but I understood Firuza's caution, and once I entered the lavish room and saw a table covered in tiny egg and cheese pies surrounded by sausages and fresh-baked bread, the inn didn't seem so tawdry.

We greeted each other in the way we'd both hoped, with barely a word said until we laid exhausted in each other's arms.

Then, after we'd exchanged news and compliments, I sat up and eyed the elaborate picnic.

"This is a feast for a prince."

"Or a princess," she laughed.

Something about the way she said it caught my attention.

"Neither of us fits that description."

She looked at me. "Where I grew up, not every woman had the luxury of an education, much less the freedom to become an astronomer. You Ilarian women do not realize how lucky you are."

"Lucky? Because we get to go to school? Don't people everywhere force their daughters to do that?" I'd tried to be funny but she answered without the usual undertone of laughter in her voice.

"In my homeland, only the daughter of a ruler would be given the leeway to become a scientist. Yet I was so sheltered, I didn't realize that most women my age already bore the burden of caring for a husband, a home, and several children. Study the stars? They were lucky to find time to wash their faces."

"You ran away?"

"I did. After a marriage had been arranged for me. It wasn't a horrible one, either, and such things were common. I was old enough, yet I was so set in my ways that I couldn't bear the idea."

"Why not tolerate him, take herbs, and have no children?" I asked. "That would have been easiest."

She laughed. "We had no Velka, and no herbs. Child after child was the lot of every fertile woman."

I sucked in my breath. No Ilarian was forced to marry or bear children, though most chose to do both.

"And after you left, that's when your land was attacked?"

There. I'd brought up the one thing I'd wanted to never discuss with her.

She nodded.

"After nearly a year spent eluding my father's soldiers and enduring hardships I'd never imagined, I returned home to beg forgiveness and accept my lot." She gave a sad smile. "I grew tired of constant hunger."

"But home was gone?"

"Nothing was left on the palace grounds except for the skeletons." She closed her eyes and I didn't want to conjure up the images she must have seen.

"Let's not speak of it," I said.

"I'd rather not. Would you hold me instead? Please."

As she snuggled against me, trembling with her reawakened memories, I wondered about this unseen side to the confident woman I adored. This side was filled with sorrow. Fear. And need.

I did my best. I wrapped my arms around her and let her head rest on my chest the way my sister had once done for me. After a short time she sobbed, softly, while I stroked her hair and murmured whatever comforting words came. I tried humming a lullaby my mother had once sung. Funny, I didn't remember my mother as the lullaby-singing type, yet there it was, the song I needed.

Firuza's body relaxed as I sang and eventually she fell asleep in my arms. I must have dozed off too. Later, when we woke hungry for our supper, neither of us mentioned Firuza's early life. But this time when we parted, we made specific plans to meet in K'ba over the Keva holiday.

The Good Fortunes stood on stage, ready to perform on the eve of Noruz. People filled the large tavern, their happy faces eager to hear us. None of the lookouts I'd recruited had seen Ura anywhere nearby.

I felt better than I had in anks. A phenomenal woman, perhaps a princess, had chosen me to confide in. To be with. To love.

My fellow musicians picked up on my good mood, and our music started out strong. Zamarran banged on his largest drum and Feene's fingers flew over the strings of his cittern, which had become his instrument of choice for most songs. He and I harmonized as Mirva wove her most intricate of melodies through it all.

Then one of the lookouts I'd hired ran through the side door and onto the stage.

"You need to leave now. The Mongols are here. The invasion has started!"

What?

People in the crowd began to yell.

"They're here!" "Get out!" "Take Cover." "Run!"

"We're as safe here as anywhere," Zamarran said as the crowd forced its way out through the two narrow doors. "Let's stay put."

"How did this happen? How could we not have known?" I asked the others. "Don't we have scouts ready to send messages if something is seen?"

They shrugged.

After the hall emptied and nothing more happened, we made our way outside to get some answers. Frightened people filled the street, heading in different directions. Some begged others for help. A few looted the abandoned merchants' stands. The only thing missing from the chaos was an actual Mongol.

"Where are they?" I asked a man walking past us.

"In Pilk Center," he said. "Ten of them are outside the offices of the Ruling Prince of Pilk."

"Only ten?"

Zamarran and I looked at each other.

"Want to go back inside and practice?" I asked.

"Might as well," he agreed. "It's a big empty hall and a shame to waste the space."

~ 7 ~

A Well-Worn Legend

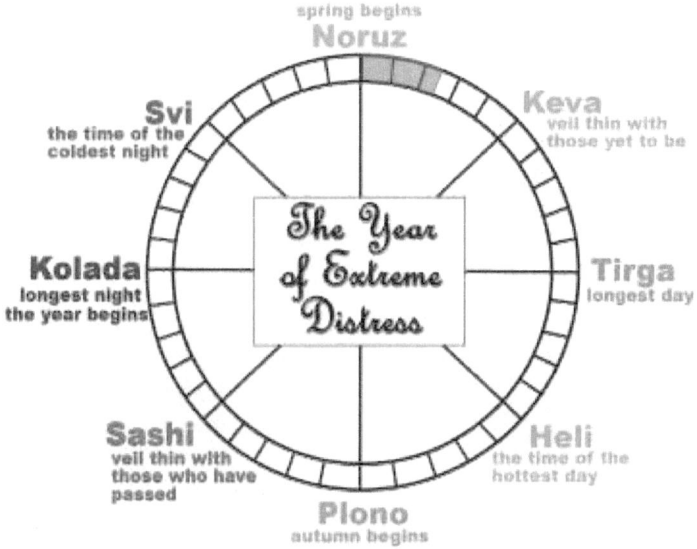

The day after the invasion that wasn't an invasion, I learned that ten Mongols had entered Ilari and scouted our roads, settlements, and defenses before they made their way to Pilk Center to articulate their demands.

We heard that our would-be overlords intended to return on Kolada, a mere three-quarters of a year later. They specified how many wagons we should have waiting for them at the realm's easiest entrance along the marshes in Bisu. They itemized the amounts of smoked meats, preserved fruits and vegetables, grains dried for storage, and barrels of wine they required. Our tribute would be yearly and predictable, and the rest of the time we would be left alone to live as we pleased. It wasn't a bad deal as far as servitude went.

I didn't know how those in other lands reacted, but my knowledge of crowd behavior led me to believe most nations greeted such an ultimatum with anger, not relief. I suspected many envoys were executed on the spot while the crowd screamed for their blood.

Ilari's leaders showed more restraint. Rather than boast of our military prowess and threaten back, they told the envoys we were but a small and gentle nation and would give the demand for tribute serious consideration. This level of cunning surprised me. I had not realized our Royals were that smart.

For I had no doubt it was subterfuge. I couldn't imagine Ilari agreeing to give away our precious wines, meats, cheeses, and produce. Not to anyone. Ilarians had a long history of being free. No, worse than that, Ilarians had no recollection of being anything *but* free. We knew of the bloody history of other lands but had given little thought to why we were so fortunate when they were not.

Now I asked the question. Why were we?

Scholars explained it away by pointing out the natural protection provided by our rivers, marshes, and mountains. But other nations had such geographical features too and a body of water or steep terrain hadn't kept them safe for centuries.

I thought a half-forgotten legend provided a more realistic theory.

The details of this old story had been worn away by time, leaving only the vague information that our realm once possessed far stronger magic, powerful enough to allow the Velka, or their ancient precursors, to hide us from potential invaders.

However, tales of small exchanges with members of the outside world also filled our past. Our own historians had recorded some of these encounters in great detail and we studied them in school. Scholars often pointed this out when refuting this theory.

Yet, each encounter had involved only three people or less, so some enterprising modern Ilarians theorized that subtleties in the old magic had allowed a few explorers and traders to come and go but kept large groups from finding us. Convenient, but it did fit the facts. The most popular subset added that only the pure of heart, or those with noble motives, could qualify. This nice add-on sounded like wishful thinking.

Yet, if this legend contained some truth, why had we lost this ability? Did a lone Ilarian back in history pruck something up so bad? Or had our protection faded gradually as we no longer needed it? Or wanted it? Or appreciated it?

Could we bring it back? Perhaps that was exactly what Ryalgar was doing, even if she didn't know it. Maybe reigniting magic consisted of a lot messier hard work and a lot less dramatic pageantry than people thought.

Maybe I and my singers would be part of this restoration. The idea made me smile.

We performed for a full house on the night of Noruz. Many musicians had left town in fear, but plenty of people anxious for the distraction we could provide remained in Pilk Central.

On the night after Noruz, I settled into my room, tired from an exhausting evening, when a late-night visitor appeared at my door. Tall and thin, with long pale blonde hair, my sister Gypsum had an other-worldliness to her appearance even in the daylight. Showing up unexpectedly at night, with me in my nightgown and the lamps flickering behind her, she seemed more ghost than real.

I had two younger sisters in school in Pilk, but neither's place of learning was near the taverns, so I seldom saw them. I suppose I should have tried harder, but I wasn't all that close to either one.

"Gypsum?" Perhaps I imagined her in the shadows.

"I need help."

"Are you hurt?" I overcame my hesitancy and stepped closer. No blood. No bruises.

"I'm fine. I've dropped out of school and I don't want Mom and Dad to know. I've nowhere to sleep for the night. Can you help me?"

I hadn't been home since mid-Svi, but back then my parents thought Gypsum was a happy student set to wrap up her learning later this year. Yet, Gypsum generally kept her thoughts private. She could have been planning this for a while.

"Why?" I asked. "Don't you like your classes?"

She laughed. "Classes aren't the problem. You don't have all night to listen to why and it will take that long to tell."

I gestured for her to sit on my bed and I pulled her stuffed rucksack in behind her as I closed the door. How could I spend all night listening to her story? I needed sleep. Feene had two new songs to go over in the morning, and I had to be alert to do that.

"It's okay," she said as I sat next to her, before I had a chance to make my excuses. "Just let me stay here tonight. Then someone will get me transportation."

"Who?"

"It's better if you don't know."

"Where?"

"It's better if you don't know that either."

"Are you sure you're doing the right thing?"

"I'm positive. Don't try to talk me out of it."

Gypsum's famous defiance made its way into her eyes and the jut of her chin.

"I won't," I said. "I've been working towards moving off the farm too. I just haven't gotten around to it."

She raised an eyebrow. "You? Mother's favorite? She'll be devastated."

"You know what she told us about marriage?"

Gypsum's laugh was bitter. "Oh yes. We all know it well." Her voice changed to the tone of a mimic. "It's just as easy to fall in love with a prince."

"Yeah, well, I seem to have fallen in love with a princess."

Her mouth dropped open. "You? Really?" I couldn't gauge her reaction until she added "Pruck. That's fantastic."

"So now. Where is it you're running away to?" I asked. "Someone in the family ought to know, and I won't tell a soul about you if you won't tell anyone about me."

Gypsum understood the nature of our bargain.

"Okay." She sat up a bit straighter. "I'm joining the reczavy."

I didn't know what to say.

The reczavy lived in tents. They existed on the fringes of society. They got by with tips for performances and selling small items, mostly toys and joke gifts they made. I couldn't think of a worse existence. Even the Velka had stone lodges and decent meals.

Much of the realm focused on the reczavy's frequent nudity and alleged sexual promiscuity well into adulthood, although people knew little about what actually occurred in their camp. Was Gypsum joining for sexual reasons?

I looked at her. She waited for me to show her the same acceptance she'd shown me. Well, why not? If this was what she wanted …

"Pruck. I think that's fantastic, too!"

The next morning I left her sleeping when I went to work with Feene. When I got back to the room she was gone. I should have asked more questions when I had the chance.

Well, whatever else people said about the reczavy, I'd never heard of them harming one of their own. Or harming anyone. She'd be safe, and once she got miserable, she could leave.

Spring began to warm the city as the Good Fortunes performed in Pilk nearly every night. Zamarran got us excellent bookings as the uncertainty caused by the Mongols' ultimatum increased everyone's need for entertainment. While I settled into a routine of practices and performances, the conclusions I'd drawn about Ilari led me past worrying and on to realizing I couldn't disregard this inconvenient threat.

I started to write down ways Ilarians could work together. How could we fight the evitable panic? How could we share information? I needed to learn more about the scouts who had failed to see the Mongol envoys enter. How could we prevent such a surprise in the future? Somebody had to be thinking about communication. Connecting to crowds had become my whole life. My people needed me in ways they didn't even know.

I also undertook a second task, though my heart led the way on this one.

I wrote love letters to Firuza. All sealed, of course, none to be recited by a messenger. In those letters, I spoke of my attraction for her, and my affection, but I also asked questions. Questions I had no desire to ask her in person.

Had her realm received such a visit from an envoy? Did she know if the invaders honored the date given for compliance? Did she know if they had spared other nations who complied?

She responded with reassurances of her love for me, but at first she ignored my questions. I persisted. By the third letter she wrote me back of things I suspected she never wanted to speak of.

I learned what she'd heard about the horde after she ran away. Of what she saw when she returned to her homeland. Of what she learned from others afterward when she wandered off, living by her considerable wits as she sought a new home.

I believed that the writing of these things helped her to heal. I hope they did.

She also wrote me of the legends others told about Ilari. Some called us an imaginary place, made up by those who wanted to believe in somewhere perfect. Their detractors pointed to acquaintances or distant relatives who had met an Ilarian or at least knew someone who had.

Some foreigners knew we were real, but they also believed magic once protected us, just as our own legends claimed. Some even thought such magic protected us now and only allowed the pure of heart to enter. Sadly, I knew this last bit to be nonsense. Groups of thieves crossed into Ilari all the time and had to be expelled by our Svadlu.

Then I read Firuza's next words. She described in her beautiful penmanship how she rode her horse along the marsh, feeling in her bones that she'd found this fabled land and that it judged her worthy and granted her entry. Thus anointed, she'd made her way to Pilk and studied our language and customs as she slowly parlayed her knowledge of astronomy into a teaching position.

She added that she now wondered if our magic protection had allowed her in because she brought unique ways of helping the realm survive.

Hmm. In the privacy of a letter, my logical science teacher believed in more whimsical illusions than me.

One evening we performed at The Crested Lark, a much smaller venue than usual. A handful of well-off and important guests occupied the few tables. We'd been asked to play mostly instrumental music to allow for conversation amongst the classy clientele.

We had a private area behind the stage, where a large curtain shielded us from the eyes of our audience as we got ready. Or maybe, it allowed our audience not to have to look at the likes of us while they dined. Either way, I appreciated the privacy while we prepared.

We peeked around it of course.

"Do you know any of these people?" I asked Zamarran.

He nodded.

"The man on the far left is named Kazimir. He's the chief commander of the Svadlu. Not a particularly well-liked man. He dines tonight with his second in command and his second's wife. The three of them eat together a lot in the better restaurants."

"The head of the Svadlu is unmarried?"

"He is. There's a tragic story of rejection by some woman he loved. Now, do you see the tall lady with the harsh hairdo at the table next to them?"

I looked. A thin woman, perhaps ten years older than I, wore her hair in a tight bun atop her head. The look wouldn't have flattered anyone.

"That's Hana. She's from one of Pilk's best families. Everyone knows she's had political ambitions since she was young. Wanted to help run the realm but didn't find avenues open to a politically ambitious woman. So she joined the Velka and now she's in line to lead them someday."

I'd seen her during my visit to the forest, but I hadn't realized she was, so to speak, in line for the throne. I'd gotten the idea there wasn't much warmth between her and Ryalgar.

"And the woman with her?" I asked.

"An old school chum of hers, I think. She keeps company with Royals and other important people."

"How do you know all this? It's fascinating."

He grinned. "No. It's useful. If you want to make a musical group successful, the more you know about important people, the better."

I had to agree. If I wanted to learn to influence Ilarians, to help them act wisely and well in an emergency, then the more I learned about those who ran the realm, the better.

"The next table is two of the top professors from the advanced schools. One teaches mathematics and the other philosophy. And the last table ..."

"I know the couple at the last table."

"I thought you would." Zamarran gave me a light sympathetic touch on the arm.

Nevik, the prince my sister had once loved, sat at the final table his new wife, the foreign princess he'd chosen over Ryalgar.

The woman wore a beautiful gown in soft shades of purples and pinks and she had exceptionally long shiny black hair which she wore loose, much like mine. Unlike mine, hers hung flat like a shiny curtain that swayed as she moved her head. Her face would have been pretty if she'd looked less unhappy.

She and Nevik avoided each other's eyes and barely spoke.

When we pulled the curtain back to begin our performance, I watched the way each of these important players responded to me.

Kazimir kept talking as though nothing could be more important than what he said. His second gave me a nod and a small smile of encouragement while his wife dutifully listened to her husband's boss.

Hana rolled her eyes at the appearance of Ryalgar's sister, and her eager to please friend pointed to something on stage and whispered to Hana. They both pointed and giggled. One of my band members must have spilled food on their clothes or something.

The two professors gave me a passing look. I wasn't of interest to them.

Nevik gave me a big grin and a couple of hearty claps as I picked up my psaltery. His wife glared at him, then turned in her chair so her back was to him and she faced a wall instead of the stage. Oh my.

Both Mirva and Feene struggled without the encouragement of a crowd, but they managed. Zamarran had brought in a wider range of percussion instruments than usual, most of them softer and more melodic. He entertained himself by trying them out in different combinations.

I only sang two songs, both short ballads, but I got some satisfaction when the two academics paused to listen to one song, and Nevik's angry wife turned her head to hear me better when I sang the other.

We received a smattering of applause as we finished our last number.

"Please don't make us ever do that again," Feene said once we were backstage.

"I agree," Mirva said. "I couldn't wait to be done."

Zamarran turned towards me.

"We don't perform at The Crested Lark for fun, or even for the money," I said, "although it is excellent. These performances serve another purpose. The Good Fortunes have a role to play in shaping Ilari's future. We prepare for it here."

Mirva and Feene both looked confused but said nothing. Zamarran didn't look confused at all.

"I'll book us here as often as I can," he said.

~ 8 ~

A Bird in Flight

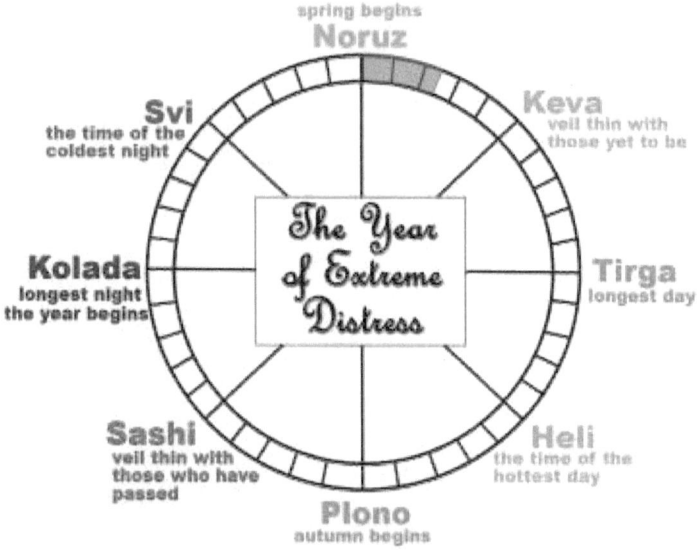

I was in Pilk longer than I expected. As I rode up to the farm, my father worked on the front porch, repairing a railing that refused to stay mended. He looked up at me, hot and dusty from my ride.

"If you haven't enough coins to send us a message to let us know you're safe, I'll send extra with you next time."

"I told you when I left that I didn't know when I'd be back."

Before he had a chance to counter me, my mother came out to offer me a cup of water.

"This strange thing happened in Pilk over Noruz," I explained to them both. "After that, people couldn't get enough entertainment. We got last-minute bookings every night, ones too good to walk away from." I turned to her for understanding. "I'd have a sent a message but every day I thought I'd be coming home the next."

"Your father worried," she said.

"We know all about the strange happenings in Pilk," my dad added. "We were there when the Mongol envoys arrived."

"You were there?" The spring sun warmed the day but my insides turned cold. *What were my parents doing in Pilk? I hardly needed them nosing into my business.*

"Your sister Sulphur became a Mozdol," Dad said. "We thought you'd like to attend."

My sister? An honorary prince? How in the Goddess's name had Sulphur managed that?

"You told us you'd be in K'ba, so I rode out there and searched everywhere for you and Olivine. No one had seen either of you girls. Why were you in Pilk instead?"

My father's tone hadn't softened and I understood, given his frustration. I only told them I'd be in K'ba so they'd be less likely to contact me. Messengers charged more coins to cross the desolation.

"Our booking got changed. Look, I'm sorry, okay? I never thought you'd care which place I was, or I'd have sent word."

Even I heard the defensiveness in my voice. Lucky for me, Coral followed my mother out the front door with the baby sleeping in her arms.

"You're here?" I said.

"Visiting for a few days," she answered, "and hoping to see you." She looked at each of our parents for permission to interrupt. They both backed off, probably thinking they could complain about my absence later. She nodded towards the garden and I walked with her.

"He's really growing," I said looking at the bundle in her arms as we left the porch.

"He better be, the way he eats."

We both glanced over our shoulders. Neither parent had followed us, and we were no longer in earshot if we spoke softly.

"I stayed here waiting for you. Ryalgar has these grandiose plans for us but she knows nothing about what we're doing or why it works. It scares me. We need to find out more about this effect we have on animals."

"I agree."

I bet I had more concerns than Coral. As a luski, a woman with the gift of coercing others with her voice, she knew why she was part of this mechanism. I didn't. Singing was a non-magical talent used by humans, birds, wolves, and more. Sure, music held power, but not by sorcery or enchantment. Why was I part of this equation?

We agreed to start by experimenting with animals in the barn. I set up a sitting area with blankets, stools, and a small table half hidden behind the hay. Then we gathered up creatures likely to respond.

To our delight, the goat would eat anything upon command, the cats would groom themselves after a few notes, and the rabbits had sex with little encouragement. No animal would do something it didn't want to do and every other living thing ignored us, except for some disturbing insects that watched as if they couldn't decide what to do. I exhaled with relief when they finally flew away.

As in the forest, the animals ignored us when we didn't work together, and responded when we did. Maybe I got their interest, and then Coral shaped that attention into compliance? Maybe. We finished our experiments with as many questions as answers.

"I can tell you have things on your mind," my mother said as she and I enjoyed a cup of watered-down afternoon wine on the porch. Coral had left the day before, and in a few days I'd make the long ride out to the K'ba settlements where I'd perform for the Keva celebrations.

"Of course I do, Mom. I feel a responsibility for the Good Fortunes. People like our old stuff, but they also want to hear something new. I'm always writing a song and it takes a lot of work."

"I wasn't talking about your music." She gave me one of those direct-in-the-eye meaningful looks and waited.

I ignored it.

"You're not getting any younger, Celestine. That beauty of yours will fade. Best to have secured a husband before then, don't you think? While you can still have your pick?"

When I didn't answer, she charged ahead.

"I haven't forgotten what you said at Coral's wedding, you know. I hope it's something you'll outgrow, but if it isn't, then you need to find the *right* sort of man. One who's, uh, less interested in the physical, perhaps. Some are that way. You could find one who loves music!" She brightened at this last idea. "Now's the time for you to secure a situation you can live with." She paused. "No, he doesn't have to be a prince."

When I still didn't answer, she sighed.

"Okay. I've heard some men will look the other way if their wife occasionally plays around with a girlfriend. If she keeps him happy too." My mother's scrunched face betrayed her discomfort with such an arrangement. "Perhaps you could find such a situation before your options become more limited."

This was *not* a conversation I expected. The varmin thing was, I knew mom cared about me. Concern for my welfare prompted her increasingly bizarre suggestions.

If the world tolerated what I wanted, she'd accept my choice as readily as she'd accepted Ryalgar joining the Velka. Or Sulphur joining the Svadlu. Heli, she might prefer my choice to either of those.

No, Mom didn't object to my loving a woman. She objected to society ostracizing me. If I entered into a sham marriage like mom described, I'd have status in society as a wife. My other option was living life as a spinster while perhaps sharing my home with a "friend." Tongues would wag and I'd always be looked down upon by some. The situation wouldn't help my popularity as a singer, but then again I didn't think marriage to a man would help either. The ideal female performer was young, beautiful, and unattached, and I could only be those things for so long.

So I was a bird in flight, and no bird can fly forever. Sooner or later I'd have to land somewhere.

Was I lucky a marauding horde had given my people an ultimatum they had five eighths of a year to satisfy?

Give us tribute or die.

You'd think such a threat could keep people's minds off of my sex life.

"I'm uncertain, Mother. About what I want." I tried to choose my words with care. "With this thing, this invasion, staring us in the face, it's hard to make life-altering decisions."

"I suppose," she said. "But I hear some young people are rushing into marriage because of it."

"But not me. I'm going to focus on my music and hope to raise the spirits of the people. And I'm going to do what I can to help Ryalgar between now and then."

Mom tilted her head back and looked into the blue afternoon sky. "Don't tell me she's somehow involved you with her crazy ideas, too."

"They're not all crazy. I'm going to help her with my music. It's reasonable."

"And after this horrible thing passes? You'll worry about your future then?"

"I will. I promise."

Pruck. I hated to admit it, even to myself, but a small part of me hoped the invaders would just burn Ilari to the ground so I'd never have to deal with all this.

The next day a messenger arrived. My father once again worked on the porch. He'd now removed half the rail on one side, seeking to replace all the rotted wood. He held a tool in his mouth and directed the messenger inside with a nod of his head. The messenger saw me watching him through at the door, came inside, and stood.

"Please. Proceed."

The young man stared at his hand, then he made a dramatic motion, moving his palm from his chin up to his forehead, the classic gesture indicating he now wore the face of the person who wrote the message. Most delivery people managed it with far less drama. This guy had to be new.

"I, Zamarran, herby notify you, Celestine, that I have secured another performance at The Crested Lark for two nights hence. We have a small but influential audience. Please make haste to Pilk. Be prepared to go from there to K'ba for our additional performances."

He extended his palm in front of his face again, lowered it from his forehead to his neck, and bowed with a flourish. Perhaps he was desperate for a larger tip? Who knew what troubles plagued others. I reached into my pocket for a second coin.

He took both coins and held them to his chest. "I'll never spend them, my lady. Rather I'll tell the world these two coins came from the amazing and beautiful Celestine, given to me by her own hand." He bowed again and left.

"What the Heli was that about?" my dad called to me from the porch as the messenger rode away. "Is that how all your fans behave?"

"I hope not."

I left the next morning after cramming clothes into my worn saddlebags, thinking I needed to have bigger ones made. I'd grown clever with mixing shawls and scarves to appear to wear something new each night, but even these techniques left me struggling to appear as fashionable as my audiences expected.

I opted to use my best clothes for our first night at The Crested Lark. This more sophisticated crowd would be harder to fool with shawls and scarves.

"Good evening. The Good Fortunes are delighted to be back." Last time I hadn't spoken from the stage, but this time I insisted on it. "Fear not. I will not interrupt your meals with prattle, but only wish to know if there is a song or two we could please you with."

I examined the audience. Tonight we had only two large tables. On one side sat a group of Mozdols, decked out in their scarlet capes and medals. I recognized Kazimir, their leader, and his second. No wives dined with them tonight. As the men joked amongst themselves, I tried to imagine Sulphur dining with them, as one of them. Try as I might, I couldn't see it.

Davor, the man who was still technically my sister's husband, sat with his back to me, perhaps hoping I'd not recognize him. It was impossible to miss his full head of shiny black hair atop his stocky frame. During our days together in the barn, Coral had confided to me that they were husband and wife now in name only and would divorce after the threat of invasion passed, as he'd fallen for another woman. What a shame. Sweet Coral deserved so much better.

At the other table sat much of Pilk's royal family, including Nevik, my sister's former lover. His dad, the current ruling prince, wasn't there, nor was his mom. However, Nevik's wife sat next to him while his older brother and his brother's wife sat across from them. A sister, a young princess, sat at one end of the table, and an even younger third brother sat at the other end looking uncomfortable in his fancy clothes.

Everyone knew Nevik's wife was pregnant, though it wasn't yet obvious. Everyone also knew the wife of the older son was not, and that her husband would lose his chance at the throne if the situation did not remedy itself. The two wives never looked at each other as they ate.

"Sing 'The Beauty of a Lone Rose,'" Nevik called out to me. I froze. Ryalgar loved that song, and surely any man she'd spent time with knew as much.

"Please," he said when I hesitated. I considered refusing, but what would that accomplish?

"Very well. A song for the prince,"

I turned to my group. Zamarran had picked up on my hesitation and it puzzled him, but we rallied and performed it as well as we could. I didn't ask the crowd for more requests.

Backstage as we gathered our things to leave, Nevik stepped behind the curtain.

"Madam, your music is excellent," he said to me. "Would you allow me the privilege of walking with you to your inn?"

"Your wife? Your family?"

"They'll see to each other," he said. "I told them that I've some musical questions I wish to ask of you."

"Very well." I turned to the others. "Do you mind if I start back now?"

"Please." Zamarran spoke for them all.

Once we were outside, I dropped the polite veneer.

"I know we've never met, sir, and you are a prince, but I also know what you did to my sister and I've nothing to say to you."

He shook his head. "That is why we are walking together. If you're going to frequent the places in Pilk where I dine, I need you to stop glaring at me. It's awkward."

"I don't glare at my audience," I said.

"You sure did when I requested that song."

"It's Ryalgar's favorite."

"It's my favorite too, and she and I continue to enjoy it together."

"I don't understand."

"Your sister and I...we remain much in love. We see each other whenever we can."

I looked at him in horror. Despite the freedom permitted to the young and unmarried, most of us took marriage vows seriously. I couldn't believe my sister would participate in such a torrid arrangement.

"My marriage is not one of love, it never has been, and your sister knows it."

"Right. What woman hasn't heard that line before?" Was this man just another Davor?

"No. The farce I've been saddled with was arranged by our parents. She hated the idea worse than I, yet we were both ordered to make it seem real, so it wouldn't sway public opinion against our families. Ryalgar has known about this from the start. The woman I am forced to call my wife has an agreement with me and she loves another as well."

"Are you serious?"

"Yes and I beg you to verify this with your sister. I love her with all my heart. And she loves me."

Well, wasn't that a surprise?

We'd reached the inn where I stayed.

"Celestine. Before I bid you good night, let me say that I regret I never got the chance to meet you when Ryalgar and I were publicly courting. I enjoyed the sisters I got to meet. Your family is wonderful. Please. You're becoming quite the figure here in Pilk so I don't need you as an enemy. In fact, I could use you as a friend."

I didn't know what to say.

"*If* I find your story to be true, we'll talk again." Then the side of me that handled our promotions kicked in. "And if it's it true, I could use a friend, too."

~ 9 ~

Why We Make Music

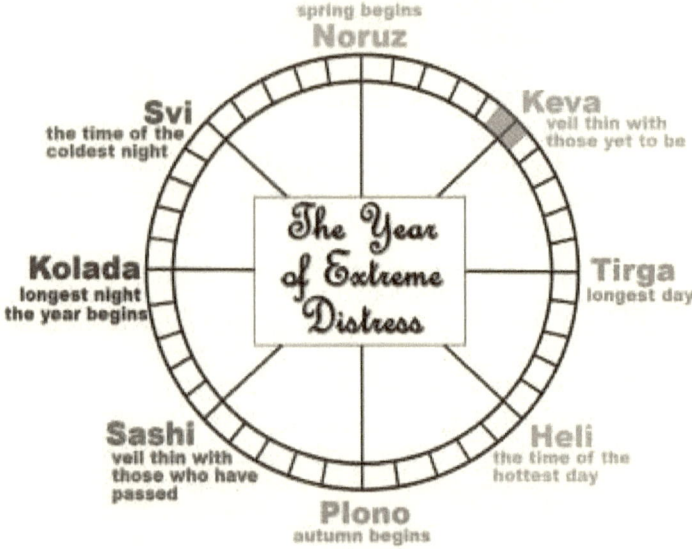

spring begins
Noruz

Keva
veil thin with
those yet to be

Svi
the time of the
coldest night

*The Year
of Extreme
Distress*

Tirga
longest day

Kolada
longest night
the year begins

Heli
the time of the
hottest day

Sashi
veil thin with
those who have
passed

Plono
autumn begins

Some people think that visiting is the same as talking. It's not. Talking is something you do. Visiting is something you do *with* someone.

I talk on stage because I have to. It's work, not fun. I enjoy visiting, however. The nice thing about conversation is that it lets you make a friend. The nice thing about a new friend is that they introduce you to more people, and then you can visit with them too.

By late Noruz of that year, I had *lots* of friends in Pilk, and they were happy to answer my questions.

By noon the next day, I learned that a quarter of my friends suspected the Royals of Pilk had coerced their second son into a marriage arranged a decade ago to secure rights along the Wide River. Half of them had the impression the Prince and his wife lived under an arrangement in which they each had a lover they preferred, although everyone thought the couple had taken care to see that the princess carried her husband's child.

About a third of those who believed the Prince had a lover *also* believed that his lover was a Velka.

Given I started by talking to forty-eight people, that meant that two of them thought Prince Nevik was seeing a Velka on the side. Half of *those* people (in other words one of them) were sure the particular Velka was my sister.

Why did it surprise people that math was my second favorite subject in school, right after music?

"I just assumed you knew," my friend said when I asked why she hadn't told me sooner. She was one of the ladies-in-waiting in the castle, straddling the line between companion to the royal family and hired help. "I don't gossip about it," she added. "I like your sister. Arranged marriages are barbaric and I'm glad everyone is getting the love they deserve."

"But you're sure it's Ryalgar and Nevik?"

"I'm certain."

It looked like I owed Prince Nevik an apology and an olive branch. Unfortunately, I didn't get the time to deliver either before we left for K'ba.

The four of us hadn't traveled together before, or I might have noticed it sooner. I'm perceptive about these things, but I am also uncommonly focused onstage and when we practice. And Mirva was an unusually shy young woman. And Feene was an odd sort of young man.

Yet, as we rode to K'ba, the signs were obvious. His hand lingered on her shoulder as he took her bag. Because her flute took up hardly any room, she carried the snacks for us all. Each time, Feene got offered his first. It was kind of cute, really.

The glances they exchanged were quick but clear. I knew how longing looked because I knew how it felt. I felt it too, more so now with every step we took in the direction of Firuza.

She and I saw each other in the street. It was in more of a cobblestone alleyway, really, and it happened as I brought my horse in to be stabled. Firuza had come outside to see if I'd arrived.

She hesitated when she saw me, glancing at people who trailed behind me, leading their horses.

I didn't care. Best they knew what I was and best they saw the reason why and how much she meant to me. So I ran into Firuza's arms and held her, shaking with relief and delight that we were once again together.

It was she who began to kiss me, I'm sure it was, because Mirva walked behind me, her shoes clanking on the stones, and I could hear Mirva's footsteps stop as Firuza's lips touched mine.

Feene preferred soft slippers when he rode, so I have no idea what he did.

Zamarran's gait was unmistakable, and he strode right up to us and tapped me on the shoulder.

"Come on now, they have rooms inside for that," he said. When I broke free from the kiss and looked at him, he grinned.

"Don't keep us waiting, Celestine. Introduce the person who inspired those longing ballads you've been writing for the last half year."

He turned to Firuza before I could speak. "You've done wonders for her music."

She gave a flustered laugh. Zamarran could come on a little strong.

"Inside, over some ale," I insisted. I looked behind Zamarran. Mirva and Feene were holding hands and looking at us, not the least upset.

"Drinks it is," Zamarran agreed.

"It's just different here," Firuza said as we waited for our ale. "I love Pilk and the school and the students but everyone there is so conscious of what others think. So careful. Here, I feel like I can be whoever I am. No one cares." She turned to me. "I'd like to spend more time here with you."

"Better talk to her manager about that," Zamarran suggested.

"Oh?" Firuza arched an eyebrow. "I didn't know it was possible to manage her."

He laughed. "Only barely. But she allows me to make the bookings for us, and, well, I just want to make sure you understand, I can be bribed."

"Okay, gentle giant," she said. "What's your preferred currency when asked to ensure that the Good Fortunes perform in K'ba at least once every eighth?"

"I'd say getting treated to dinner with you two lovely ladies and getting my fill of a fine dinner wine with it. All the better if the other two band members get fed as well," He gestured at Mirva and Feene. "They're both too skinny to be musicians."

Their laughter blended into the conversations around us, and the clatter of plates and mugs, and the smell of roasted meats coming from the doorway that opened out to the fire pits.

For one wonderful interlude, I didn't care who said what. I sat there, holding a mug of ale in my two hands, feeling safe, loved, and fully accepted, perhaps for the first time in my life.

Practice filled my afternoons, performances filled my evenings, and my late nights overflowed with the fun and affection that true intimacy brings. After four such glorious days, Firuza had to return home to her teaching. Zamarran promised her I'd be back in K'ba for Tirga, if not before.

The next day Mirva and Feene didn't show up for practice.

"That's not like them." I reached for my psaltery and knocked over the rest of my ale by mistake. I flung the cheap metal mug onto the floor in frustration.

"A little off today?"

"I suppose. What's it to you?"

"Everything," he answered. "Your well-being, at least as it manifests on the stage, is *everything* to me. That's why I asked Mirva and Feene to take the afternoon off. Besides, I thought they could use the rest." He rolled his eyes.

"Okay. What's on your mind?"

He took a long sip of the ale he still had. "The downside of love."

"Aren't we poetic today?"

"Don't give me a hard time, Celestine. You're smart. You sang your best these past few days. How will you do tonight?"

"I'll do fine. I don't have to have everything going perfectly to sing well." I glanced at his mug. "I don't even have to have ale to drink."

He pushed the mug towards me. "Help yourself." Then, as I took a swig, he added, "Okay. How well do you think Mirva's piping will flow into Feene's music once they have their first fight? They will, you know. All couples do."

"What are you saying? None of us should have personal relationships? That's ridiculous."

"No, but I'm saying our primary relationship should be with our audience. Don't get me wrong. I think Firuza is tremendous, and I'm happy for you. I'm happy for Mirva and Feene, too. But I can see what's coming from both situations and it's not going to be pretty."

"Well then, it isn't. We have to be able to have lives." Something bothered me. "What's eating you. Some lovely lady reject your overtures last night?"

He didn't reply.

"Oh, was it a handsome lad, then?"

"Neither. I don't make overtures to people and I don't see why I have to. How come everyone is so prucking eager to push me into someone's arms?"

"Everybody wants to be with somebody, Zamarran."

"No. Not everyone does. I don't, and I'm getting prucking tired of the entire world deciding they know what I need."

"You're serious?"

I looked closer. The defensiveness in his eyes looked all too much like my own when people asked why I hadn't found a man yet.

"You are," I said.

He nodded.

I'm sorry, Zamarran. People shouldn't make assumptions about what others need or want. Believe me, I understand that."

"Then understand that I'm not so selfish that I expect everyone else to be like me, you know. It's just that I want this band to be great. Okay? And yes, it would be nice if people stopped pushing me."

He stood up, took one more swallow from his mug, and handed it to me.

"Here. Finish it. I'm going for a walk."

I watched him go, thinking how Firuza would always influence my music, for good or for ill. Mirva and Feene would often struggle to keep their squabbles from affecting a performance. And, whether he knew it or not, Zamarran would sometimes bring our group down as he struggled to fit into a world that didn't understand him.

When Zamarran returned from his walk a short time later, I still sipped on his ale as I stared at the wall. The lack of emotion in his face told me he'd shared more with me than he wished, and I'd be ill-advised to bring it up. So I didn't. We said goodnight as though the conversation had never happened.

There was no solution. A band was made up of people. All people had problems of one sort or another and no one could change that. But then, if we didn't struggle and suffer, we probably wouldn't create music in the first place.

Our next performance went horribly, and it had nothing to do with relationships.

We were at a different tavern, in a part of town that catered more to locals. Feene and Mirva made eyes at each other through the first few numbers as they outdid themselves. I rose above my sorrow at Firuza's departure and sang like the nightingale she called me. But when the time came to address my audience, the evening took a turn for the worst.

"How is everyone tonight?" I yelled out above the typical bar noise.

"Great!" "Drunk!" "In love!" The usual answers came. Then, once they quieted down, a woman in the front row gave one I hadn't heard before.

"Scared."

The room got quieter.

"Why does everyone keep pretending?" she said. "We have a little over half a year to live, and we all know it." She turned around to face the others behind her, some of whom were now trying to hush her. "What is wrong with you people?" she persisted. "How can you pretend none of this is happening?"

I didn't think, but responded on instinct, as I usually did.

"It's okay. Don't be afraid. We *can* prevail over these Mongols."

Much of the room looked at me with skepticism.

"Our soldiers grow stronger, they train every day," I added.

My words weren't having the desired effect. More of the audience looked at me in disbelief.

"You must know better," a man in the back yelled. "You can't be that stupid."

"Well, yes, I do know these invaders are fierce, but I also know our realm has other ways to defend itself too." I hadn't meant to drag Ryalgar's efforts into this, but I had to get this performance back on track. "My sister, and others, are looking hard for ways to supplement the Svadlu. We can all help."

"No!"

"Not on your life!"

Cries begin to emanate from the audience, cries sounding suspiciously like boos. What was wrong? I'd never been booed!

"I told you not to let the sister of that pruska perform in here!" an older man shouted to the proprietor above all the commotion.

"What did my sister do?" I shouted back at him.

"It's what she will do," he yelled. "She'll get every one of us killed. She's the leader of the reckless fools. She's the reason we'll all die!"

I couldn't have been more confused. Zamarran reached out to touch my arm.

"There are some issues here in K'ba I should have discussed with you. And I would have, too, but I never dreamt the Sage Coalition had grown so strong."

"The what?"

Zamarran ignored my question as he stepped in front of me and spoke to the crowd. "Please, good people. Let's put politics aside and enjoy the music. Forgive our lovely singer. Celestine isn't as informed about current events as many of us. It's not her way." He shrugged. "She's too busy paying attention to her clothes."

That made me furious. I was plenty informed and I didn't appreciate his inference about my stupidity. But as I saw the understanding chuckles from many, especially the men, I realized what Zamarran had done. He'd saved what he could of the performance.

Mirva, smart lady, started to play her flute with a slow, soothing song of peace. Feene began to strum along. We'd do an instrumental now of course. Zamarran walked back to his drums, selecting the softest in his arsenal. Me, I knew enough to step into the shadows and play softly. I didn't have many fans left in this room.

Several people walked out during that song, including the man who'd called me a pruska. We played two more and by the time we finished them the tavern was less than half full. It was time to stop. When we took our final bows, most people kept visiting as if they didn't notice.

We crept out the back entrance, humiliated.

~ 10 ~

A Free Lunch

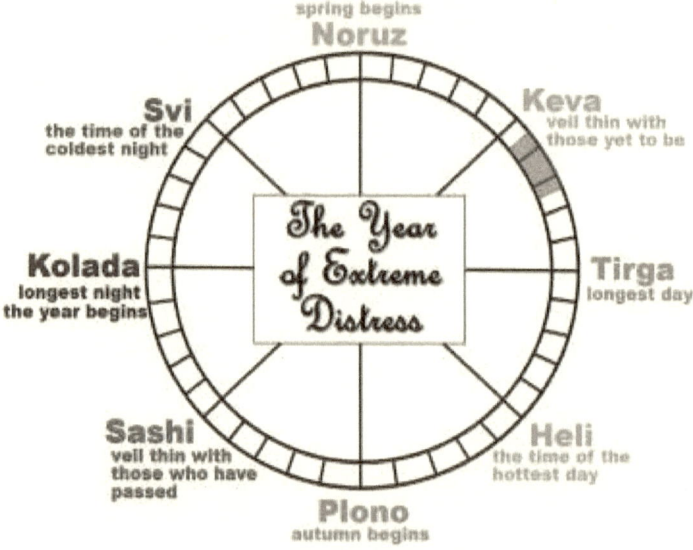

I didn't want to be seen arguing on the street, so I held my tongue as we walked. The others kept their silence too, mindful, I supposed, of the late hour and inadvisability of calling attention to ourselves. Once we crossed the threshold of our inn, I turned to Zamarran in fury.

"How could you not tell me ..."

"You begged me to book us in K'ba."

He held up his hands to ward off my anger. I think the big guy was scared of me.

"I had concerns, yes, because I heard of this thing," he said, "and I worried a few might hold your sister against you. Believe me, I had no idea an entire tavern would turn on us."

He was so distraught I couldn't stay mad.

"This movement, what did you call it, where did it come from?" I asked.

"It's called the Sage Coalition," Feene answered in a far calmer voice. I thought of him as being from Pilk because he studied there, but his real home was somewhere out in the dry nichnas. In Eds maybe? He seldom spoke of it.

"I grew up at the other end of K'ba, the unpopulated part, near the forest," he said as if he sensed my question. "And yes, a few families do live there alongside the reczavy, and mine is one of them."

That had to have been an interesting upbringing.

"This coalition isn't a bad thing, Celestine. It grew out of information that those who pay the tribute don't have such a bad life, while those who fight back often have no life at all," he said.

"You support it?!" Mirva sounded aghast. Wait. She was from the mountains of Tolo and Tolovians were notorious for not liking to be told what to do. I doubted a single person in Tolo would support paying the Mongols the tribute they demanded. Did I sense a first big fight looming on the horizon?

"I don't support anything at this point," Feene retorted "except gathering all the facts and considering them carefully. What do you support?"

"Well, I certainly don't support anyone who boos Celestine for what her sister is doing."

"Children. Please." Zamarran tried to usher us all out of the entryway and into the tavern, where a heated discussion would get less attention. "Let's focus on the band for now, okay?"

We all quieted down.

"If this had gone differently, we could maybe have stayed neutral and performed here in K'ba. But now, I think we're best served by being elsewhere. Until ... Look, I've got this idea. Some vineyards in Lev now offer food and lodging and I think I could convince proprietors that providing music is the next step."

"I've never been to Lev." Feene liked the idea.

"The hills there are gorgeous in the summer," Mirva told him.

Zamarran looked at me.

"Sure. Why not. It'll be good to get out of the heat of Pilk in the middle of the summer."

He knew why I had no enthusiasm for his idea.

"I'm sorry, Celestine. You and Firuza can still find a way. I know you can."

I didn't answer. Of course we could. It just wouldn't be as often or as nice.

That night I dreamt. Coral insisted we all dreamt but if I did, I seldom remembered mine. But that night my mother held my hand. Firm, because she cared for me. Gentle, because I was little and she didn't want to squeeze too hard. I knew these things in the dream. I think Olivine was on her other side.

A man stumbled in front of us. Maybe drunk. He stood up cursing her and called her a pruska. I had never heard the word. Her face went pale as he said it.

The dream ended then, or actually, it morphed into me being on the stage in K'ba except the room was huge and the crowd went so far back that I couldn't see where it ended. Everyone booed me as I ran from the stage and as I did, I realized I was naked, too.

Then I woke up and remembered the incident with the drunken man. It, or something similar, had really happened. Afterward, later in the day and back at our house, I'd crawled onto my mother's lap for comfort. I was maybe five, kind of old to do that, but Mom let me.

"That man called you a very bad name, Mommy, didn't he?"

She nodded, and I saw tears forming in her eyes.

"Why does it make you sad?"

"No one has ever called me that before." She laughed, a sharp little sound I didn't hear often. "At least not to my face."

"It's okay, Mommy. I know you're not one."

At those words, she threw both arms around me and sobbed. I sat as still as I could until she finished. Even then, I knew people had to cry until they were done. She lifted me off her lap then like nothing had happened and she never spoke of it again.

Funny. I never asked her about it either.

Musicians hang out with all sorts, and we're certainly no strangers to coarse language. Yet for all that, to this day, I'm not sure exactly what it means to be a pruska.

Back in Pilk together, we had no bookings for days. Zamarran worked to remedy that and to look into his idea about the vineyards in Lev. I stayed at the inn writing sad songs and plucking notes on my psaltery. I didn't want to go back to the farm. I felt like a failure. I'd been chased off stage, with my charm and talent insufficient against a group fearing my sister's actions would cause their deaths. Understandable, I guess.

Except, we had no reason to think we could take these invaders at their word or that any amount of capitulation would spare us. Why were these people so sure they were right? Why was everyone always so sure?

Ryalgar's plans grew more solid all the time, yet I'd failed to defend her. I'd failed to defend my band. And I'd failed to accomplish the one thing Firuza wanted, which was to ensure my presence in K'ba on an ongoing basis so she and I could make some sort of life together.

Now, I not only couldn't perform in K'ba, I probably shouldn't even set foot in the nichna as a guest.

Were there any more ways I could have failed? I didn't think so.

I sought out Firuza in Pilk. What else could I do? I had to tell her how things had gone, and I needed the comfort of seeing her. So I sent a messenger to ask if I could come to her house. Late in the day, she sent one back to guide me there. He carried no message other than to follow him and to watch my footing in the growing dusk.

He led me to a small stone building near the classrooms where she taught. It was more private than the large group housing most of the students used, yet still in a public location. As soon as I entered, she greeted us with a single candle. I could feel how uncomfortable my presence made her, and I already regretted putting her in such a position.

"Leave us," she told the messenger. I saw sorrow in her eyes when she turned to me.

"Sit, please. You must understand. You can't come here again."

"I know, but I need to tell you what happened."

"Something in K'ba? After I left?"

I nodded. She sat in a chair across from me and listened as I told her of my last evening there.

"Don't blame yourself," she said when I finished. "This isn't your fault. They'd have turned on you soon enough, those morons. What makes them think they can trust the Mongols? Yet, I understand their fear."

"I do too."

"And so you should. But please, there are other things to fear as well."

She paused and swallowed as if preparing her throat to force out the next words. "You and I, we shouldn't speak openly in Pilk. We should only communicate here by sealed messages."

"Can't we even interact in groups, with others?" I asked.

"No. Affection between two people is so obvious. I'm sorry, Celestine, I wish I could be bolder, but I can't." She looked down and added in a whisper "You probably deserve someone braver than me."

"You are brave." Then when she didn't reply. "I don't want someone braver than you. I want you."

She kept looking at her hands and said nothing for so long that I thought I should leave. Perhaps she'd finished saying all she would. But then she looked up and spoke.

"Perhaps Pilk *would* accept us, but I've lost so much in my life, I couldn't bear to lose this home, too. Not even for your love." I'd never seen her look sadder.

I could have argued with her, and I suppose another lover would have. But I didn't, because I knew her fears made sense. No matter how many open-minded people encouraged us, we'd encounter those meddlers certain they should force us to behave the way they thought we should, or pay the consequences. People like that were scattered about everywhere and they always found people like us.

My livelihood came from being liked. I'd already struggled with Ura's manipulating my audience, and I withered inside when I remembered how the K'basta hated me. I didn't have the temperament to deal with being despised by a whole segment of the population.

So. When Firuza said we shouldn't meet, she didn't only look out for herself. She looked out for me, too.

I accepted her edict and cried all the way home as I walked through the darkness.

Over the rest of Keva, the days grew uncomfortably warm and my mood grew more foul. I saw Firuza from a distance a few times but our eyes never met. Why should they? I couldn't live in K'ba, I couldn't even visit. What sort of future did she and I have?

My lodging had used up most of the coins I'd brought. More were hidden in my room back on the farm, but I still didn't feel ready to go back to Vinx and face my family. I sent a message home telling them I was well. My father was right, it was the least I could do. When a messenger arrived at the door of my small room a day later, I assumed my parents had sent a response.

The messenger raised her palm in front of her face and began reciting.

"Prince Nevik of Pilk requests your presence at lunch today. Noon at the Crested Lark. He has questions regarding your music and hopes you will do him the honor of humoring him with your answers."

Would I attend? Of course I would. It was a free lunch at The Crested Lark and I owed his princely highness an apology for insinuating he'd treated my sister like a cad.

I searched the room to find my cleanest frock.

Nevik stood to greet me and waved off my curtsey as though it didn't matter. Today the intimate dining space at the Crested Lark was set with many small tables for two and all were filled. I'd heard it was difficult to get a seat here for lunch.

The occupants of every table stopped to stare at the prince dining with the cabaret singer.

"You wished to ask me questions about music, sire?" I projected my voice to carry to every table.

Nevik smiled. "Yes. I've been told you have the expertise to assist me. Please. Sit."

Others turned back to their meals, satisfied nothing particularly interesting was happening after all.

"Clever," he muttered.

I shrugged. "Do you actually play an instrument?"

"I do. I prefer the lute. I played it as a young lad until my father decided fencing was more appropriate for a prince. Now I do both poorly."

Some women wouldn't have liked his self-effacing good humor, but in a world full of men who strutted and growled, I found him charming. I suspected Ryalgar did too, including ways I did not. Despite our differences, I applauded her taste.

"You owe me an apology," he said. "You've had plenty of time to unearth the truth."

"Yes. My sister kept this well-hidden from me and most of my family, and I'm sure she did it out of concern for you. It appears your love story with her is complicated and yet you two have found a way."

"It's hardly the life I'd have chosen to share with a woman," he said. "Yet, my loss may be the realms' gain. She's amazing and her plans to save Ilari grow more complex with each day. I think she may succeed."

"The people in K'ba don't think so." It slipped out before I gave it any thought. "Are you aware of the situation out there?"

He blew a short puff of air out his mouth. "Oh yes. The Sage Coalition." There was a hint of an eye roll. "They are a bit riled up, but there's nothing they can do. We *will* defend Ilari, no matter how scared they are."

"I hope Ryalgar's plans go as well as you surmise."

He set down his eating utensils and gave me his full attention.

"That's exactly why I called you here. Your sister, she puts on such a confident air to others, but I know her heart. She and I saw each other a few days ago and, strictly between us, she's frightened by what she's set in motion. She smart enough to know the chances we're taking and to understand what rests on her shoulders."

This was supposed to make me feel better?

"She keeps up this act of being strong with everyone. The Velka. The Svadlu. All of your family and the farmers and the people in Pilk who judge her every day. I worry for her. She needs some support."

"Sure, I'd like to help, but ..."

This prince had the wrong sister. Coral was the giver of hugs. Sulphur was the fighter. Olivine and I, well, we didn't do much of anything helpful..."

"You do the one thing that can give her strength."

"I do?"

"Yes. She needs to know people support her. Lots of people. Think about it. We only have so many archers, oomrushers, and luskies ... But you, you can assemble masses of singers and bring them to these practices of yours. Get the whole realm singing if you can. Surprise her with the sounds of the crowds that show up to support her."

"Well, the singers I'm using now have already insisted they outnumber the luskies."

He chuckled. "I can understand wanting that. But go bigger. Much bigger. Let Ryalgar know she has the support of the people when she sees your numbers. Let her hear their support in every note they sing."

I didn't have to think about it long.

"You know what? I can do that."

~ 11 ~

What I'm Going to Do About It

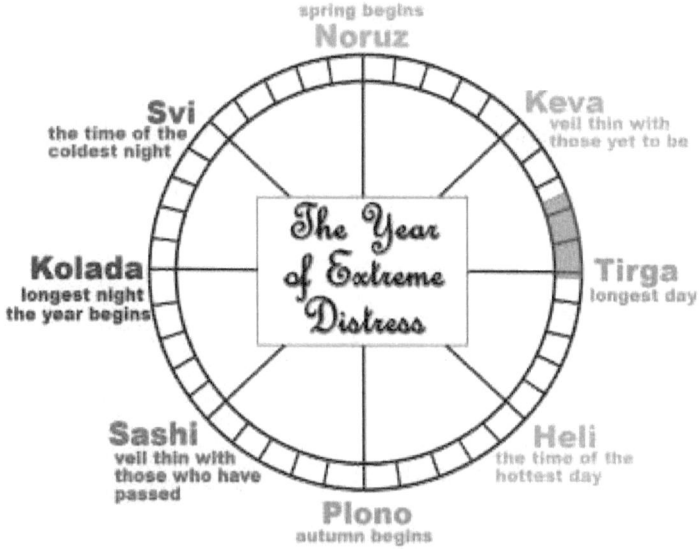

After my lunch with Nevik, I knew I had to go back to Vinx. I needed to be in touch with Ryalgar's evolving plans and be sure I knew what she expected of me. And, if I was to keep my promise to Nevik, I needed to recruit a lot more of us. I could hardly do so without a better understanding of the role of singers.

I stuffed my impressive array of dirty clothes into my overflowing saddlebags, paid the proprietor the rest of what I owed her, and headed to the large outdoor market in Vinx.

Back in late winter when we'd tested our theories out a second time, I'd brought several of Vinx's singers with me because I appreciated Feene's help and wanted him to feel comfortable around the luskies. He had said having more of us there would help. Today, I sought out those singers.

Vinx offered little in the way of gathering places, but it had one inn and a tavern located next to the market. Here, I knew I'd find those musicians.

"Celestine!" "Where have you been?" "Too famous now to come home and sing with us?"

The jovial tones told me I'd been missed, not resented, and I joined my oldest of friends for a glass of wine and conversation. When I mentioned the need for us to get together and practice, they surprised me.

"For Ryalgar? We already practice together. Didn't you know?"

"No. I'm surprised Coral didn't tell me. I thought she and I would set this up together."

The woman caught my undertone. "Oh, don't blame Coral for not telling you. She's got nothing to do with this."

No? Then who did? "Ryalgar called for singers?"

Several of them laughed. "Not that one. Your sister coordinates this from deep in the forest but she picked some of her new Velka friends to come out here and work with us."

"They're pretty nice."

"The one who handles us is a little bossy, but she gets things done. And she's a friend of Ryalgar's, so we tolerate her, you know."

Perhaps I had met her when I was in the forest.

"What's her name?"

"Hana. From Pilk. Wears her hair on top of her head in this tight ugly little bun."

Oh yes. Hana. The woman in line to lead the Velka. And the one who'd been so rude when the Good Fortunes performed at the Crested Lark.

"You're *sure* she's a friend of Ryalgar's?" I asked.

"Oh yes. She talks about your sister all the time."

"Come find out for yourself. We're having another practice in two days and she wants you there. She asked us how she could get ahold of you."

"I'll be there," I said. "Thanks."

Two days later I stood outside the barn of a nearby farmer, watching and waiting. I'd arrived well before noon, anxious to learn about the underpinnings of this endeavor I'd promised to lend my voice to.

Hana showed up first and went to put her horse in the barn. When she came out and saw me her eyes widened and her lips turned down just enough to let me know she wasn't happy to find me waiting for her. Perhaps she liked to be the first to arrive. Maybe she wanted to be bossing around an entourage when she met me.

"Celestine. I'm so glad you made it!" Within a heartbeat, an expression of warmth replaced what I'd seen. "I have to apologize for my friend's behavior at that wonderful little lunch concert at the Crested Lark. You are *so* talented." Hana gave a little helpless shrug to let me know her next comment embarrassed her before she said it. "My friend Ketevan had a bit more lunch wine than she should have. It makes her unruly."

My sisters can do many things which I cannot. They are a talented bunch. But I think I'm the only one who could do what I did next.

"Oh Heli yes," I said, flopping my hands forward in an exaggerated gesture of understanding. "Musicians have plenty of people like that. Doesn't it just embarrass the scump out of you?"

"Oh, I'm so glad you understand." She put her hand over her heart. "I didn't want us to get off on the wrong foot."

"Oh Heli, no." I waved my hand dismissively back at her. If this animated conversation kept up much longer my wrists would get tired. "I'm *so* glad Ryalgar found a Velka to coordinate all of this. I know the last thing Coral or I wanted was *that* responsibility." My hand went over my heart, matching her gesture in a sign of comradery. "And any friend of Ryalgar's is a friend of mine."

"That's so charming. You girls certainly do seem to stick together."

I heard the question she implied and I gave her the answer she wanted.

"Well, now, this whole defense of Ilari has got to be the main thing, doesn't it? Can you believe the likes of *us* are part of a defense plan?" I put my hand over my heart a second time, confirming our unspoken commonality. "Sister loyalties are wonderful, but until our realm is safe, we follow your lead."

"You are as wise as you are talented." She beamed.

I beamed too. I'd just out-schemed a schemer.

By the time the others arrived, I'd become one of Hana's favorite people. I stood with the singers, doing whatever she asked. Coral arrived a few minutes late, this time wearing a mask like the other luskies. It sent the message that she wished to hide her identity even though strands of bright orange hair stuck out, identifying her to anyone who cared. But I respected her desire for privacy, and only gave her one brief smile.

Hana paid almost exclusive attention to the luskies. I guessed she considered them the important component and us sort of an add-on. We didn't even involve the horses that day but focused entirely on the various ways the luskies could issue commands. Slow. Fast. In groups. Singly.

We sang along with whatever Hana did and in return, she asked little of us.

I had one other mission to accomplish at this gathering, and it was best saved for the end.

As we walked into the barn together to gather our things and get our horses, I shouted out to Hana. "Oh and please don't worry about the small number of singers here today. I already know I need to recruit many more and I'm going to get started on it next thing."

"You are? I think this number is plenty."

"Oh no. Ryalgar worries about our ability to rise above the noise of all the horses. We singers will make the commands carry on the wind so they can be heard."

She scrunched her brow in disbelief.

"I figured you'd be all for it," I added. "It will make *our* part of the plan the largest, and therefore the most important component."

The brow relaxed part way.

"I'd have started sooner but I feared we needed a leader before our numbers grew too large. But now …" I gestured towards her, hoping Zamarran's information about her once having had political ambitions was correct.

"I see. Yes, of course. Of all of Ryalgar's deputies, I *am* the one best suited to handle a massive group. By all means, do as you've been instructed, but keep me well informed."

"Oh absolutely." I gave her a big grin over my shoulder as I mounted my horse.

Most years we had pleasant weather during the Tirga holiday but this year the heat had us sweating by noon. By mid-afternoon most of us wanted a summer nap. Others cursed the unseasonable warmth, but I'd listened when Ryalgar spoke of the cold mountains our attackers called home. I thought the heat was our friend, keeping our foes far from us in our sweltering misery.

In the past, I hadn't minded that a musician had to work around the holidays. In fact, being busy during holidays had made my life simpler. This year, though, I wished Firuza and I could run away together for a few days, going somewhere cooler and more private. I almost asked Zamarran if I could miss one performance, but I held back.

Firuza and I had only exchanged one set of messages since I showed up at her home. The first one, from her, assured me she cared for me and hoped I'd be welcome again in K'ba once all this passed. Perhaps then we could pick up where we left off. The answer from me assured her I cared for her, too, and until this passed I was open to exchanging more messages, having secret rendezvouses in Faroo, or meeting casually in public in unsuspicious ways that would allow us to be together.

That had been two anks ago. She hadn't answered yet.

Did her silence make me doubt her love for me? No, it didn't. But it told me that the courage she showed, standing in front of a large hall teaching students about the stars, was only one part of her. Her other parts were damaged by a world that found her desires intolerable. They were fearful of a world in which she'd lost everything, more than once. I thought I'd have no more courage than she did if I'd lived her life, so I made the sad decision to leave her alone, to give her time to come to terms with what, if anything, the two of us could ever have.

When Zamarran gave me the schedule of our Tirga holiday booking, he looked at me with one eyebrow raised.

"Any conflicts?"

"No."

"Good, then. We'll finish this holiday with plenty of shiny new coins."

By the eve of Tirga the heat hadn't let up and most of the customers at the tavern seemed more interested in quenching their thirst than in listening to us.

I began with a ballad as lethargic as I felt and knew right away I'd taken the wrong approach. I tried to pick up the pace and the others did their best to follow, but there is only so much life one can, or should, poor into a song about a dead lover.

Mirva and Feene had been exchanging barbs since our afternoon practice. I gathered that their philosophical differences about the Sage Coalition had opened the doors to all the various ways a daughter of cantankerous Tolovians could disagree with a K'basta boy raised in the shadow of the reczavy.

Once the performance started, they resorted to glares.

I usually waited until after we did two songs before I spoke to the audience, but not tonight.

"So how's everyone feeling?" I shouted out after my ill-chosen ballad.

"You know what Tirga is?" a man standing in the rear shouted back.

"Prucking hot!" yelled an older man up front.

"The start of two eights of heat," said a woman next to him.

"No," he yelled back. He stomped his way up to the little stage we crowded upon and slammed his mug of beer down. "It's exactly half a year from Kolada. Half a year till those varmin show up!"

I didn't know what to say. The Sage Coalition held no influence in Lev, so I didn't expect another disaster like the one we'd had in K'ba. But just the memory of that performance made me freeze. I didn't know how to respond.

He looked me in the eye. "What are you going to do about it?"

I said the first thing that popped into my head.

"I'm going to scream with my music."

As I said it I knew it was exactly what the crowd needed. What Mirva and Feene needed. And Zamarran. And me too.

I picked up my psaltery and picked the first few notes of the liveliest song I knew. My instrument was far too lyrical for the sound I wanted, but I hoped my band would pick up on it so I could concentrate on the vocals.

Zamarran went first, going for a huge drum with a bass that made the small room shake. Feene grinned and let his fingers fly in response, forcing squeals I didn't know his cittern could make. His look to Mirva was a dare. Her eyes said she accepted the challenge.

I've never heard a piper do what Mirva managed next. That little bit of metal came to life with a screech and it never stopped wailing.

The song I started had words and I knew them well, but they hardly fit what we were doing to the music. So I used them as a starting place to shout out frustrations I didn't even know I had.

I'm not sure everyone there considered the sounds we made to be music, but we were loud, you had to give us that. Zamarran's big drums somehow kept it all together and every so often we all returned to a refrain and managed enough of a melody to make it work.

I noticed some of the customers left, and a few of them covered their ears with their hands as they did so. But others replaced them and soon the tavern was packed and it appeared we had a crowd gathered outside in the street, too. Some yelled along, or tried to sing, or clapped or banged on nearby things. It was quite the commotion.

We didn't stop, but ran one song into the next, using our livelier jigs and reels as our starting points. Finally, Zamarran began to slow things down, going for a softer sound. He was right, it was time. I joined him. Mirva followed suit. Feene rolled his eyes at us to say he was nowhere near ready to quit, but he accepted the inevitable.

Once we went silent, the crowd stilled as well. The man who'd slammed down his mug had stood the entire time at the front of the room, and now he had a giant grin on his face.

"*That's* what I'm going to do about it," I said to him. "Thanks for asking."

The back of the room laughed and clapped their hands together and others joined in. They grew louder, pouring the little energy they had left into thanking us for the energy we'd spent.

It was both the worst and the best performance of my life.

~ 12 ~

The Meaning Behind the Words

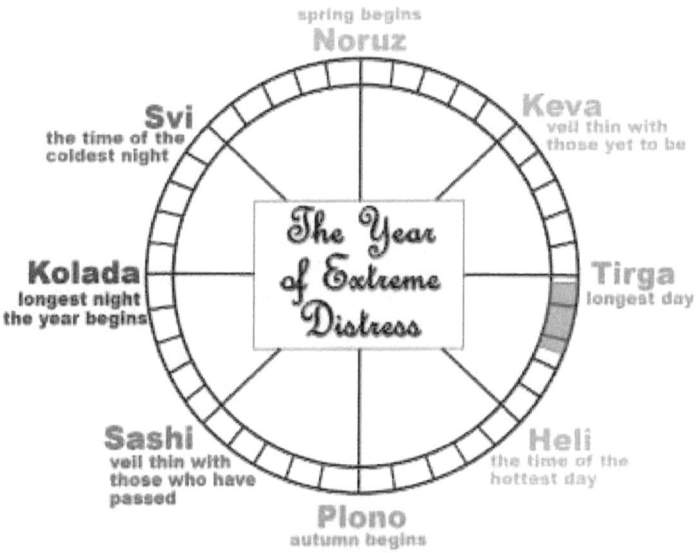

spring begins
Noruz

Keva
veil thin with
those yet to be

Svi
the time of the
coldest night

The Year
of Extreme
Distress

Tirga
longest day

Kolada
longest night
the year begins

Heli
the time of the
hottest day

Sashi
veil thin with
those who have
passed

Plono
autumn begins

I needed a luski friend because I needed someone to help me find answers. Coral taught school and cared for Votto, leaving little time and less patience for more experiments with me, but I didn't know another luski. Well except for Ura, the woman who'd tried to coerce me into hiring her, but I was hardly going to turn to her for help now, was I?

Then I remembered the luski who came to visit Coral in the forest before she gave birth. I'd met Ewalina, a tall, thin woman with hair that had greyed early and that she kept cut short around her face so it fluffed out. Coral said she lived in Pilk and worked with doctors at one of the centers of healing.

I'd seen that hair on one of the luskies at practice. If I nosed around the medical building, I thought I could find her.

She frowned when I found her at work and invited her to dine with me

"People recognize you. They'll ask me why I spoke with the famous singer Celestine," she told me as we walked outside. "And your efforts with your sister are no secret. I can't afford to have people draw conclusions."

"I didn't mean to cause you trouble. I thought you could tell anyone who asks that I needed medical information about the human voice. And hearing."

"You want my expertise as a medical assistant? I thought …"

"Yes, I need to know more about luskies too. But tell others about the medical part. Please. Will you help me?"

She gave me a cautious nod.

The next step was getting Feene to help us. He stayed at the same inexpensive inn I did, so I knocked on his door to ask. He got up from his nap to open it and I explained.

"Please. It has to be someone I trust, so she can trust them, too. You're the only one who qualifies."

"I don't want to be alone in a room with a luski."

"You won't be alone. I'll be there at all times, I promise. Will you help me?"

He gave me a cautious nod.

The final step was to find someone with a dog. Dogs were the closest thing to horses, nearly as intelligent and at least as inclined to please the people they cared for. And they fit better into a small hotel room than a horse. I figured me, Feene, Ewalina, and a dog could get some serious answers.

Zamarran stayed down the hall from us. He'd recently adopted a light brown shaggy mutt named Popover and he brought the dog with him everywhere. Popover wasn't that big and he seemed friendly.

"Could I borrow your dog for an evening?"

"Ask him," Zamarran said.

I felt foolish turning to an animal and saying "Will you help me out tonight?" but when Popover responded with an eager bark that could only mean yes, I had my crew.

"So what is it you want to know?" Ewalina asked.

I sighed. Where to start.

"Tell me about sound. How do our bodies make it? Why is singing different from talking? How do ears hear? Do animal ears work the same way as ours?"

Ewalina answered my questions as best she could while we sipped on a deep red dinner wine and nibbled on the little pies I'd bought. I'd splurged for the ones filled with duck meat and turnips. Popover enjoyed two of them and Feene listened with more interest than I expected.

After I'd exhausted what she knew about hearing, I brought out soft cheese and candied fruit for dessert. Time to move on to the magical issues.

"I need to know if the quality of the singing matters. And the number of singers. No, wait. What I really want to know is why we're even necessary. How can I ask people to risk their lives doing something that makes no sense in a battle?"

She nodded. "It baffles us too. Frankly, we'd prefer you weren't involved. We'd feel safer. Less observed."

She turned to Popover. "Such a sweet dog must be all tired out from all that eating and playing. Sweet doggie wants to rest, right?"

I could detect the timber, even though it wasn't aimed at me.

Popover put his front paws on Ewalina's lap and gave her a lively face-licking. She brushed him away. "That's not sleeping," she said.

I put my index finger up to my lips to hush the other two.

"Sleep, sweet doggie, sleep," I sang in the worst voice I could produce. Popover ran over to me and put his paws up in my lap. He licked my face, too, but I think he was trying to quiet me.

"Sleep, sweet doggie, sleep," I sang in my most melodic tones instead.

He stopped trying to lick me and thumped his tail hard on the floor.

"Better, huh?" I asked him.

Then Feene shrugged and gave singing a try. Popover ran to him and licked his pants leg. It looked like Feene had spilled some of the pie on his clothes.

"Okay," Ewalina leaned forward, eager to get some answers. "Let's do non-melodic together."

She used her timbre and Feene and I sang in our worst voices. Popover looked at the three of us, confused.

"Now a better version."

We'd barely started when Popover lay still and closed his eyes. He wasn't sleeping, but he was pretending to. I think he wanted to make us happy.

We tried a few more variations and some conclusions became obvious. Two singers got faster compliance than one. The better we both sang, the better Popover responded.

"So we *do* need more of us, and everyone should sing well. That helps."

"Yes, but we still don't know why you singers matter," Feene said.

"Only Popover knows," Ewalina laughed, "And he's not talking."

Feene stared at her and, in slow motion, his mouth dropped open.

"You're right," he said. "He's not talking. He doesn't use words. And *that's* what doesn't make sense. How does the dog know what you want? I mean, he *doesn't talk*. How does he know you're not asking him to eat? Or take a scump?"

"Relax, Feene," I said. "Animals understand human orders all the time. Simple ones anyway."

"Yeah, but this dog doesn't know the word 'sleep'."

"He might," Ewalina said. "But you've touched on a bigger issue. Has anyone realized that if the horses of our attackers *do* understand human commands, they certainly won't be in Ilarian?"

Feene's concern hadn't bothered me, but Ewalina's words hit like cold water. Of course our attackers didn't speak our language and no one thought they did. Why had we assumed their animals would?

"Wait. Let's not panic," I said. "My sister and I got cats to groom themselves in our barn and we got goats to eat rubbish and I don't think either animal understood the words we used."

The three of us stared at each other. This reasoning led to some uncomfortable conclusions.

Feene said it first. "That only leaves one option. Animals have a way of detecting intent, and it's got to involve more than words. Are you really going to tell people your plan is based on animals reading human minds?"

I laughed. "That's overstating it. They must pick up on simple things. As people do. We all can often tell when someone is lying or that they're sad even when they deny it. There's tone, gestures, and, I don't know, maybe a little more."

He interrupted me. "I hope you're right. Because if you're not, hundreds of Mongolian horses are going to ignore you, having no idea what your commands mean."

"I do think she is right," Ewalina said. "How many of our horses understand the command to buck? It's not one they're trained with. Yet look at the results we got with Ilarian horses."

She had a point.

There was only one thing left to do. We needed to try to sing Popover to sleep while using another word he knew. That way we'd find out if he obeyed the word or the intent. What word did Popover know?

"He loves to chase the sticks Zamarran throws," Feene offered. "Concentrate on sleep but say the word f-e-t-c-h."

It was harder than I expected to sing one word and think about another, so no wonder Popover stared at us in confusion. He kept looking sideways, expecting to see a stick fly by. He liked to fetch. A lot. But when no stick came, and the three of us got good and focused on slumber, he gave up and yawned, laid down, and closed his eyes. His snoring was one of the most delightful sounds we could have heard.

"I think you ought to remain vague about how the animals know what you want ..." Feene suggested.

Ewalina and I both nodded. "Yeah. If anyone gets too curious about it, send them to me," I told her.

I planned to leave Pilk the next day, but in the morning a messenger arrived with an official Royal Summons. I'd never received one before. He did his hand motion thing and began.

"You, Celestine Renata Glonti are hereby commanded to appear at the Royal Court of Pilk tomorrow at noon."

There was no question mark.

"May I ask for what purpose?"

"Yes. You will be providing a musical lesson for the second prince of Pilk. He has decided to resume playing the lute."

I wasn't happy about changing my plans and was less happy about being commanded to do something I'd have done cheerfully if asked. However, people didn't refuse a Royal Summons and I was a little curious. Whatever Nevik wanted, I doubted it had to do with playing the lute.

"Thank you for coming!"

Nevik motioned me into the parlor as he would a visiting friend.

"What can I do for you, *Your Highness*?"

"Please. There's no need for that. I called you here out of concern for your sister."

I'd offended him with my formality. Good. Somebody had to educate this man. I was willing to do it.

"Are you aware I was *ordered* to appear here?"

"For Heli's sake, no! I never asked anyone to do that. I think I told them to request your presence …" His voice trailed off in confusion.

"Perhaps others in the palace assume ordering people to see you is what you want. *Your Highness*."

"Stop with the Highness scump, will you?"

I smiled.

"Okay," he said, "I'll look into it. Perhaps my requests may get translated into commands sometimes." He hesitated. "Do you think any of my invitations to your sister were delivered in such a manner?"

"It's possible …"

He tilted his head to the left.

"You're on my side, aren't you?"

I softened. "I am. If you're going to be my sister's secret lover, I'd as soon you made her happy."

"I'd like to make her happy, too. And I could use someone on my side."

Yes, he probably could.

"So what's bothering you, other than your poor ability to play the lute?"

"I've seen your sister again, and her state of mind concerns me. She spends most of her time holed up in that lodge in the forest, in her room, studying all the ways this whole invasion could go horribly wrong. She dares not show her fears to anyone, especially to the other Velka who are risking everything to follow her. Can't you do more for her?"

"I think you're in a better position to provide her with counsel and a loving ear."

"Only when both she and I can get away," he said. "It's not as often as we'd like."

"Well, I am trying to recruit more singers, as you asked. Just last night I secured the support for doing so."

"Excellent."

"I'll try to think of other ways. Knowing she has the support of others will help her, you think?"

"I do. I've done all I can to shield her from the nonsense going on in K'ba. I fear she'll lose heart if she learns of the extent to which she's being vilified there."

I winced. "I'm no longer welcome in K'ba either, after making the mistake of publicly mentioning Ryalgar's plans. I had no idea they felt so strongly."

"I'm sorry to hear it."

We'd both sat as we spoke, and now he leaned forward and looked into my eyes.

"I, I just appreciate knowing you're my ally."

Nevik didn't know that Ryalgar and I had never been close and I was ill-equipped to advise him on how to keep her spirits up. I was better suited to rousing the masses to support her ideas, so I'd concentrate on that.

He stood, walked over to the table, and picked up an old lute.

"I better make some sounds with this, lest others doubt my reasons for having you here." He plucked a few strings. His technique was awful. I couldn't resist. I stood and joined him.

"Here. Hold your hand more like this." I reached out and curled it, then turned it slightly. He tried again. Better.

We both glanced up to see a young woman with long dark hair passing by the door. She paused as she saw us.

"Well, if you're going to learn to play the varmin thing, why not get your lessons from the best?" she said.

Although she spoke Ilarian with a heavy accent, she got the words right. I wondered if she'd been forced to learn our language to prepare for her lot in life.

I curtsied. "Your Highness. I don't generally give lessons, but if you have an interest, I'd be happy to make an exception for you as well." I turned to Nevik. "Perhaps you'd like to study together?"

She looked at me. "Thank you, but I think not."

She looked at him. "Enjoy your lesson."

Many messages hid behind her few words. I felt like Popover, ordered to fetch and sleep at the same time while trying to discern the meaning behind the sounds I heard.

~ 13 ~

A Little Wild Music

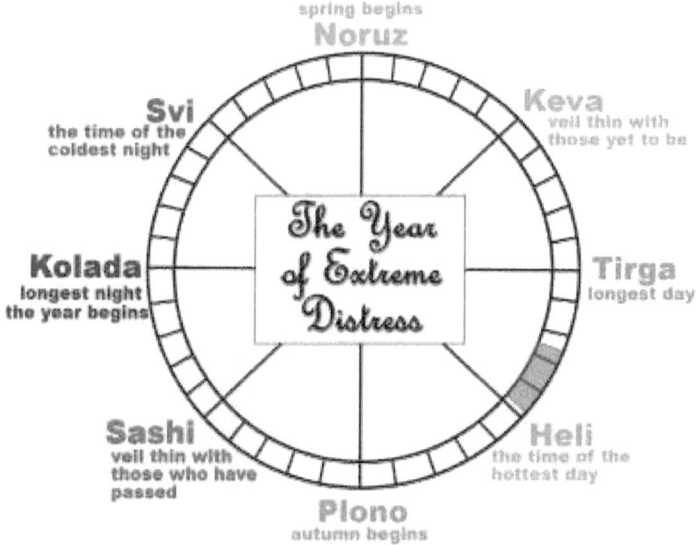

Tension crept into our next practice with Hana. Coral showed up late with her baby and a child she watched for a friend, and they made it hard to get anything done. I understood Hana's frustration with Coral as they bickered. To be fair to my sister, Hana did annoy everyone, but she bothered the luskies more because she demanded more of them. We mostly objected to how she ignored us.

Coral challenged her because she refused to behave as if Hana ran the show. I knew Hana ran things and opposing her right now didn't help anything. She could kick Coral out if she became frustrated enough with her, and that would hurt everyone.

I decided to approach Coral after practice and see if I could nudge her off of her path of self-destruction. I caught up with her as she prepared to put the little girl up on her horse.

"Hey, big sis. What's with you and the lady in charge?"

Coral gave me a funny look. "What do *you* think she's up to?"

Although I didn't particularly trust Hana, I didn't think she was up to anything other than making us better at throwing the people who wanted to kill us off of their horses. I said so.

"Stop worrying," I added. "She's done nothing but get us organized."

"I suppose. Maybe she doesn't like me because I'm Ryalgar's sister."

That glaring mistake told me Coral needed a friendly shake.

"Uh, I'm Ryalgar's sister, too. Remember?" A red flush of embarrassment crossed Coral's face. I ignored it. "And she seems to like me fine. Maybe *you're* the problem."

Coral's body stiffened, but I knew she'd think more about it later. Meanwhile, I'd keep a close eye on this ambitious woman. Hana had decided I was the good sister, but at the first sign of trouble I could become a far worse enemy to have than Coral.

I let Zamarran know I had to be at these once every ank. He agreed and as a particularly hot Tirga wore on, the practices became an ongoing part of my life.

Hana impressed me with her themes for our meetings. She always had us look into obstacles we might face. We worked at overcoming noise from the wind. We practiced while being further from the horses than we'd hoped. She continued to treat us singers as assistants to the luskies, but otherwise, I had no quarrel with the way she ran things.

I felt impolite staring at the luskies, so I averted my eyes from them at each practice. I'd noticed Ewalina's fluffy hair early on, but now I avoided her, honoring the luski code I'd learned. Always part as strangers. The few times when I had to find Coral to exchange information, I tried to not see the others. At one such time, when I scanned through the luskies looking for Coral, I saw it. The small mole in the middle of the chin.

Luskies wore the kind of masks sometimes worn at parties or balls. It covered the lower forehead, the area around the eyes, and ended above the nostrils. Most people's hair, chin, and mouths weren't that distinctive, so the masks hid most identities, although my sister's bright orange hair made her impossible to miss.

But I'd seen this perfectly centered mole before. I raised my gaze and recognized the intense eyes behind the mask. A grin spread over Ura's face.

"Did you wonder what happened to me?" she asked.

"Hardly." I admit it shook me to know I'd been spending time with her every ank and didn't know it.

"I've found better things to do than ask for a place in your silly band," she said. "I've found people who want and accept me."

"I'm glad." I meant it. If she was busy doing this, then I needn't worry about sabotage. "This is good work for you."

The grin turned towards a smirk.

"*Good* work? Hana says I'm much more important than you. Luskies matter in a way singers don't. Now I'm so glad I'm not a singer."

It seemed childish to me, but if thinking she was better than me kept her out of my life, I was okay with it.

Hana saw us talking and walked towards us, giving me a disapproving look.

"I thought you knew we discouraged socializing with the luskies."

"I do, but she and I have met before." When Hana didn't respond, I added, "I was just leaving."

Hana turned to Ura, her wrinkled brow full of worry. "Was she bothering you in any way?"

"A little," Ura said.

"Come sit with me. I'll get you some water; it will help you calm down.

Hana put a motherly arm around Ura and as they walked away, Ura glanced over her shoulder and gave me a big smile.

Maybe I hadn't given Coral's instincts enough credit. Something about the combination of Ura and Hana made my skin crawl.

In the heat of that summer I spent more time sweating on a horse than I would have liked.

I rode over to Pilk to practice with the band, to hope for a message from Firuza that never came, and to perform. Then I rode back to Vinx to check in with my parents and help on the farm, to attend a practice with Hana that usually took all day, and to visit with the friends I grew up with. Many had joined my cadre of singers and those less musically talented now helped me recruit. Maintaining contact with them was essential.

Then I rode back to Pilk in the heat, my coolest summer frocks crammed into my new extra-large saddlebags. The inn I stayed at knew my drill. They always had a cool basin of water waiting for me, along with a well-watered-down afternoon wine. After both, I felt ready to begin it all again.

Zamarran worked around my schedule, and Mirva and Feene's too. Feene no longer came to practices with me. I noticed he often went home to see his family now and guessed the coming invasion made us all more conscious of spending time with those we loved. Although he and Mirva remained a couple in Pilk, she never went back to K'ba with him. She rarely visited her own people in Tolo, either, but when she did it was always alone. Had they agreed to wall off their families to keep the peace with each other? Not a good recipe for love in my opinion, but who was I to give relationship advice?

When Zamarran told us he'd scheduled a performance during lunch at the Crested Lark in two days, we all groaned. The heat made daytime concerts miserable, and we enjoyed performing for large crowds. Our fans called the rowdy music we'd played on the night before Tirga our "wild music." Though we couldn't sustain a full evening of such riotous sounds, most venues now wanted some of it. One or two such songs had become our signature.

Of course, the elite lunch patrons at the Crest Lark would not agree. A subdued recital had been requested.

I arrived expecting to be in front of people who made me uncomfortable. However, I didn't expect to be singing for Coral's husband and his new girlfriend. The two of them sat at the center table, their entwined hands removing all doubt about this being a business meeting or a reunion of old friends.

And I certainly didn't expect his new girlfriend to be Hana's best buddy, the woman who'd heckled the Good Fortunes last time we'd appeared here. Her name was Ketevan, and Hana had claimed she drank too much that day. I doubted it.

To Davor's credit, as soon as we came on stage he pulled his hand away, placing it in his lap like a little boy caught sneaking pastries in the kitchen. It didn't matter; I'd had plenty of time to observe him from behind the tapestry.

A large table on his left was filled with Svadlu officers in their saffron capes. No crimson-caped Mozdols, no Sulphur. But a few of the officers were women and that made me more comfortable. In my experience men behaved better with women in their company.

The smaller table on the right included the foreign princess married to Nevik and three other women who fawned over her the way people do over Royals.

I couldn't help but give Zamarran a look of irritation. Why had he booked us here? I took the stage.

"This is a year of extreme distress," I said, opting to speak before we played. Zamarran nodded his concurrence. "All the more for those who bear the burdens of leading us." I bowed my head to the princess, who looked at me in surprise. "And all the more for those who bear the burdens of defending us." I gestured towards Davor first, and then the officers.

Feene had a look *of why are you cozying up to them* on his face. He needed to understand that a good lead singer always gets the audience's backing.

"This is your concert, meant to lift your weary spirits. Tell me, what music would bring you solace?"

No one wanted to speak.

"Please. We beg of you."

"Nothing sad, okay? No ballads," an officer said.

"How about a little of your wild music?" one of the saffron-caped women asked.

I turned to the other two tables.

"I wouldn't mind hearing it," Davor said. "Like to know what all the fuss is."

The three women with the princess looked at her for guidance.

"I suppose a little," she said. "Just enough to acquaint us with it." She gave a small shrug. "One has to understand the masses."

I turned to my group and, holding my hand out flat in front of me, I pushed down. *Tone it down.* I got three nods of understanding. This would be barely-wild music.

We practiced together more than most ensembles because both Zamarran and I insisted upon it. That very moment was the reason why. We'd learned to take cues from each other, and ways to vary what we did.

Zamarran took the lead and we all wove melodies of strength and valor, from songs we knew, around and over barely articulated screeches of fear and grunts of anger. The tune always led, always won, but the undercurrents of chaos left no doubt about danger and the narrow margin of victory.

Zamarran gave the cue to come together and we finished it with the melody to a popular song about the beauty of Ilari. I swear, I saw a couple of the officers wipe their eyes.

Davor stood.

"I'm surprised. That was odd, but uncommonly moving. Thank you for sharing this."

Even the princess and Ketevan didn't look totally displeased. Given that one of them had wed the man my sister slept with, and the other now slept with the man another sister had wed, I was willing to call anything other than outright hatred a victory.

As Heli approached, I grew more irritable in the heat. I wanted the comfort of contact with the woman I loved. I couldn't go to her house, under any pretext, and speaking with her at school would be worse. Sending a message was my best option because messengers were sworn to secrecy about the messages and the identity of their clients. However, I didn't dare. People did all sorts of things they swore they wouldn't and I had no reason to think messengers were all that different.

Meeting in a public place would start gossip. Meeting in a private place could do worse. I thought our night in Faroo had gone unnoticed, but she made it clear she wasn't willing to risk such a rendezvous again. She would only see me in K'ba, the one place I couldn't go.

I had to find a way to see her, or at least to let her know my feelings had not changed.

I considered standing outside her window and declaring my love but that would hardly please her. I *could* pay someone to do it for me, someone who would approach her in public on my behalf and give her a carefully crafted message only she would understand.

But it had to be someone I trusted.

Honestly, that group only included my sisters on a good day, and Mirva, Feene, and Zamarran on most days. The nature of Firuza's worries meant that a public declaration of love from Mirva or any of my sisters would be no more welcome than mine. So who was the best choice?

"I couldn't possibly," Zamarran said. "I mean I'd do this for you ten times over if I thought it would help you, but I'm nearly as well-known as you and I don't disguise easily. I'd just muck things up more. You should ask Feene. He'd be good at something like this."

Feene raised an eyebrow when I asked.

"How badly do you want to spend time with her?"

"More than anything."

"Then I'll do better than declare my love for her in a way she'll know comes from you. I'll beg her to come with me, to visit my family near the reczavy, to celebrate Heli."

"You're going home for Heli?"

"I wasn't. Mirva and I were going to join the group skinny dipping in the river, but I think she'll understand. And, if we're lucky, so will Firuza. She can pretend to be intrigued and agree to join me, knowing there's more to the story."

"And then what?"

"Did you ever wonder why you hardly ever meet old reczavy?"

"Not really. I can't imagine them getting old."

"Well they do, just like everyone else. Have you ever met former reczavy?"

"No one that admitted to it."

He laughed. "You're right. Some leave and keep quiet about their history. Some form small groups, people who have grown older together, and they make their own camps, still loving each other but more in the way of people their age. Others eventually want families. They set up their tents and raise children, but stay close to the greater group. They're not reczavy, but not really not reczavy if you get what I mean.

I thought I did. Maybe more than he intended.

"Feene, is that how you grew up?"

"Sure is." His pride in his origins surprised me. "I was raised with more love than most kids ever know."

He must have caught my expression because he looked alarmed.

"Oh great Goddess, I didn't mean it like that. Children are cherished by the reczavy, allowed to have the childhood nature intended. I was never mistreated, certainly not under the guise of love."

"I'm glad to hear that." I sought a subject change to ease me out of this embarrassing territory. "Will you join them someday, then?"

He shook his head. "I never expected to. It's just, not, well, not what I fancy, I guess. I always wanted one woman who wanted me. And I think I might have found her except she's none too happy about my upbringing and I'm not exactly crazy about hers."

"Yeah. I'm aware of the problem. So if Firuza agrees to run away at Heli with you, then what?"

"I'll get word to my folks to ask if the reczavy can put you two up in a guest tent or something."

"Wait. You don't have to involve your parents. You just get Firuza there. I know someone living with the reczavy and she owes me a favor."

He didn't look like he believed me. "*You* know someone in the reczavy?"

"Yeah. My little sister. I'll contact her to set this up."

The one group I trusted to deliver a message was the Velka. Those ladies were varmin serious about discretion. I found a young one at the nearest market.

"I love your music," she said. "That wild stuff makes me feel so alive."

"Thank you. Then can you help me get a message to my sister?" I asked.

"Ryalgar? Of course. I'll see her tonight."

"No, not her, but tell Ryalgar I said hi."

"Oh, okay, then the luski in Vinx?"

"No, I see Coral every ank at practice."

"Of course you do. The Svadlu then? She's not far from here; you can walk over yourself."

"No, not her. But I should do that and say hello." Heli, this girl knew more about my family than I did. "I need to get a message to…"

"The artist? The one in K'ba? Strange stuff going on out there …"

"Yes, I know. No, not her. The one who is …" I paused. The mere mention of the reczavy by name embarrassed many. "She lives where the forest meets the edge of K'ba. Can you get a message there?"

The young woman laughed. "One of us goes there every few days. Ryalgar coordinates with that sister. The reczavy play a major part in our plans."

My parents had failed to mention this. Then again, I understood why it would be a touchy subject.

"Write out your message," she said. "No problem."

She was right. Two days later I had a response from Gypsum. She'd prepare a guest tent where I and anyone of my choosing could celebrate the holiday in complete privacy.

~ 14 ~

What an Astronomer Can Do

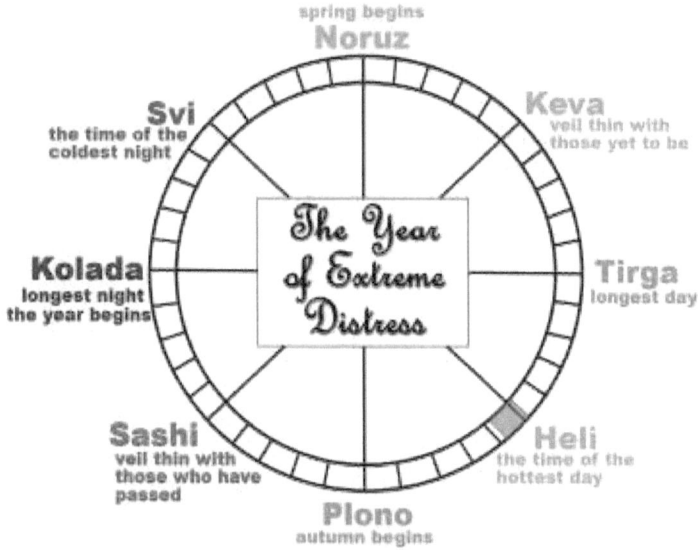

I could tell from Feene's walk that he'd been successful. No one bounces like that when they've made a mess of something.

"She knew I was in your band," he said by way of introduction.

Of course she did.

"Didn't you disguise yourself?"

"I tried. She saw right through it. Do you think she's been sneaking in, watching our performances?"

The possibility hadn't occurred to me. She seemed so nervous about being associated with me in any way. But … maybe? I felt my heart lighten at the thought.

Feene had joined me in the small, stuffy practice room where I worked. He sat down to tell me more.

"She let me know that she accepted my invitation for a holiday celebration because she assumed I delivered it for another. She'll ride with me to K'ba the day after tomorrow. I'll drop her off with you and I'll give her a public ride back to the city after the holiday." He gave me a grin. "She can tell her associates how much fun a younger man was."

I glared at him.

"That was supposed to be funny. You're the one she wants, Celestine, and I'd say she wants you a lot." He shook his head the way one does when a bewildering thought occurs. "No one should have to go to these lengths to celebrate with the one they care about. Why are you hiding like this?"

He'd done me a favor, so I gave him an honest answer.

"If I wasn't so famous, and if she wasn't so fearful of losing her place her in Ilari, maybe we'd say pruck them all and do what we pleased. I know some do. But … not us."

He reached out and put his hand over mine.

"After Kolada," he said, "let me introduce you to the people I grew up with. You two might find a home with them, a place where others would leave you be."

"Oh, I don't think …"

"Why? Because you need to sing and be in the city? She needs to teach and study the stars? Compromises can be made. I don't think you should accept misery as a given. Not for your whole life."

I had to laugh. "I didn't think I was, but okay. After Kolada, I'll look harder at my options."

At first, the worn tent with its old blankets seemed a shoddy place for a love as beautiful as ours. But after Gypsum got us settled in, my desire for privacy overtook my preferences for elegant surroundings.

It was only the fourth time Firuza and I had been together, but it felt like we'd become a couple. I'd learned the things she liked. To do to me. To have done to her. Already we knew exactly how to bring the other to a crescendo of pleasure. Repeatedly. It had to be the rare man who could do *that* for a woman, understanding parts he didn't even have.

By the second day, the tent had gone from barely acceptable to kind of cute and then all the way to being a charming hideaway. Funny …

Of course, we did more than please each other. We shared food and wine and on the morning of our first full day we walked along the border of the forest, enjoying the stark beauty of the scraggly trees meeting the desert's edge.

We finally spoke of the future, but only of the near future, of the next three eighths and what would happen when they ended.

The Mongols terrified Firuza and I couldn't blame her. She felt sure our Svadlu would never prevail over fighters so fierce, yet unlike the audience who had booed me in K'ba, she desperately hoped our Royals wouldn't choose surrender. She distrusted our invaders at least as much as she feared them.

"What do you want Ilari to do then?" I asked as we walked.

"I hoped Ilari would be spared," she confessed. "I wanted the tales to be true. But if the Mongolian envoys could deliver their ultimatum, then this land lacks magic strong enough to hide it from its foes and we are as vulnerable as my original homeland once was."

"What do you want Ilari to do?" I asked again.

She gave a soft little shrug. "I've lain awake many nights pondering that question. Probably as many nights as I've lain awake craving you."

I gave her a closer look in the morning light. The previous night's campfire and candles had hidden the dark splotches under her eyes. She appeared not to have slept well for a while.

"I've made a decision," she said. "Only recently. I'm going to help your sister in every way I can."

"I thought you wanted no contact with me…"

"You needn't be involved. I can do this on my own."

Firuza looked so determined. Hard eyes. Jaw jutting out. I hated to ask my next question, but it needed asking.

"You teach astronomy. What is it you think you can do?"

She smiled and reached into a deep pocket in her skirt and pulled something out. It was a tube, about twice as long as my foot and thinner than my fist, hammered out of metal.

"What is that?"

"Look through it." She demonstrated, then handed it to me.

I put the thinner end of it in front of one eye and looked at the sky. It was a clear day, and the blue I saw through it looked no different than the blue I saw without it. Then a bird flew past and it filled the sky before it flew on.

"This device turns me into a long-eye like my twin! Where did you get this?"

"I made it."

"How can you make such a thing?" *Did my lover possess magic powers of her own?*

"You grind the glass so it makes a little hill or depression. Then what you see through it is different than what really is. Smaller, or bigger, or warped if you do it wrong. It's tedious, but it can help those who see poorly. I put several such glasses inside this tube because I've always wanted to fly to the moon, and I thought if I could get enough of them lined up it would look as if I had done so."

"Does it?" *This was incredible.*

Her warm laugh reminded me of when I'd first met her.

"I planned to let all you students use it when I taught my class about the moon last summer but there were so many of you I didn't want to risk breaking it. But tonight we'll use it together. You can see for yourself."

I held the device against my heart.

"I wondered why no one had reported the Mongol envoys entering Ilari," I said. "I suspected we didn't even have scouts watching. But with this …."

"With this you can see an invasion coming from a long way off …"

"Maybe an astronomer *can* make a difference."

I returned to Pilk happier than I'd been in anks. It wasn't just the time with Firuza, or the long naps we'd taken in the afternoon heat. Her ideas for helping Ilari gave me hope. The courage I saw in her commitment let me imagine that once we vanquished the monster of her nightmares, maybe she would find the courage to love me openly, or at least to love me discretely.

Nothing raises one's spirits like deciding they aren't facing certain death or a life of misery.

Both the heat and Zamarran's almost continuous bookings had kept me in Pilk, but I knew I needed to travel. My experiments with Ewalina, Feene, and Popover had convinced me that more singers, and better singers, would increase the luskies' effectiveness. I needed to rally Ilarians to support Ryalgar's plan, lest this horrible Sage Coalition grew larger. And nothing brought people together like singing. Nothing filled people with hope like music. I had access to, and expertise with, the best tool for inspiring crowds. I needed to start using it.

I now sent a letter once an ank to Ryalgar telling her of how many singers we'd added. I hoped her spirits lifted as she saw the list grow. Despite Nevik's wishes that I comfort Ryalgar more directly, I knew I wasn't the sister who gave hugs and she wasn't the one who liked them. My reports would work, for the two of us.

"You're already traveling to Vinx every ank for your practices," Zamarran complained. "And we lose three days out of every nine. Now you need more time?"

He set his ale down on the table with more force than was needed. I got the point.

"I'll combine the two trips and be gone for four, at most five days each ank. I've got to get to every nichna and soon. It's important. More important than the Good Fortunes."

"*Nothing* is more important than the Good Fortunes," he said. I opened my mouth to argue but the look in his eyes stopped me.

"How much better would your recruiting go if the Good Fortunes traveled to every nichna in Ilari with you? And if you not only recruited before and after our performances but at our performances too?"

"You'd do that?"

"Nothing is more important than the Good Fortunes," he said with a laugh. "Let's let them show their worth."

I leaned forward to study his face. He meant what he said, despite the laugh.

"*Can* you book us everywhere?"

"As far as I know. If we can do music in the vineyards, why not perform in the middle of a farmer's field? Actually, we could accommodate more people outdoors than in the biggest tavern."

The way he tapped his fingers on the table betrayed his growing enthusiasm.

"I'll try to get the Good Fortunes in front of every single person in the realm," he said. "Except for those rantillions in K'ba of course. But other than them, we'll reach everyone."

Zamarran's dog Popover stayed at the inn even when Zamarran left town. Other musicians looked after him, and the innkeepers had gotten fond enough of the little mutt to stop telling Zamarran that the dog had to go. Popover did have endearing eyes and a way of making friends and getting fed.

One of his oddest friendships, though, was with a small black cat. I guessed this stray kitten had attached itself to Popover for food and protection until I noticed the little creature's cunning and confidence. Her regal air implied she thought she protected him. I had to wonder.

Her coal-black fur matched my hair and perhaps that's why I took to her. I fed her and played with her and soon she spent nights in my room when I was there, so I called her "Night Sky." By early Heli, people referred to her as my cat and I suppose by then she was. That or I was her person. Yeah. It was more like I was her person.

The day I had my conversation with Zamarran about recruiting singers from around the realm, I retired to my room with a queasy stomach. Perhaps insisting good singers could save the realm affected my digestion. I knew I stretched the truth. Others may have thought me unaware of the severity of the dangers we faced, but I knew what I did. I understood how the confidence of one person can inspire more confidence in all.

Ilari didn't need more people wringing their hands and saying we were doomed. I'd purposefully adopted a public certainty about Ryalgar's success and it didn't bother my conscience at all. However, it had begun to bother my stomach.

I hadn't seen Night Sky for a few days and I was relieved to find her waiting for me. How had she gotten in? Night Sky had her ways.

She gave me an expectant look and I fumbled in my pouch for cheese, singing an old song about a woman making cheese as I searched. After a few notes, Night Sky meowed. Not an impatient *come on, get the food* meow, but more of an *I'm singing along with you* meow.

I found a tiny piece of old cheese with bits of blue on it and a few threads stuck to it as well. I laid it in front of her and she turned up her nose like she did when she considered my offerings below her standards. Annoyed, I repeated the song in an ugly voice. She responded by turning her butt towards me and flicking her tail in anger.

Ah, I hadn't meant to sound that *offensive.*

I sang it again in my sweetest tones. She turned around and meowed back, then nibbled on the cheese. Two bugs on the window sill stopped crawling and looked at me as well.

"So, you all like my pretty singing better, huh?"

Night Sky cocked her head to one side as if she was surprised I didn't know that.

"Is it true that my song lets you know the luskies are worth listening to?" I asked.

I didn't get an answer. The two bugs flew off and Night Sky turned back to the remaining cheese, already bored with our exchange.

~ 15 ~

A Visit to the Vinx Castle

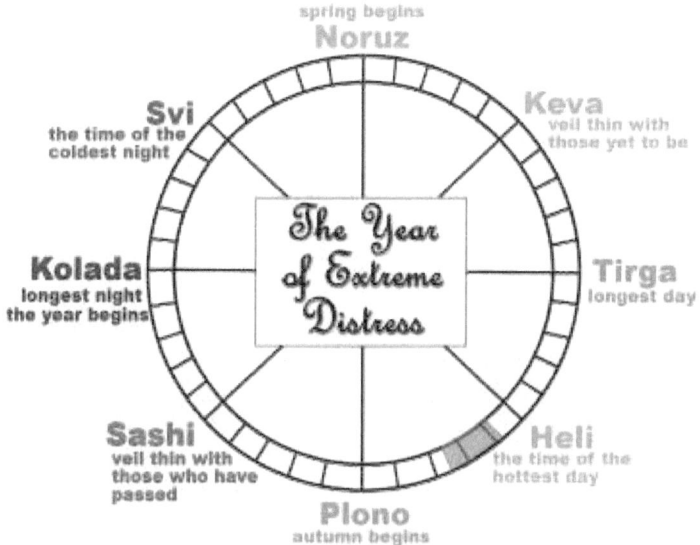

Our idea seemed so brilliant that Zamarran and I didn't consider Feene and Mirva might not want to travel around the realm recruiting for Ryalgar.

"What makes you think I want to be part of shutting down the Sage Coalition?" Feene said. "People I love believe in them."

"What do *you* believe?" I asked.

"I'm still deciding."

"And I'd like to stay out of this," Mirva added. She crossed her arms then gave Feene an uncomfortable look over her shoulder as she turned away.

"What do *you* think Ilari should do?" I asked her.

"Honestly? I don't think it matters. Ilari is doomed. I suppose I'd rather see us go down fighting."

"You seem calm for someone who thinks we're all going to die soon," Zamarran said with a roll of his eyes.

"Oh, I don't think *I'm* going to die. Do you know how hard it is to find people high in the mountains?"

"So you're going back to Tolo when this happens?" he said.

She nodded, tightening her arms closer against her chest. "Tolo will survive. Just ... probably not the rest of the realm." She gave Feene a meaningful look. "I'm hoping I won't be going to Tolo alone."

"Well then. I guess this ends the Good Fortunes," I said. "Because Zamarran and I are going to do this, with or without you two. Right Zamarran?"

I knew it would pain him to agree.

"It doesn't have to be all or none," he said. "We can schedule performances in Pilk in between our travels. With no recruiting. Would you be willing to perform at them?"

Mirva shrugged. "I don't have anything else to do. Sure." She looked over at Feene. This time he turned away from her. "Ah, Heli," she said. "I might as well go with you while you recruit, too. What you're doing won't hurt anything, and you'll sound better with me. Besides, I could use the coins."

"Great. Then we're glad to have you." And I was. Three of us was better than two.

Feene looked at the floor.

"Then I need a few days to go home," he muttered. "To say goodbye."

He had everyone's attention.

"They all know I perform with you, and some have heard that I even helped you. Once you start doing this, I won't be welcome, not unless I renounce you completely and move back to K'ba, that is." He looked at Mirva. "Alone."

Finally, the two of them turned and stared at each other. I could feel the hurt and the longing that passed between them.

"I'm not willing to do that," he added. "Because I'm thinking of spending Kolada in Tolo."

A smile grew on Mirva's face. I think she wanted to throw herself in his arms and only held back to let him finish.

"Once whatever happens finally happens," he added, "I hope I'll be able to go home again. Maybe even bring you with me," he said to Mirva.

"So you'll perform with us in Pilk then?" Zamarran clarified.

Feene answered him after blowing out a long breath. "I'll travel with you, too," he said. "I'll play and sing but I won't help you recruit. Can you live with that?"

"Of course we can."

The Good Fortunes began with one of Ilari's most difficult nichnas. Actually, most of them were difficult in their own way, but only the Zurians occasionally captured visitors and tried to ransom them for additional land. When Zamarran made our booking he insisted our hosts guarantee us safe passage. They promised, leaving us merely nervous instead of outright scared.

Their guide met us at the edge of the forest and led us through the dense growth. The travel on foot was harder than riding the Velka's small donkeys and the trees closed in on me several times forcing me to shut my eyes and steady myself. I kept waiting for a clearing like the Velka had, but the Zurians didn't live that way. They tucked their tiny wooden houses right against the trunks, removing almost no trees.

The one exception was the home of their Royals and I sighed in relief when we arrived. The land around this comparatively spacious home was partially cleared, leaving enough space between the remaining trees for people to congregate.

Their ruling prince came out to greet us before we began, his every step filled with purpose. He marched up to me and before I could get in a decent curtsy, he picked up my hand and kissed it.

"We are honored to have someone of your talent and beauty visit us. But before you begin, I'd like to say a few words."

True to his station, he turned his back on me and began talking without waiting for my reply. Yet, I had no quarrel with his words. He beseeched his citizens to consider lending their talents and even their coins to support the efforts of my sister. He went so far as to suggest that those lacking musical abilities should consider aiding the farmers and herders or find other ways to help.

"Today, we are all Ilarians, and we must step forward and behave as such." He had a fine bellowing voice which must have served him well in his role.

I noticed Mirva looking at the ground while he spoke. Perhaps her *I'm going to go hide with the other Tolovians* didn't make her feel so proud.

Our audience seemed to enjoy the music as they craned their heads around the tree trunks to see us. In the end, dozens approached us to offer their help, including the director of the Zurian choir. I would never have guessed they had such a thing, but they did and the entire choir wanted to sing with me on the day of the invasion.

I told them we'd count on it.

How funny to find such cooperation in the most cantankerous place in our land.

Iolite's school was tucked into a fork of the Little River and uncommonly difficult to get to. As a result, I seldom saw my youngest sister.

Some assumed my celebrity status prompted me to avoid her, but no. Although Iolite suffered from a disease that made many people uncomfortable, she never made me feel that way. Her gentle nature was tempered with a wisdom that made her seem almost elderly, and with a childlike love of adventure. I often wished she and I were closer.

The trip back from Zur took us near her school, so I sent the others ahead, thinking I'd surprise her and we'd spend the night visiting. The last letter from my mother told me Iolite had been slow to finish her studies and wouldn't be home until well into Heli. So I rode onto campus to find her.

"Again? What is this?" a young woman who shared Iolite's lodging greeted me at the door. "Yesterday we sent away your parents' messenger. He wouldn't believe us that Iolite left in the spring, after finishing early. He searched our house, and then the entire campus."

"What? That's impossible. She told my parents ..."

The girl twiddled a cloth in her hands and now she began wrapping and unwrapping it around her fingers as she avoided my eyes. "I've no idea why she lied to her family. I don't know what to tell you." She looked up. "I promise you, she's gone and has been for a while."

"But ... don't you have any idea where?"

Her eyes went back to the cloth in her hands. Twist and wrap. Twist and wrap.

"No. No idea at all."

"Okay. Thank you for your time."

The next morning, back at the inn in Pilk, a message came from the ruler of Vinx. As per our rules of succession, young Prince Giorgi was given the reigns of my nichna when his son turned two years old. I'd heard leadership intimidated him, and his parents ran things behind the scenes. I supposed it wasn't uncommon for one who took over the throne while still more of a boy than a man.

What could he want with me?

I laughed as the messenger delivered his words. He wanted to please his mother. She'd liked my music, and her birthday approached. Would I write her a song and perform it for her six days hence?

Well, at least this young man had the grace to request my music rather than to command it.

I began my response with a curtsey I knew the messenger would mimic.

"Your Highness. I, Celestine Renata Glonti would be honored to fulfill your request."

The messenger nodded, then surprised me by delivering a second message.

"This answer is for you if you accept. Please know that your sister Sulphur will accompany you. She requested an audience at our palace, and her cause will be best served by combining your visits."

Well, wasn't that interesting. What business did my Svadlu sister have with the Royals? And why had this boy-prince decided to help her by adding me into the mix?

I guessed I'd find out.

A few days later Sulphur and I met to share afternoon wine, and I learned she needed the Vinx Royals to intercede with the Svadlu regarding issues she had with the other Mozdols.

She learned I was part of Ryalgar's plans.

We were both surprised.

This sister and I didn't communicate much but it didn't matter. We were sisters, and we helped each other when needed. So we made plans to travel together to the Vinx Castle, then I went back to my room and wrote a happy-birthday-to-a-wonderful-mother song.

Upon our arrival, Lady Patela greeted me with the adoring look I'd come to associate with fans. I'd gotten used to it from common folk, but finding it on the face of a Royal jarred me. I curtsied anyway, suspecting that no matter how much she adored me, the usual rules still applied.

Lest my pride overtake me, though, Prince Giorgi's young twin sisters appeared to neither know nor care who I was. They jumped up and down with excitement at meeting Sulphur, the Lady Mozdol, and begged her to let them touch her sword.

I had only to watch Lady Patela's face when she thought no one looked to understand why Prince Giorgi had requested my presence. Perhaps the lad was cleverer than people realized, for his mother distinctly disliked Sulphur or something about her. Did she object to women in battle? It mattered not. I understood my assignment.

I let Lady Patela lead me into the house and show me around as I asked about the running of the royal household and shared tidbits about my music. I also mentioned how much I admired my unusual sister.

"She's easy to misunderstand her until you know her," I whispered. "She has such a tender heart under that tough exterior."

I felt the chill recede a small amount.

A servant showed me to my room to refresh myself. Good thing. I needed to revise my song. I'd written something my mother would like. Pleasant yet dignified. Now that I'd met Lady Patela, I knew I could do better.

By the time I performed Prince Giorgi's birthday gift to his mother, we'd all had our share of full-strength red dinner wine. I'd filled my song to overflowing with all the ornate hearts and flowers I could put into music, and Lady Patela melted into happy sobs and asked me to sing it again.

"This is the greatest birthday of my life," she declared. Everyone beamed as we dug into the fabulous dinner of roast mutton and more fancy vegetables than I'd ever seen at one table.

Mission accomplished.

When Giorgi's young wife expressed fatigue, I understood her exit meant more serious discussions would begin. I could have stayed, but now that Lady Patela was content, I made my excuses and settled into the feather bed for an exquisite night of well-earned rest.

Sulphur and I left the next morning. The air was cool and the sky blue, but Sulphur scowled as she rode.

"Your meeting with the Royals went poorly?"

"Not at all. Couldn't have gone better. I appreciate the way you, uh, I don't know what to call it. Interceded on my behalf?"

It made me happy she'd noticed. But something else bothered her. I didn't have to ask many questions to learn that she hadn't been able to round up the volunteers she needed for Ryalgar's plans.

"Why didn't you mention this sooner?"

"To you? Why would I?"

Maybe I ought to let my sisters know what I could do.

"Sulphur, I have a following. A big one. If I want to get the word out about something, I can do it."

"You can?"

"Give me specifics. How many people do you need? What kind of people? Where do you need them? I'll write a song for it."

"You'll do what?"

"I'll give you a jingle that gives the meeting time and place and makes people want to go."

"If you think it can help, sure."

She had no idea.

~ 16 ~

On Tour

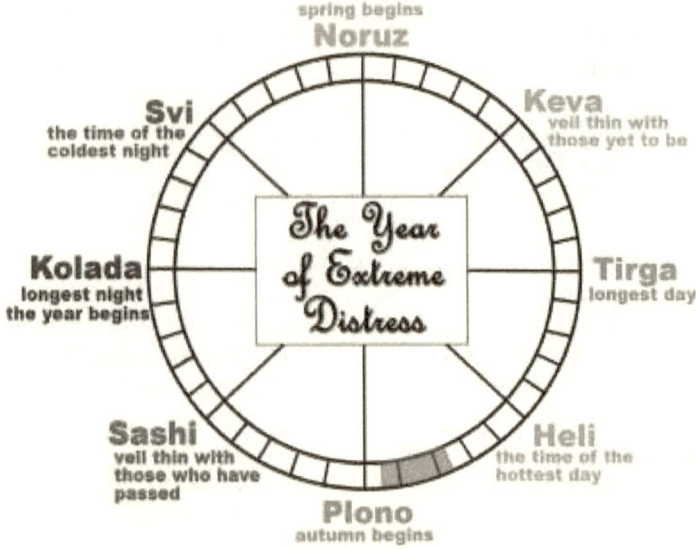

The morning after I returned to Pilk, I sat on my cot plucking notes on my psaltery. A simple tune would be best. Sulphur had given me the particulars, so the words almost wrote themselves.

By the big brown barn in Bisu
On the ank's second day
Come stand up for your nichna
Make the Mongols go away.
Bisuites and Scrudites
Come do what must be done
Arrive at dawn, learn to fight

The battle can be won, so ...

I sang the little jingle in my head until I knew it by heart. I'd designed the notes so they didn't conclude but rather lifted on the word "so." It ran the end of the song back into the beginning, making it hard to stop singing it.

Now I had to get the song out there. Could Zamarran schedule us in Bisu and Scrud over the next few days? Sure he could.

Mirva and Feene rode side by side to Bisu, singing my jingle as we traveled. They reached out for each other often, sometimes holding hands as they rode. I thought it was cute.

Because Bisuites produced our coveted beef and cheese, they lived far apart so their cows could graze. Their nichna sat below the cliffs of Vinx, bounded by the desolation of Scrud on one side, the steep Canyon River on another, and the marshlands on a third. Bisu's other claim to fame was the narrow entrance into Ilari along the marshlands.

Our arrival for a concert said that Bisu mattered, and the Bisuites liked the message. When the crowd gathered for our first performance, they sang along and tapped their toes and I had no doubt Sulphur would have as big a turn-out as she needed. We performed once in Scrud, too, holding a concert in the middle of nowhere, surrounded by dirt. Scrud had fewer people but I think most of them came and they brought the same enthusiasm.

I had a different plan for Vinx. Zamarran set up a large show for us in the Vinx market where I introduced my jingle and announced that the Good Fortunes would play at Sulphur's practice sessions. Want to hear more music? Come sign up to fight.

I settled the other three in at Vinx's inn, then I rode out to the farm, knowing it had been too long since I'd been home. Again. However, when I arrived this time, no one complained. Mom hugged me and shooed me inside as though my showing up was normal and Dad shouted hello from the barn as though he'd seen me yesterday.

I learned that worry about Iolite and Gypsum preoccupied them. They'd discovered that my youngest sister had disappeared from school to work with the Svadlu, while Gypsum coordinated one prong of Ryalgar's plan. Apparently, I was considered safe and out of trouble.

After we returned to Pilk, Zamarran scheduled us for lunchtime again at the Crested Lark. I was exhausted and wanted to sleep in, but I suspected he wanted to check on the politics of Pilk before we headed out for our long journey to recruit singers in Tolo, Lev, and Kir.

Peeking out from behind the curtain, I studied the patrons. They were all female. Perhaps our men now considered themselves too busy saving the realm to enjoy their lunches? I knew varmin well they consumed food and drink somewhere, but perhaps not where the public could see them.

At one table sat Nevik's wife, clearly with child. Hana and Hana's friend Ketevan flanked her on either side. The last time I'd seen Ketevan she held hands with Coral's husband, but perhaps that relationship had soured. He struck me as the sort of man who changed girlfriends often.

The fourth woman at the table had her back to me, but I knew who she was. Ura had managed to get a lunch invitation with the princess at the Crested Lark. How had the little weasel managed that?

Although Hana and I continued to flatter each other at practices, when the curtain went up her scrunched face signaled her displeasure with finding me here. Well, I wasn't any happier to see her and her friends.

I blew out a long breath. How could I win over this crowd? I stepped forward to speak.

"I see we have an audience of all women today." The guests looked around, some of them surprised to notice the fact. "How refreshing. We can speak of important business now that the men aren't here to prattle on about nothing."

A few of the women laughed, a few looked at Zamarran and Feene with discomfort.

"Oh don't mind those guys. These two are smart enough to understand what I mean."

Zamarran had the presence of mind to nod and give me a slight bow. The women relaxed.

"I'm not just making a joke, you know. Before we start I want to acknowledge the power and intelligence we have in this room. Hana? May I tell those who don't know you what you do?"

"Oh I hardly think ..." Her tone held no real resistance, so I introduced her as a key leader in our defense plan. Then I acknowledged the presence of the lovely woman likely carrying the next heir to the throne of Pilk. I spoke of her in my softest tones, but she held her body stiff. Her lack of comment or even eye contact told everyone she rejected my public peace offering. Very well.

I complimented Ketevan for her influence in the social circles of Pilk and invited her to introduce the next table. Yes, I know my snub of Ura was petty, but honestly, I couldn't think of a single attribute of hers to praise.

Ketevan preened as she introduced the next two women, whom she knew, of course. They took their time introducing table three, who happily introduced table four. As the crowd's gaze moved away from the first table, Ura and the princess exchanged a look of contempt, for me I presumed.

After a few musical numbers and an upbeat ballad, we left the stage. We'd gained new fans including a chancellor at one of the places of higher learning, two wives of Mozdols, and a woman in charge of the Pilk Royal treasury. Not bad for half a day's work.

Zamarran gave me another slight bow once we were behind the curtain.

"How do you feel the crowd's needs like that? I'd think you were a sorceress if I didn't know better."

"I'm certainly not that."

How could I be? I'd expected Ura's reaction but not the comradery it gained her with the princess. Nevik's wife was the most important woman in the room, and my charms held no sway over her.

The next morning I wanted to sleep in but a messenger summoned me at dawn to meet Firuza at her school. The location indicated a business meeting, not a rendezvous, so I dressed in suitable clothes and followed the young woman there.

Firuza stood in front of the building where she taught, wearing the formal grey wools of a teacher. Her long dark hair blew in the wind as she held a looking glass in each hand. She moved one until the reflection of the rising sun burned into my eyes. I turned my head away.

"If you were further away it wouldn't be so bright," she said.

"You called me here to shine light in my eyes?"

"Yes!" Her face glowed with excitement. "It's a clear day and I needed to show you another way an astronomer can help your sister." A few students gathered around and Firuza gave them looking glasses and sent them off to various rooftops.

"Ryalgar's people will need to get the word out about what's happening," she said. "This is the closest thing to an instantaneous message. It only works if we get attacked on a sunny day, but we should be ready to use it because if we're lucky, it's faster than anything else."

I hadn't woken up fully I guess. "I'm confused. How much can you say by shining sunshine into someone's face?"

"One can cover or turn the looking glass to make it blink off and on, using codes to transmit words. Look. I've got some of my students up on the roofs now, trying it out."

I glanced up. Yes, bright lights were blinking as us from three different roofs.

"You can make codes?"

"I can. I'll work with anyone to set this up. I … I've just been thinking about ways I could help, and I want your sister to know about this. You're here in Pilk, and you're my best shot at getting word to her."

I noticed Firuza said the last part loudly, so anyone could hear.

"This is great. I'll make sure she knows. Do you have any ideas for a cloudy day?"

Firuza shook her head.

"Well, I do."

She took a step back and looked at me. "You?"

"Entertainers use flags all the time. We hang them outside of taverns to communicate about rehearsals and canceled performances. The higher one hangs them the less everyone has to walk to get the message."

"So you could have a series of flagpoles, barely in sight of each other, and change flags to pass a word along?"

"Exactly. And we'd need a code for the flags, too."

"I can help with that. Would you ..." she hesitated for a heartbeat. "Would you like to go somewhere to get breakfast wine? So we could talk over the codes?"

"Are you sure?"

"Yes. I mean, this is for the cause. Your sister. My expertise." She smiled. I smiled back.

"Let's go get some breakfast wine together. For the cause."

The Good Fortunes left two days later for our longest road trip. We planned to perform in the farming nichna of Kir, the wine-growing regions of Lev, and then the mountains of Tolo.

Zamarran had been giving me odd looks ever since our lunch concert at the Crested Lark. He didn't seem annoyed with me, or smitten, thank heavens, or anything else I could put my finger on. I finally wondered if he decided I did have magical powers for dealing with a crowd.

If I did, I'd know about it, right?

I ignored his looks, thinking he'd regain his senses soon.

Kir went well. Word of what was happening in the eastern nichnas had spread, and Kirian farmers wanted to plant bushes and dig ditches to aid my father's road crew. Mirva began a journal for me, with names and ways to contact people. I suspected my father would be grateful for all the help he could get.

The Levish were less inclined to commit to manual labor, but I got several new singers including three duos who each sang in fabulous harmony. By the time we got to Tolo we were tired and ready to go home, but with only a single concert there we stuck it out. The Tolovians liked our music and, much like the Bisuites, they appeared more grateful than most that we had trekked into the mountains to perform for them.

We had one notable attendee. The wife of the ruling prince of Tolo sat front and center and never took her eyes off me as I sang. I knew she had been born to herders in Bisu and as a young woman had caught the eye of a crown prince from across the realm, managing the sort of dream match my mother had hoped for her daughters.

Despite the audience's enjoyment, when we got to the end of our performance and asked for help with Ryalgar's plans, the crowd shouted a lot of excuses. The battle would be too far away.

Tolovians needed to care for things at home. Others merely looked away as we asked.

The ruling prince's wife, however, kept her eyes on me as she walked up to us.

"We do plan to do our part, you know," she said. "Just not the way you have in mind." At our surprised reaction, she continued, speaking loud enough to be heard. "My husband is not here because today he negotiates with the other ruling princes on a plan to evacuate your tiny children, your elderly, your ill, and your pregnant. Some will shelter with the Velka or the Zurians, but most will leave their homes two anks before Kolada and journey here."

She gestured out to the audience. They had quietened down to listen. "My people have agreed to feed and shelter your vulnerable and to keep them safe for as long as *we* remain safe. It is no small thing for us to give."

No, no it wasn't. I'd given no thought at all to the needs of those who could not fight.

"That's a lot," I said. I turned to the crowd. "One more song for all of you then," I said. "A song of thanks. We didn't know about what you've already agreed to do."

"Play us some of your wild music then," one man yelled. "Yes!" others shouted.

"Wild music it is," I yelled back. "Wild music filled with our thanks."

I looked at Mirva. She had tears in her eyes.

"Did you know your people had agreed to this?"

"No. I'm surprised but proud of Tolo."

Mirva took the lead as Zamarran, Feene and I held back. She'd done some amazing solos before, but I've never heard a flute played as well as she played it that night.

I thought the evening would end uneventfully, but soon after I retired Zamarran knocked on my door.

I cracked it open. "I'm in my sleeping shift." He gave me the same inscrutable look I'd shrugged off on the trip into the mountains.

"Find a robe or a blanket. Please. I need to talk to you before I lose my courage."

My first guess was that he'd grown frightened of my supposed sorcery in front of a crowd and talked himself into leaving the band. What a mess. I grabbed a shawl and let him into the room. Small drops of sweat ran down his face even though the night was cool.

"Are you ill?"

"I'm fine. I'm ... I'd like you to marry me."

"What? That's insane."

"No. It's an incredibly sane idea. You have a problem. I solve it. You solve my problem too because everyone will stop trying to find me a wife. Neither of us will expect what the other doesn't want, and we can save money on rooms and won't get upset at each other's travel schedules, and we actually like each other."

I didn't know what to say. Everything he said was true, but ...

I touched his face. His skin felt clammy. "You're sure you're not ill?"

"Just say yes." Pain radiated from his eyes, telling me how difficult this was for him.

The varmin thing is I might have agreed if he'd asked a few anks earlier. I didn't want a husband but Zamarran was the most decent man I knew, and his arguments made sense. I'd have agreed, thinking I had no future with Firuza.

But only days ago she'd invited me over to talk about messages and looking glasses, and we'd gone out for breakfast wine and talked about flags and codes. She'd promised we'd meet again as soon as I returned.

So now I had hope. Hope for the life I wanted.

"I'm sorry, Zamarran. I love another, and I want to be with her. I'm sorry."

He left without answering me.

~ 17 ~

Better Communication

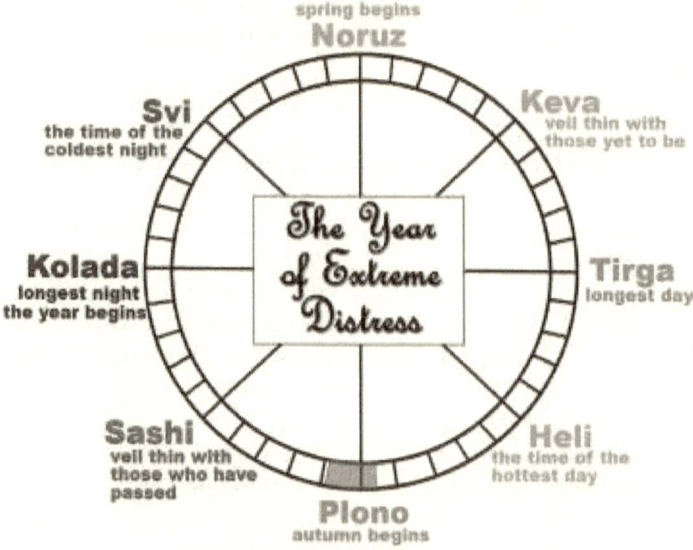

We arrived in Pilk hoping to rest for a few days before we rode over to Faroo to perform. Back at the inn, I learned that issues between Coral and Hana had exploded while I was gone. The other singers were now furious with Hana because she threatened to expose the luskies' identities if they didn't aid her in various schemes to give her more power within the Velka.

Coral's response surprised everyone. She cooked up a story that luskies could work together to force a person to do things against their own will. It wasn't true and the singers knew it, but the luskies managed to get some half-drunk lad to drop his trousers in a bar to demonstrate their combined power to Hana.

Now they planned to give her an ultimatum. Never ask anything of us or we will make you do horrible things to yourself. The luskies wanted the singers to join them at this meeting, providing backup and a show of solidarity. It was tomorrow. Would I be there?

I worried my presence would distract Coral. She'd undertaken a role to which she was poorly suited and having someone there who knew her well could make it harder. On the other hand, I could dive in and help if things went awry.

I decided to go but hide in the background unless she needed me.

I woke at dawn, but getting out of Pilk central and riding over to the wall bordering Gruen took longer than I expected. Even galloping partway, I arrived late.

Coral spoke, surrounded by the luskies and singers I'd worked with now for anks. I'd never seen any of them so agitated.

"Our last choice is to put on a second demonstration for her," she said as I slipped into the shadows, moving in closer so I could stay hidden yet hear.

"Surely you don't want to make another poor drunk lad drop his trousers?" someone said.

"No, I don't. And I don't think it'd work a second time either. We have to make her harm herself. Not seriously, just enough," she said.

"We can't do anything like that," another replied.

Wait. The luskies planned to harm Hana to make their point?

I had my misgivings about the woman. She enjoyed controlling people and her self-importance annoyed us all. But this?

"… we've got the power of suggestion on our side." Coral elaborated. "Everyone throws in all the timbre they've got, getting her to scratch her face. We start slow but build up. Then I come in with the threat to turn it bloody and leave scars if she doesn't promise to leave us alone."

That was disgusting.

I whispered to the singer next to me. "What did Hana do to deserve this?"

"She threatened to get your sister's baby taken away from her."

Oh. "How could Hana make that happen?"

"She said she'd tell Davor that Coral is a luski. Claimed her friend Ketevan could convince Davor to take the baby for its own safety. Hana owns your sister with those threats."

I wasn't the only one with misgivings. Ewalina, Coral's teacher with the fluffy hair, confronted Coral. "You're turning into the monster I promised you'd never become," she said.

The male luski from Tolo added, "And you'll turn the rest of us into freaks with you."

I stepped forward to defend my sister, sure I could turn the crowd around, but she spoke before I could.

"No. You're just helping me put on a show. I need your theatrics. If we do this, I'll be the only monster in the group. I promise."

"Aren't you afraid if you do this once, it'll be easier to do it again?" someone asked.

"Right now, I want Hana's ambitions behind us, so we can focus on defending Ilari. Ask me your question again, after Kolada."

No one said more. They accepted what she'd said. It had to be done.

"Let's go," Ewalina said to the others. "We've got work to do."

I watched the luskies, and a few of the singers, mount their horses and ride away as a group, presumably to confront Hana with a lie they hoped would scare her into better behavior. Coral rode at the rear, both pariah and savior, escorted by luskies on either side.

My doubts turned into a strange sense of pride in Coral. My tenderhearted sister had grown fangs.

I took my time riding back to Pilk, enjoying the warmth of the morning sun on my back as I gave more thought to Coral's situation. Circumstances had forced her into behavior I thought she was incapable of. But what about Davor? Did he suspect Coral was a luski? Would he care? Would he choose to take little Votto away and settle down with Ketevan and raise a baby?

Wait. I knew the answer to that last question. Davor might dislike me, but he liked other women too much and he cheated on all of them. Of course he didn't want to commit to raising a child with any one woman. And I doubted he'd want to see his son raised by an angry ex-girlfriend.

Hana couldn't make good on her horrible threat no matter how hard she tried, but Coral was probably too upset to see that.

Zamarran said little to anyone after I rebuffed his marriage proposal but his spirits lifted as we rode over to his home nichna of Faroo. Its eastern part bordered Pilk and had many inns and taverns, so our performances there on the Plono holiday didn't create much fuss.

He invited four of his friends to accompany us on to our other two concerts, both to be held deeper into Faroo. We planned to perform in the fishing lowlands along the lower part of the Wide River and then to move on to the far western edge of Faroo to hold a concert in a large settlement centered around ferries handling trade with lands to the west.

I found his friends' presence odd. None of us had ever brought guests along. Then I realized these "friends" had been hired to provide security. The parts of Faroo away from Pilk had more thievery, and rumors circulated about fights and even murders in the furthest settlement handling trade with the westward nations.

"Was this a bad idea?" I asked Zamarran as he strapped the drums he traveled with onto the back of his horse.

"Not anymore," he answered, nodding his head towards his "friends."

The first night we learned that much of Faroo along the lower Wide River already participated in Ryalgar's plans. Gypsum intended to drive the Mongols into the river where the adept swimmers of Faroo would capture both horses and warriors. They'd trained for this all summer; we just hadn't known it.

I felt much like I had in Tolo when I learned of the Tolovians' promise to safeguard our small children.

Truly, this entire endeavor could have benefitted from better communication.

Well, if we ever got invaded again …

I didn't feel unsafe along the lower river, but when we moved on to the border town filled with traders from the west, the feeling changed. Most Ilarians offered a lone traveler hospitality but we avoided contact with groups of outsiders. Here, among many non-Ilarians for the first time in my life, I understood why.

These others appeared to operate by different rules. Listening to them, I gathered that they thought anything they could get away with was okay. Constraints came from penalties for breaking rules or from the threats of others. They only behaved well if someone else forced them to.

I know that sounds odd, but *it* is what I heard. I couldn't wait to leave.

Then I discovered Zamarran had grown up in this settlement.

"I thought ..."

"I know. My parents live along the border with Pilk these days, and I learned long ago not to tell people I grew up here." He gave me the first smile he had in days. "I'd like to show you what I spent most of my youth doing. Would you go somewhere with me this afternoon?"

I followed him on foot through the trash-filled streets to a large wooden building. In Vinx, it would have been a barn, but here it was a warehouse for storing goods awaiting distribution. A deafening amount of noise poured out through the windows.

Inside, twelve men of various ages, many of them bearing a strong resemblance to Zamarran, pounded on percussion instruments of all sorts, including a few I'd never seen before. Many of them played several at once.

"It's a family drumming group?"

"Exactly! The males in my family, and some of the women too, have done this for generations."

"I've ... I've never heard of anything like it."

Most of them had stopped so Zamarran and I could talk.

"Do you think you could use drummers as well as singers?" a cousin of his asked me.

"Of course we can. Somehow."

And with that, Ryalgar's efforts, which we now all called the Chimera, gained twelve drummers. They'd join us a few days before the invasion.

Feene, Mirva, and our bodyguards spent that afternoon in a local tavern where they learned that lands to our west had received ultimatums similar to ours. Their deadlines came later, which fit the theory that the Mongols would move westward.

Something bothered me after I heard that. If traders carried news here, then they also carried it back home. News circulated, slowly and inaccurately sometimes, but it made its way to the ears of those who cared. Yet, the less anyone outside of Ilari knew of the Chimera, the better.

"You don't want to ask for help after we sing?" Mirva said when I explained my concerns.

"We need to ask for something because they expect it. But I thought we'd just ask for money. Or maybe talk about how we're training herders and farmers to fight and we'd love help, but leave out the rest."

"They might have heard of it all by now anyway," Feene said. "Zamarran has to have told people things."

"Only family," Zamarran corrected him. "Mine knows how to keep quiet. And not many Ilarians come this far west so there's less communication with the rest of the realm than you'd think." He turned to me. "You're right. We'll talk up how we're here to build a citizens militia because the Svadlu aren't up to the job. If anyone asks about the sorcery they've heard of, we laugh at them and say it's wishful thinking. Only swords and knives will save us. The people here will accept that."

So we did. After our modified request for help, we even got a few coins, and some of them from non-Ilarians, too.

"Hey. The more of them you kill the less we have to worry about," one man said as he dropped coins into the purses our bodyguards carried through the crowds.

At least two other men tried to take coins back *out* of the purse, but our bodyguards acted swiftly to stop them.

As we rode home, Zamarran turned and gave a small bow to the nichna of his birth.

"That, ladies and gentleman, is the real Faroo."

A messenger woke me at dawn the day after we arrived back in Pilk. This time I guessed right. He'd been sent by Firuza who seemed to favor early morning meetings.

Soon, I stood at an eating place near campus catering mostly to teachers. Firuza called to me from an outdoor table. She had two goblets of breakfast wine, two plates piled with pastries and sausages, and an armful of papers she held close to her chest.

"Thank you for coming to hear the information I need to get your sister."

So we still played that game.

"Have you made progress with the codes we discussed?"

"Much progress. But I need more information from you about these flags."

She pulled out sketches and we talked, ideas tumbling from our mouths. How about this? Could we try that? When I looked up, midday neared. We'd eaten every bite of the food and talked the morning away.

"Ryalgar has to know about this soon," I said. "It would be best if we could explain it to her together. Can you ride with me to Vinx?"

"Of course. When?"

"This afternoon?"

She looked surprised. "Today? Now?"

"Well, yes. It's that important. We'll stay at the small inn near the Vinx market. It's close to the main entrance into the forest and tomorrow morning we'll send a message through the Velka asking Ryalgar to come to meet with us. Or to bring us in to talk with her, whichever she prefers."

"I'll get to meet Ryalgar? Maybe go into the forest?"

I hadn't realized that would be such an enticing opportunity.

"Well, yes. Bring your moon glass and your mirrors. You two need to talk."

We arrived at the small inn before dusk that evening.

"Celestine! What an honor to have you're here."

I'd seen the proprietor at many a concert and remembered her son from my basic schooling.

"Thanks. Today I travel on my sister's business, bringing the Chimera a much-needed expert."

"Of course. We'll send dinner up to your room then, so you ladies can work. We're rather full now. Do you two mind sharing?"

"No problem," I said before Firuza could answer.

That night we finalized many more things in our communication plans, then retired for the day. What we did afterward was entirely our business.

As soon as we woke we sent our message to Ryalgar and by mid-morning Firuza and I rode little donkeys towards the Velka's lodge. Firuza's eyes were wide as a child's as we rode.

I'd made a bold move, insisting on an immediate audience from the coordinator of our realm's greatest effort. But pruck it, she was still my sister and we brought her tidings of importance.

By midday, we sat on the Velka's front porch and Ryalgar beamed with excitement as she held Firuza's moon glass and spoke of setting up a house on cliffs where Ilarians could keep watch and Firuza would oversee our scouts.

I got a warm feeling inside from knowing the woman I loved had become an essential part of our plans.

~ 18 ~

A Bigger Problem

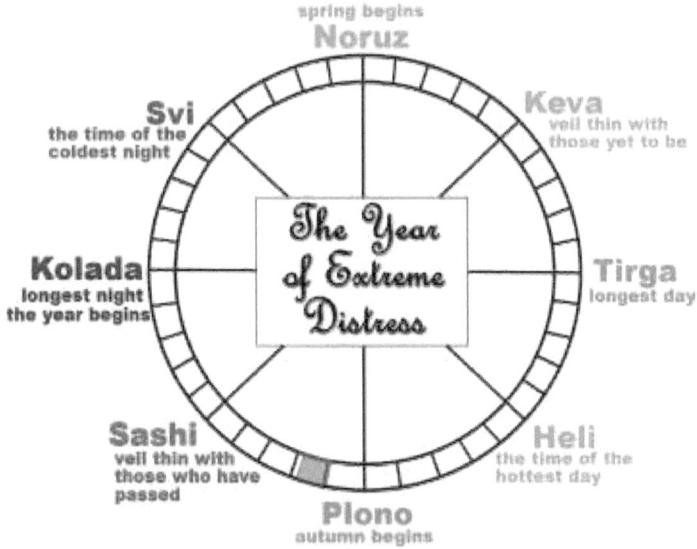

Later, I imagined the two of them talking.

In my mind, Ura would always start the conversation by saying something like "She was mean to me from the first time she saw me."

Hana would respond with "You poor dear. It probably was your lovely eyes. Celestine strikes me as the kind of woman who can't abide anyone being more attractive than she is."

Ura would wiggle in satisfaction when she heard that. Then she would whine. "Why does she have so many fans. She's not *that* good."

"No, no, she isn't. She almost seems to bewitch her audience, doesn't she?"

"No one should do that," Ura would say.

"Well, maybe we can do the realm a favor and stop this undue influence she wields. What do you think?"

Of course, maybe no such conversation ever happened. I had no way of knowing. All I knew was that after we returned from Faroo, the problems began.

The morning after I got back from the Velka, Zamarran and I met to decide if a concert in Eds was worth the risks of traveling through K'ba to get there. I already knew I didn't want to go.

He waited for me at an outdoor table at our favorite tavern near the inn where we stayed. Plono gave us a bright blue sky with a hint of gold in the leaves. I felt at peace with the world, at least whenever I forgot about the Mongols.

"The Crested Lark told me they won't book us for the rest of the year," he said as I sat down.

"Really? Are they shutting down until … until this is all behind us?"

"I don't think so. The man alluded to our falling out with the Royals as the reason. Said he couldn't afford to lose their patronage. Did we have a falling out with … anyone?"

"Not that I'm aware of. Did you ask Mirva and Feene?"

He shook his head. "Can you imagine either of them getting crosswise with a Royal?"

"Not really. Did he say more?"

"He said he'd rather not mention specifics but it ought to be obvious. How can we have angered important people and not know it? Don't you have royal friends you can ask?"

I nodded. I had two of them.

"Lady Patela would fill me in, but people in Vinx don't always know what goes on here. I do know a prince in Pilk who asks me for musical advice."

"Right. Your sister's former boyfriend."

"Yeah, only it's more complicated than that. Look. I can only tell you this because I trust you. Completely."

I saw a flash of hurt in his face, but it vanished as fast as it appeared.

"Ryalgar still sees Nevik. He loves her. His parents arranged his marriage to the foreign princess years ago. Some people know of this but most don't. His wife, she loves another, too."

"She does? What about their child then? The one who will rule Pilk?"

"Oh, it's Nevik's baby. He says he's sure. They, uh, took care to make it so. Once she has his son, she'll return to her lover's arms."

"Ouch." Zamarran saw it in a way I had not. "So Nevik is getting love right now while she carries the child of a man they made her marry? It must seem terribly unfair to her."

I hadn't considered her point of view. It *was* unfair. "Do you think she tires of their arrangement? Or at least of the one-sidedness of it?" He didn't have to answer. Of course she did.

"Why would she take it out on me?"

"That is the question, isn't it?"

"I'll try to find out."

Before I had a chance to talk to Nevik, two other places refused to book us. The Brown Stag said some patrons objected to our wild music. The Thirsty Owl, our old stand-by, told Zamarran they wanted to bring in more variety.

Nevik might not know why this was being done to me, but I had to ask.

How does one summon a prince? I decided to do it the same way he summoned me.

"You wish me to deliver this to Prince Nevik?"

The messenger's right eyebrow went up as he repeated my words back to me. "I have further important musical information for you regarding your study of the lute. Kindly send word as to where and when you can meet with me."

He looked me in the eye. "This message? From you to the prince?"

"Yes." I put the customary coin into his hand and added another. "For your additional trouble."

He shrugged and took both coins. "As you wish, madam. I will return with his message *if* there is one."

The same messenger interrupted our practice later that afternoon.

"I didn't expect to be back, but here I am. He says he will see you tonight in this tavern at sunset."

It wasn't much, but the fact that I got a response at all told me Nevik wouldn't let his pride get in his way of helping Ryalgar.

He sent a man ahead to ensure both I and a suitable table awaited him. We couldn't have the likely heir to the throne just wandering into a tavern, could we?

"I trust this is important," he said as he sat.

"I don't know, to be honest, but it could be and I felt it best to keep you informed."

That earned a curt nod.

"First, I saw Ryalgar a few days ago. We spoke of plans for sending messages around the realm. She has left the forest finally and visited the ongoing practices and seen the large numbers clamoring to help her. She seems more comfortable now with her responsibilities."

"I agree. We've spoken, too, and I think she's accepted her role as leader. I'm sure the messages you sent her helped. You have my thanks, Celestine. But why this meeting?"

"My ensemble is having trouble booking performances."

His back straightened and his chin raised. "You expect me to help your band as a thank you?"

"Pruck no."

I don't know which one of us looked more offended.

"Nevik, we're wildly popular right now. There is no reason, none at all, that multiple taverns should ban us. The first one that did, we think they spoke the truth when they told us it was at the request of Royals."

"But that makes no sense. You've several fans amongst us, and no enemies as far as I know. What other reasons were you given?"

"Just lame excuses. I wanted to talk to you because if someone in your family *is* trying to hurt me ..."

"... then I may have a problem, too."

"Exactly."

He sipped his fizzy green afternoon wine slowly, though it would grow dark soon and be time to change the beverage.

"I'll ask around. If there's anything you should know ..."

"I'm available to give you a lute lesson."

"Perfect."

The four of us were in the stable, getting ready to ride over to the small Pilk settlement along the Wide River for our next performance. I couldn't have been more surprised when Firuza entered with her horse. She'd never come to the inn in Pilk before. Her eyes had the red, swollen look one gets from crying for a long while.

"Can we talk somewhere private?" she asked me, ignoring the others.

"Of course. Uh … we were just about to leave town for a short ride." I turned to the others, seeking their permission with my eyes. I received it in nods from them all. "Would you like to come with us?"

"We three will leave now," Zamarran offered. "You two take your time and follow us."

She nodded. "Thanks. That's perfect."

We let them start down the street, then followed at a distance, moving single file through the crowded thoroughfare that led out of town in the direction we needed to go. We didn't speak until we left the city behind and could ride side by side over the wide well-packed dirt path that connected Pilk Central to this outer settlement.

"I thought our visit with Ryalgar went well," I said as she pulled her horse up next to mine.

"It went perfectly," she said. "To get the see the Velka lodge, sit on their porch. I never thought that would happen to me."

"I think she'll use all of our ideas."

"I'm sure of it. I'm trying to refine the mirror codes for her now, but …"

"… so what's bothering you?"

She slowed her horse down and moved closer, lowering her voice though my band members were far ahead and no one else rode anywhere near us.

"What I feared has happened." I could see tears forming in her eyes. "And we've been so careful."

"What do you mean?"

"I mean the teacher who coordinates the science classes spoke with me this morning about his concerns."

I didn't like where this was going.

"He said another teacher had made him aware that I exhibited unwise behavior in my personal life and this needed to be addressed."

"What?"

"He went out of his way to tell me that his concerns had nothing to do with the accompanying rumor that I preferred women sexually. He insisted he didn't care about that part."

"Right."

"That's what I thought. He said it had been brought to his attention that I'd been seen with the daughter of a teacher and such a friendship was frowned upon. I told him you hadn't been a student for over a year and asked him how long you remained off-limits as a friend after completing your studies. I don't think he liked the question."

"I can't believe this."

"Oh, it gets worse. He said that given the rumors about my sexuality, the friendship caused more concern. Understandably. The teacher who called this to his attention has a daughter your age, and the man cringed at the idea of my seducing his daughter as well."

"I bet he did." I laughed but it wasn't funny. My hands were calm on the reins, but my stomach churned with distress.

"He said my recent trip to celebrate Heli with a young man finishing his studies substantiated the pattern of unwise choices regarding relationships with students."

"What? He objected to your celebrating the Heli holiday with Feene? He's done with school *and* he's a guy, so I never thought anyone would care."

"Well, the real objection is that someone discovered that Feene and I spent the holiday with the reczavy. *That* is considered an inappropriate destination for any teacher, and my apparent attraction to both men and women raises suspicions that I enjoy whatever bizarre practices occur where the forest meets the desert in K'ba. People who do that, whatever *that* is, probably lack sufficient moral fiber to be examples for the young people we oversee. I've been asked to take a leave of absence until the end of the year."

"Oh, Firuza. I am so sorry. I thought having Feene take you there was a good idea."

"Well, it looks like wasn't."

"So now what?"

She shrugged. "The only good part of this is that I'm free to work on our communication stuff full time and to be at the lookout house in Vinx as soon as they'll have me.

Ryalgar had wanted Firuza out there as early as the Sashi holiday but Firuza had worried about her teaching obligations. But now ...

"Sashi begins in a few anks," she said. "I'll do my best to put this mess out of my mind. I've got lookouts and long eyes turning to me for direction. It's a big responsibility to be the watcher for the realm."

"It is. You should be proud, Firuza." I meant it. "Once Sashi starts, I'll be in Vinx often, getting ready for my part in the Chimera. I can come out to the lookout place, and we can see each other there."

She gave a long sigh as her eyes filled up with water again.

"Maybe, but not the way you'd like. I can't risk people deciding I'm not fit to oversee the lookouts, either."

"No one will decide that ...."

I said it, but I knew her worries weren't unfounded. There were some in Bisu, probably in Vinx too, who weren't tolerant of people like us. Some might stand in the way of Firuza doing what she needed, and Ilari couldn't afford squabbles of any kind. Not now.

"Any idea which teacher made such a fuss about you?"

She shook her head. "He wouldn't tell me, of course, but he did let the daughter's name slip. It's not a common name, so I suppose I can find out."

"What's the name?"

"Ura."

My stomach did a complete somersault.

I had a bigger problem than I'd realized.

~ 19 ~

A Sashi Toast

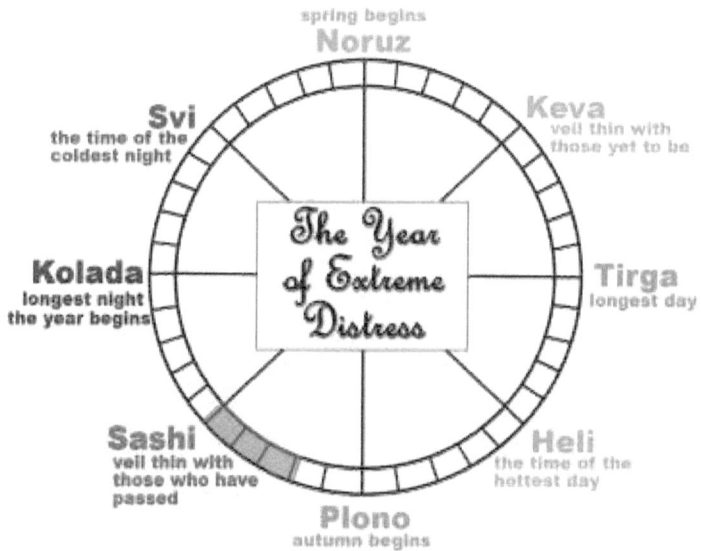

The concert along the river went well enough and when I returned to my familiar little room at the inn in Pilk the next morning, Night Sky waited for me. After chewing on the bit of dried meat I gave her, she rewarded me by curling up in my lap while I read the three sealed letters the proprietor had handed me when I walked in.

This was more mail than I normally received in an entire eighth.

The first letter, from Coral, assured me her bluff had worked and Hana had agreed to never pressure the luskies again. Good news indeed.

Firuza's beautiful script adorned the outside of the second letter. Inside, she told me that as she'd ridden back to Pilk after our conversation yesterday, she'd decided she couldn't stay here another day after what had happened. By the time I read this, she would have gathered up her things and left for the inn in Vinx. She'd make her home there until the house on the cliffs became available.

This wasn't such good news. I'd been hoping to see her in Pilk, of course, but my discomfort went deeper. Of all the nichnas in the realm, I wished she'd picked any but the one where my family lived.

Then I rebuked myself. It made sense for her to be in Vinx where communication with the Velka was easy, and she could spend her days scouting the area from which she'd command our lookouts. And, if I yearned for her to be bold about our relationship, then I had to be as bold as I wished her to be.

The third letter contained the seal of the Pilk Royals. Inside was a written request for a lute lesson. Lucky for me, it was for noon, and if I hurried I could still make it.

With Nevik's letter in hand, guards at the palace allowed me into the private chambers of the Royals. An older woman showed me into a drawing-room where Nevik waited with his lute.

I began instructing him on his hand position, playing on my instrument as I did so. He played along. Better to talk once all the servants had heard some music.

"Hana didn't cause the troubles for your band," he said finally, in a voice just above a whisper.

"Then who did?"

"Umm … my wife. She told me she asked the Crested Lark not to have you back and then she wrote several other places making similar requests."

Nevik looked as uncomfortable as I'd ever seen him.

"She used her royal status to hurt our reputation and our pocketbooks?!"

He winced. "She's entitled to do that, Celestine. Any Royal is. She seldom causes trouble, so to be honest, I think she genuinely dislikes you."

"Why? What does she have against me? Against my band?"

Nevik held his hands out, palms up, and gave the ceiling an exaggerated eye roll.

"Being pregnant has been hard on her. She's lonely. She values her friends. She recently become close to a young woman named Ura who appears to despise you and Ura probably encouraged this."

So being an important luski stopped being enough for Ura, huh?

"I gather that this Ura woman convinced her the Good Fortunes corrupted Ilari with their wild music. My wife told me the two of them decided you needed to be brought down a peg after you insulted the Royals when you pointed out the importance of women at one of your performances."

"I was trying to compliment your wife!

"Did you really say men natter on about trivia?"

"That was a joke."

Nevik laughed. "So I thought. Look, the doctor put her on bed rest until she gives birth, saying she needs quiet and no stress. On a day when she feels strong enough to write, I'll ask her to retract her requests because the realm could use your music. Will that settle the matter?"

It wouldn't. The loss to our reputation couldn't so be easily undone, but pointing that out to Nevik would accomplish nothing. So, I thanked him and left.

Part of the problem was that I knew things about Ura that Nevik didn't. Had Ura, as a luski, interjected bits of timbre into the conversations she had with the princess about my band? Coral told me luskies had a strict code prohibiting such, but Ura struck me as the sort who could justify violating any code. You know, because she'd been so wronged.

And the princess? Being lonely, communicating in a second language, and dealing with the emotional and physical burdens of late pregnancy all made her more vulnerable than most. Unfortunately, now that Ura had gotten the woman to hate me, she'd probably keep on doing so. Everyone looked for things to reinforce the feelings they had, not for things to change their minds.

Yet revealing the identity of a luski, and leading Nevik to think his wife had been influenced by one, were both dire actions. I'd keep my silence unless speaking up could do some clear good.

In truth, the damage Ura had gotten her father to do to Firuza left me even angrier than the mess she'd made for my band. Yet, that situation involved the same difficult choices. Would the school reinstate Firuza if I claimed that the complaining teacher's daughter was a luski who hated me and wanted to wreck my world and had used her powers to do so?

Unlikely. My accusations would just make more of a mess for everyone and embarrass Firuza even further.

So I continued to attend the Chimera practices every ank even though Ura did too. Many luskies now left off their masks when it was only us and sometimes they even socialized with the singers. Ura did both, placing herself in my line of vision as often as she was able, daring me to say something to her about either transgression.

I wouldn't give her the satisfaction of acknowledging her or what she'd done. The most she ever got from me was a thinly veiled glare.

At the practices, and in my correspondence with those around the realm who had agreed to join us on Kolada, many asked me why the Good Fortunes had disappeared from the better parts of the music scene. I answered that my group had been on the losing end of a misunderstanding.

People let it go, but I knew many wondered about the real truth.

At first, I waited eagerly for Nevik to make good on his promise to get his wife to retract her requests to ban us, but for anks nothing changed. Maybe she felt poorly, and he didn't want to push. Or maybe Ura argued against it and prevailed.

At least Zamarran did a great job of finding smaller and more out-of-the-way places that wanted us. We had to travel further and we made less, but as the days of Plono turned cooler and more leaves fell, we took those jobs instead.

Every ank when I came to Vinx for practice, I also stopped at the Vinx inn to visit Firuza. The first time I did, the proprietor held out a second key to Firuza's room without my asking.

"Uh…."

"I'm sorry," she said. "Did you not want to share?"

"No, it's fine with me if it's okay with her. It just that … uh …"

The woman smiled. "Don't worry, you're not obvious to others. But when a person runs a hotel they learn what love looks like. If you ask me, no one should have to hide that."

I took the key, not knowing what to say.

"Go on, go to the room. She'll be glad to see you. I promise."

And she was.

And she remained glad to see me every ank after that when I visited.

The numerical part of our defense plan fascinated me. For starters, our attackers had superstitions about numbers and Ryalgar had decided we'd face an army of a thousand.

In the first phase of our defense, our archers and oomrushers would try to stop two hundred of the attackers as they entered Ilari. One out of every five.

The remainder would ride on, entering Vinx later that morning where the forest meets the start of the Vinx cliffs. My father's road crew had created a steep new hill to narrow that entrance to a passage of only fifty paces. At the end of this corridor he'd made, a handful of reczavy would block the Mongols' entry with small bonfires. The twenty-one luskies would stand at either edge of the fires, partially hidden by the forest and shrubbery. The singers would join them.

Fifty singers attended most practices, but our numbers would more than double on that day, with the new people needing to be brought up to speed and persuaded to follow the lead of those of us who had been practicing. We hoped that the Mongols would be too busy with their bucking horses to care about the unarmed people standing around doing nothing worse than singing and making noise.

We planned to throw two hundred of these riders. One out of every four. After that, we'd put out the little bonfires to allow the horses to pass through. Then the luskies and singers would change the intent in their commands, creating a new panic to force the horses to bolt out across the plains of Vinx, reaching the waiting reczavy by early afternoon. We hoped.

But then what?

Ryalgar wanted to use the two hundred fighters who had been thrown for barter. But how could I capture these fierce warriors ready to fight on foot? Our answer had been to train twelve hundred women, men, and older children with techniques Sulphur designed wherein six of them captured a single Mongol. These amateur warriors would be hidden deeper in the forest at the start, taking care not to be seen until the remainder of the horde rode on. At least that was the plan.

Near the end of the Plono, Mirva and I treated ourselves to a trip to the market. We'd already discovered we both loved the smell of apple cider that permeated the vendor's stalls this time of year.

"How soon will you and Feene go up to Tolo?" I asked as we walked through the last of the fallen leaves.

Mirva shook her head. "We won't. He told me yesterday he'd changed his mind. He no longer plans to go with me to Tolo before the invasion."

"Oh Mirva, I'm sorry …"

"It's not like that. He won't go to K'ba either. He plans to join you. As a singer. On the day we fight."

"No. He made it clear to me from the start that he wouldn't do that."

"I know," she said. "But that's because he wanted time to think about it. Feene can't be rushed into a decision. He's made his mind up now, though, so I've decided I'll be there too."

"Mirva, please no … It's not necessary."

"It doesn't have to be. You need noise and I can play on a flute as well as others can pound on a drum."

"Of course you can, but … you're my friend."

"That's why I'll be there. With Feene. For you. Just like Zamarran."

"Why would Zamarran be there? He doesn't sing."

"No, but he's still a member of the Faroojer drumming group and he wouldn't dream of not joining them."

How could I have been so unaware? "I never considered him as part of the group when I accepted their offer. I guess I should have realized..."

"Celestine, it wouldn't be right if the Good Fortunes weren't there with you. You know it's true."

I supposed it was and I should have felt grateful. Honored. Proud of my friends. But I said nothing more because now I felt more scared than before.

The Sashi celebration would be our last holiday before it all happened, and we knew it. Firuza and I had spent lovely evenings together in the surprisingly supportive Vinx Inn, but we couldn't spend this holiday there. She had to get over to Pilk to gather the rest of her things for her move to the watch house, and I had to be in Pilk because Zamarran had gotten us our best booking since our troubles began.

On Sashi Eve the Good Fortunes played well and said little, not wanting to add fuel to anyone's complaints. Given the holiday, I expected a rowdy crowd but instead, an eerie calm overtook them. They asked for old favorites and remained wistful as we performed. A few cried at the more sentimental ones and many held each other's hands as if they wished to hang on to this life as hard as they could.

On the day of Sashi, Firuza left Pilk to move to the watch house to begin her duties. I watched her pack, subdued yet purposeful. She'd received word from Ryalgar that Olivine would spend most of the eighth of Sashi at the house with her, readying things for the days before the ultimatum. I was happy that two people I cared for would be at the same place. Even if Firuza and I had to hide our love, I could at least see them both often.

But Firuza reacted quite differently. She asked if Olivine knew about us and sighed with relief when she learned I'd yet to share something so important with my twin. Then she begged me not to tell Olivine. Not now. Not until this was over. Her request annoyed me. I insisted Olivine could be trusted but Firuza said trust wasn't the problem.

"Your sister will act differently once you tell her. To me. To you. She won't mean to, but some people may pick up on it. Please. After all that has happened, I can't take that chance. I can't even afford to be nervous about it."

I thought she let irrational fears get the better of her good judgment, but I understood that I couldn't change her mind. So even though I needed to check on the flags and other communication equipment, I promised her I'd remain silent with my twin and keep my contact with the two of them to a minimum.

How sad.

The night of Sashi itself, I felt lonely and let down. I was well on my way to both a headache and a brooding mood when Sulphur came into the crowded tavern where we played. She joined a group of saffron-caped female officers sitting against the back wall.

Somehow her random appearance at my performance breathed new life into my tired spirit. It warmed my heart to see her enjoying life. If she, a member of our army facing grave dangers, could rise above her worries to celebrate this holiday, then surely I could do the same.

At the end of our set, I joined her for an ale. We had a few laughs and drank to pleasant surprises and the hope that the days ahead would contain many more of them.

When I woke the next morning, I felt ready to face the rest of the eighth of Sashi.

~ 20 ~

A Performance for
the Eve of War

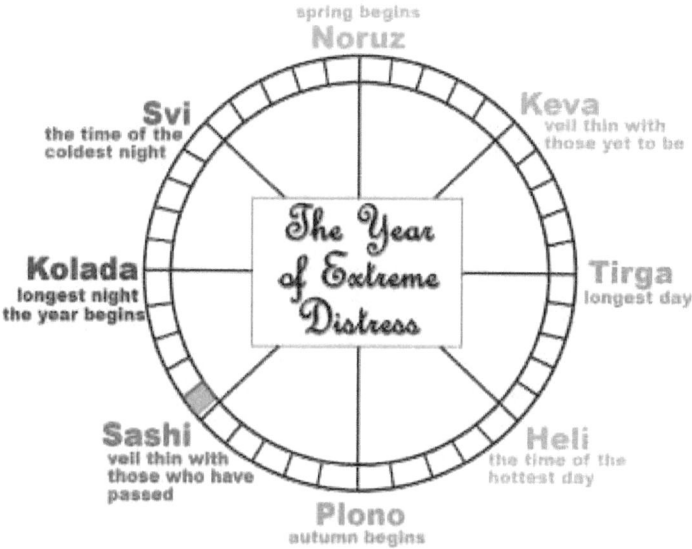

spring begins
Noruz

Keva
veil thin with
those yet to be

Svi
the time of the
coldest night

Kolada
longest night
the year begins

*The Year
of Extreme
Distress*

Tirga
longest day

Sashi
veil thin with
those who have
passed

Heli
the time of the
hottest day

Plono
autumn begins

Lady Patela sent a messenger to intercept me as the chaos of one of our biggest practice sessions quieted down. Once the hand went up, this particular messenger attempted to mimic Lady Patela's speaking voice. I found his breathy falsetto to be a poor choice.

"I am so happy to have learned that your sister Sulphur will visit the Vinx castle tomorrow night," the messenger said, adding a few overly dramatic gestures for emphasis. "And I am determined to host a dinner in her honor. Her achievement in becoming a Mozdol should have received far more attention. Please attend, despite your busy schedule, and please put together a suitable little ballad to honor your sister."

I needed to write a song? By tomorrow night?

I'd do it for Sulphur, but it might have to be a simple ditty.

The affair gave me the chance to see my parents, Olivine, Coral, and spend time with a little nephew I hadn't seen much since his birth. He sat on my lap while Coral ate, and I marveled at how the child kept getting cuter.

In the days after, that dinner would seem so peaceful, so elegant, and so incongruous with the struggles and tensions of those times. I'm grateful to Lady Patela for making us all pause and enjoy our lives, even for one evening.

Oh, and my song wrote itself, popping into my head filled with praise for my strong sister and the things she did. She acted embarrassed by it, alternating between looking at the ceiling and the ground as I sang, but her hint of a smile told me she was pleased.

Lady Patela hugged me as I left.

"You're a special woman, Celestine," she said. "I hope someday someone will write a song about you."

I don't know why her words made me cry later, but they did.

As our practices grew to include more people, I got a better sense of the enormity of our plan. I looked around, scanning the faces of the reczavy, herdhands, and farmers who had signed on to assist us. Something hurt inside of me as I wondered who would live and who wouldn't.

Was there anything, anything at all, I could do to make my part more effective? The only thing I could think of was to do my best to get riders thrown off quickly, before problems had time to develop.

Some herdhands specialized in calming young horses as they learned to let a human ride and many of these experts had helped us, doing their best not to get hurt as we honed our skills. I'd had little interaction with them because Hana didn't encourage conversation. But before I sang instructions to the animals of strangers, I thought I should ask them about staying on a horse.

Many of them congregated at a certain market stall in Vinx where hard cider, ale, and distilled spirits were sold. Today I thought I'd join them for a drink.

Eight people sat on stools sipping beverages when I arrived. The six men nudged each other as I walked up, the way men did. The two women who worked with them muttered to their friends to behave. Then one of the men looked me in the eye.

"Celestine!"

I remembered him. We'd been in basic education together. He and his little group of friends had made a year or two of my childhood miserable when they took to picking on me. I recognized now that their infantile pranks were meant to entertain each other and done without giving me much thought, but at the time they hurt.

Coral told me they singled me out because I was the prettiest girl in my class. Her logic made no sense to me. Sulphur told me they kept at it because I acted bothered and if I pretended I didn't care they'd stop. She was probably right, but I'd had no idea how to do that. Worse yet, some girls seemed to like it when the boys teased them, and my problems only got compounded by their jealousy.

Now I had no desire to speak with this annoying young man and I looked around for an excuse to move on.

"Hi. You up and left Vinx to become a famous singer! My friends and I love your music. I tell everybody how we were in school together." I could tell from the slur in his words that he'd been drinking. Something about that knowledge, and the now tattered reputation of the Good Fortunes, obliterated my normal sense of caution.

"That's nice. Do you tell them how you tormented me as a child?"

He glanced left and right, I guess to see who overheard, then he cocked his head and said, "Huh?"

"Surely you remember all the times you made me cry."

"I never saw you cry. What are you talking about?"

I suppose I did do most of my crying at home where no one could see me.

"I hated school because of you." My voice grew louder, fueled by years of pent-up frustration. "I pretty much hated Vinx because of you. Yes, I up and left and yes, I'm having a great life now so pruck all of you."

It was a colossally dumb thing to say, but it felt great. I walked away. No, I stomped away, but the rantallion got up to follow me, proving he still had no manners.

"Hey. Wait." Palms outstretched in a gesture of helplessness. "Celestine. Come back. I'm sorry. I had no idea."

I turned to face him, my hands on my hips. "You can't be that stupid."

He winced, but he didn't turn away.

"I'm *not* stupid. I wasn't the most, uh astute of children I suppose and I probably did some mean things and didn't even know it. For varmin sake, Celestine, we were what, nine and ten? I don't mistreat anyone now that I'm old enough to know better."

Maybe he didn't.

"Did you come here to yell at me in front of the people I work with?" he asked.

"No, I came here to get more information about horses when they misbehave."

He laughed at the change in subject. "Then you came to the right place. Don't you have a horse of your own?"

"Of course. But my mount is so tame and reliable. I thought we singers could be more effective if we could think like unruly horses."

"It's a good idea. So. First. An apology for whatever dumbarse things I did as a child and can't remember. Okay? I get that you remember every one of them. But if you're willing to move on, I'll talk to you about how a disobedient horse thinks."

I was too curious to say no.

"Fine. Apology accepted. Give me all the reasons a horse bucks."

"First, let's think about rearing up. Because that's what will happen first. Smoke frightens horses and your fires will cause them to stand up on their hind legs to fight off what has scared them. Bucking will happen next, or at least we hope it will. A horse bucks by kicking out his back legs, and he does it for a lot of reasons. Maybe he's in pain, or he doesn't feel like cooperating, or he feels bothered by something behind him."

He and I walked back towards the seats by the market stall, the uneasy truce growing between us.

"These are seasoned battle horses. I doubt they act up because they don't feel like cooperating," I said.

"I agree. Now, horses will keep bucking until they think they've solved the problem. So, if you want the most extreme combination to throw a rider, you want to alternate between creating fear in front of them, like you're doing with smoke and fire, and generating a general sense of annoyance that makes them buck as well. The best thing is to get the horse to think the rider is the problem. That may be difficult with horses so used to being ridden, but if you and the luskies can convince them of that, they won't rest until the rider is removed. Well, that or until they completely exhaust themselves and can't move."

"This was helpful. Thanks. And, um, I'm sorry. I'm a little on edge."

"Yeah. We all are. Don't worry about it" He gave me a hopeful look. "Can I buy you a drink?"

Oh dear.

"No, I have to get going. Thanks anyway."

In only two anks most of the realm would shut down. Classes would cease, markets would close, and all of Ilari's most vulnerable citizens would begin the long walk, or ride, into the forest or up into the mountains. People busied themselves buying supplies and securing their homes.

Zamarran surprised me with a message that I needed to come back to Pilk. He'd gotten us one last booking before the Good Fortunes went on hiatus before Kolada.

"Please. It's important," the messenger said, looking just like Zamarran would if he'd been there. I couldn't say no, so I gathered up my things and shivered through the half-day ride in the thick mist. Whatever this was, it had better be good.

Feene and Mirva waited in our old practice room at the inn.

"Where?" I asked.

"The Crested Lark. Of course." Zamarran followed me in, grinning in satisfaction. "It is a special performance, for a select group of Royals and Svadlu. We've been removed from the list of musical groups not to employ, and I wanted everyone to know it."

So, Nevik had kept his promise. Eventually.

"Any special requests for this performance?"

"Of course," Mirva said. "Ballads about the beauty of Ilari. Strong songs of courage."

"It's a performance for the eve of war?"

"More or less," Zamarran said. He gave me hard look. I took it to mean *this is not the time to be critical of our audience.* "You should be able to bring a crowd like this to a crescendo of patriotism. It will benefit everyone in Ilari if you do."

I supposed he was right. I was still a little embarrassed at my outburst in the Vinx market. Had I really told an old schoolmate to pruck off? Yes, I had. Well, this was no time to make a habit of doing that with everyone who annoyed me.

"Of course. I can do this."

The crowd dined on the finest foods in Ilari and drank its finest wines that night. Better in our stomachs than those of outsiders, right? Peeking from behind the curtain we saw the overcrowded room, stuffed with extra chairs. Candles glittered on every table, and the silver of the utensils and goblets sparkled as they reflected the flames.

Every guest wore the finest attire, as though they attended the wedding of a Royal. Earlier in the day, the proprietor had confided to Zamarran that tickets to this had turned into a status symbol coveted by Mozdols, Royals, and Ilari's most elite.

Nothing in his tone indicated he had ever banned us from his establishment. Zamarran reveled in our vindication.

I stepped on stage in my most beautiful dress, holding my psaltery, gazing at the crowd with soft eyes before I began a solo ballad. My thick coat of optimism had been penetrated by the knowledge that this could be our last performance. I would make it a worthy one.

The crowd hushed to hear me, and I began with a single, clear note which I held as they waited. Tonight, I would give them the experience they craved.

After a short ballad sung simply, Mirva joined me on stage for a more rousing song. Then Feene came out as we picked up the pace. We barely paused as helpers set Zamarran's percussion instruments on stage. Then I finally addressed the audience.

"You are here for music not words," I declared. "Honored Rulers, Warriors, and Keepers of Ilari's culture. Tonight our music is for you."

With that, we moved on to marches and reels and then a hint of our wild music which we built to a crescendo. Then the four of us looked at the audience and said nothing, just long enough to cause a little confusion. As Mirva began to play her flute softly in the background, I spoke.

"Twelve heartbeats," I said. I stepped closer to their tables and placed my hand over my heart. "Feel the twelve. Hear them in your heads and your hearts as we now pause for twelve heartbeats, one for each of Ilari's nichnas." Mirva stopped playing and we stood, completely silent, with our hands over our hearts. Many in the audience did the same.

When the twelve heartbeats had passed, we played a short medley of nostalgic favorites, with Zamarran barely audible and Mirva taking the lead, making her flute weep with emotion before it trailed off into absolute quiet. Then we stopped.

We'd done it.

The stunned silence of our audience as we finished rang louder than any applause.

~ 21 ~

Tapping on a Toy Drum

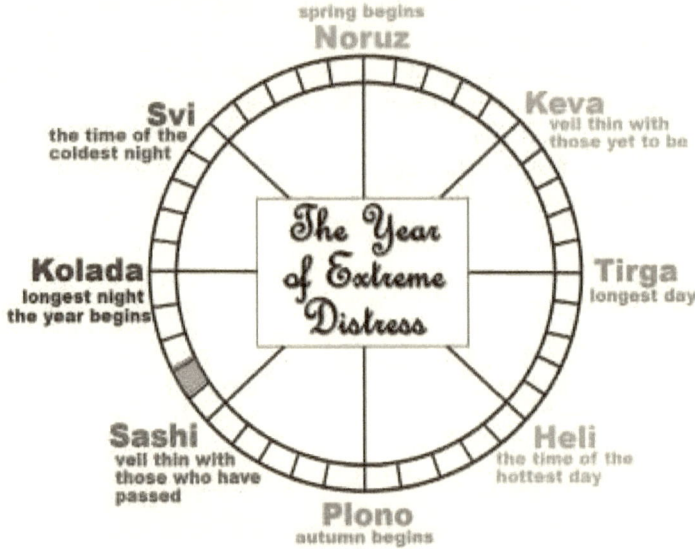

Now that I'd made the trip over to Pilk, I wanted to handle the unfinished tasks I'd left behind. Yes, they basically involved meddling in the affairs of my sisters but sometimes meddling does good. After a lot of careful thought, I'd decided I had unique opportunities to improve my sisters' lives. I intended to start with the man technically married to Coral.

"I'm sorry, miss, you can't just walk into Svadlu headquarters and talk to a Mozdol," the young but stern guard informed me, standing a little taller as he spoke. "Not usually, and certainly not now. We are busy preparing to defend the realm."

"Yes, I know." I gave him a smile filled with honey. "But he's married to my sister and it concerns a family matter."

"Davor is married?" The guard looked confused. This ill-informed soldier would have been well served to listen to more gossip.

An officer approached us from the side. His no-nonsense stride informed me I was about to be asked to leave.

"I'm sorry madam but our staff ..." He looked closer.

"Heli. You're the singer, Celestine!"

"Yes, I am."

"I, we, everyone has heard about your performance last night." He put his hand over his heart. "Your tribute to every nichna. Beautiful. Just Beautiful."

He turned to the poor guard, who really needed to get out more because he had no idea who Celestine was, either.

"What is it we can do to help Celestine?" the officer asked.

The guard started to shrug. I decided to save him by intervening.

"I know how busy you are, but I must speak briefly with my brother-in-law Davor."

"Of course. Come this way." He smiled and gestured for me to follow.

Davor looked up from his table to see me in his doorway, and his eyes widened in surprise.

"Sorry I missed the performance last night. Too much to do. Hear it was magnificent."

Nothing in his tone indicated he wished he was there.

"Thank you, but I'm here on a family matter." As I said it, I turned to the man who had brought me and gave him a meaningful look.

"Right. Of Course. I'll leave you two to talk."

"You and I have family business?" he said, making a vague puzzled gesture towards the only other chair in the room.

"We do." I moved the cape off it and sat on the edge of the seat. I wouldn't be here long. "Someone is about to try to talk you into doing something, and if you agree without thinking, or because you're upset, you'll make a lot of people's lives difficult but most of all your own."

"You care about my life?"

"No, not really. But I do care about Coral."

"You girls are something else. Most people would answer politely."

I bit back all the retorts, particularly the one that went *most people don't have brothers-in-law who flagrantly cheat on their sister.*

"Coral is a luski. She can make people do things with her voice."

"I know what a luski is." Then the rest of my words sank in. "No! Not sweet Coral."

Even as he denied it I could see his mind working to put bits of information together.

"That's what she's doing for Ryalgar, isn't it?" When I nodded, he reached his conclusion. "This is horrible."

"No. It isn't. Luskies have a staunch code of behavior and, as you would guess, Coral adheres to it more carefully than most. It's far less of a big deal than people think. But the person who plans to reveal this to you hopes you will be so upset that she can persuade you to take little Votto away from Coral."

"Should a luski be raising a child?"

"They almost all raise children. The skill has something to do with motherhood. Some are okay mothers and others are excellent ones. Coral is ..."

"... an excellent mother." He looked at me. "I recognize it. Who else would possibly raise my son?"

"The same woman who plans to deliver this news to you. She hopes to shock you into taking Votto away from Coral."

Davor continued to give me a puzzled look.

"Come on, how many women are you seeing right now?"

That earned me a glare. "Just one and to be frank things aren't going so well." Then he put it together.

"You mean Ketevan? She wants to raise little Votto? I bet Hana cooked up this idea. But why?"

"Well, Hana wants to get Coral to do things for her. As a Luski. So she's been threatening to expose Coral to you, using her threat to push Coral to cooperate. It's not working well. Meanwhile, Ketevan just wants to impress Hana."

"I hate being manipulated by women."

That made me laugh. "So do I. I thought if you and I had this conversation, it would give you time to think through what's best …"

He waved his hand in a dismissive gesture. "I get it. Ketevan pulls this off and the next thing you know she and I are raising a baby together and she wants to get married. That's what you're here to warn me about, right?"

I nodded.

"I say 'no thanks' to that plan. Not good for Votto. Not good for me."

The man was quicker on his feet and more reasonable than I'd hoped.

"Worry about something else," he said. "This is one scheme that won't work."

He studied my face before he said more.

"I got a question for you. While we're being so honest with each other. You are the first good-looking woman I've met who wouldn't even give me a little 'maybe-under-other-circumstances' smile. What did I do to piss you off when we met?"

I will never know why I picked that moment to stop living a lie. With Davor, of all people. But I did.

"You are a handsome and charming man." He smiled. "But I prefer handsome and charming women. In that sort of way."

"No. The fabulous Celestine? Likes girls??"

"Likes them a lot."

I couldn't resist adding, "Almost as much as you."

He chuckled and then the sound grew into a deep, long belly laugh.

"I would *not* have guessed that."

We looked at each other, not as a man and woman, but as two people.

"Votto means a lot to me," he said as he began shuffling things around on his desk, letting me know he didn't want the conversation to last much longer. "You're his aunt. I'm glad you told me, uh, a little more about yourself. I look forward to getting to know you better."

Who would have guessed the infamous womanizer Davor would be okay with someone like me?

So.

One Ilarian down and about fifty thousand to go.

Nevik's child had been born ten days ago, and heralds had traveled throughout Pilk announcing the arrival of a healthy baby boy.

The day after I spoke with Davor, I sought a gift for the child. I wanted something that obviously came from a musician. I found a tiny drum, made for little hands. At the palace, I asked if I could deliver the gift in person to my student.

The guard came back.

"Prince Nevik says he will see you in the drawing room."

"Congratulations on the birth of your child." I held out the gift. He smiled when he saw what it was.

"I came to say goodbye," I added. "I'll be in Vinx now until, uh, the day. I'm glad you involved me in helping Ryalgar, and I wanted to thank you for enabling us to perform at the Crested Lark one last time."

"I'm sorry I missed your performance. Those who saw it have hardly stopped mentioning it." He winced at his next thought. "You'll be out there too? In Vinx? With all the others?"

"Of course. And you?"

"I hope to fight alongside the Svadlu officers guarding the palace. Some think I should hide in the forest to preserve the Royal line, but a ruler must set a better example than that."

"Your wife and child will go to safety though?"

"Oh, they'll do more than that. She and the baby leave in six days to ferry across the Wide River to her homeland."

"Really? The new heir is leaving Ilaria?"

"It's highly unusual I know, but under the circumstances..."

"Are you sure her own land is safe?"

"Oh yes. It's far too large for the Mongols to attack."

So our Royals didn't know that those to the west had received ultimatums of their own? Why were those in Western Faroo keeping that information to themselves?

"My biggest worry is that she won't want to return," he said, "even if it all goes well here. Or that she'll insist on conditions. Conditions I can't imagine accepting."

"Involving Ryalgar?"

He nodded. "Recently my wife has spoken of changing our agreement."

"I … wanted to talk to you about that. Do you remember the woman who dislikes me and persuaded your wife to cause trouble for my band? I've reason to think she and her friends also goaded your wife into rejecting this arrangement she and you once made."

"How would you know about this?"

I recognized the delicate ground I tread on. Nevik understandably considered his relationship with his wife to be private. I, understandably, had done all I could to avoid revealing the identity of a luski. We were about to cross both lines and I didn't do it lightly.

I took a deep breath and exhaled slowly.

"This woman who dislikes me, well, she's a luski and I don't think she's a particularly scrupulous one."

"You're talking about Ura, right? *She's* a luski?"

"Yes. I don't mean to speak out of turn …"

Even Nevik knew that nice people didn't reveal the identities of luskies.

"I kept this to myself even when Ura tried to destroy me, but I speak of it now because I fear Ura influenced your wife to cause Ryalgar harm. I thought it was important enough that you knew …"

He had to have seen the conflict on my face.

"You did the right thing," he said. He picked up the baby drum I'd given him and began to tap on it with his fingers as he added "This palace nonsense drives me crazy."

"There is one more thing you should know. It may be helpful."

"Please." He stopped tapping.

"I was in Faroo a few anks ago. In the settlement by the ferries. Merchants from the west told us that every single land over there has received an ultimatum from the Mongols."

"No! We'd have heard about it if that was true."

I said nothing. He went back to tapping lightly on the drum.

"Those in the ferry settlement aren't always as forthcoming with the Royals as they should be," he admitted. "Yet I can't believe this horde of horsemen would be so bold as to threaten the large kingdoms to our west."

"I don't think these invaders see any conquest as too big. But, their tributes are due *after* ours, which means they won't be attacked until we're out of danger. As you and your princess negotiate, this could be helpful."

"Yes. It could."

He paused, considering if he needed to add more. His better judgment lost, and he kept talking.

"My wife's family forced her into an even more barbaric deal than mine, you know. Living in another land. Bearing children like a breeding animal. I wish now I'd had the sense to refuse the whole arrangement. But I didn't." More tapping on the little drum. "We Royals are raised to be obedient children."

"You have some sympathy for your wife?"

"Of course I do. I'd have to be a monster not to. She's stuck here now and she wishes to grow her influence as a Royal. I don't fault her for that, but please understand. Whether she was influenced by a luski or not, none of her demands are made out of love for me."

"I assumed as much."

"I try to give her all the cooperation as I can, except in one arena. Ryalgar will always have my love. All of it. In every way."

"Then I will continue to hope you can bring your wife and son back home, with no strings attached."

We gave each other one last awkward look and I attempted a hint of a curtsey as I turned to leave.

"Thank you." Nevik said it to my back as I walked out the door. As I moved down the hall I heard him tapping on the little drum. It sounded like a war beat and I wondered if he was thinking of the Mongols or his wife.

Six days before my mother would take Votto into the forest to hide with the Velka, I rode to Vinx.

"I hoped you'd come to say goodbye," she greeted me as she worked in the kitchen. I'd already waved to my father out in the fields as I came in.

"Of course." I put my arms around her and I held her. "I can only imagine how difficult this must be for you." I took a step back but kept both of my hands on her shoulders as I looked into her eyes. "You are being incredibly brave. You know that, don't you?"

She laughed at the idea. "No. Everyone else is being incredibly brave. Me, I'm going into hiding."

"You're saving a child by taking refuge in a place you fear. That's brave." I intended to hold my ground on this.

"Don't be silly. I'm not scared of the Velka. I suppose I resent them, but only because they took something from me, and then they went and took Ryalgar too."

"Will you be okay there, surrounded by them, dependent on them?"

"Of course I will. I can see how happy your oldest sister is and what important work she does."

"So, what did they take from you?" It was a bold question, but one I and probably every one of my sisters had always wanted to ask.

"My happiness," she said.

That seemed extreme.

"Mom, no one took your happiness. You got to have us. What more did you want?"

It was the first time in my life that my mother looked at me like I was stupid.

"I wanted to have what you have when you stand in front of a room and mesmerize them with your voice."

"You wanted to sing?"

"Absolutely not." The sound she made started as a laugh but ended as a sigh. "There is so much daughters don't know about their mothers. As a girl, I made jewelry. Beautiful pieces with colored stones. People raved about them. Then I met your father at school and he taught me the names of the rocks and promised me he'd always find more of them for me ..." Tears started to form in her eyes. "I kept it up for a long while, I was so determined. Three little girls and I *still* designed pendants and made bracelets ... People adored them. Then I got pregnant with the twins and the Velka said I had to stay in bed and..."

Why had this never come up in family conversation? Because we never spoke of those years when we were babies, that's why.

"Couldn't you make more jewelry after the twins were born?" It sounded naïve as soon as I said it.

"You know my mother died before I married. And my few remaining relatives lived in Lev. I had to depend on your father's family for help, and none of them thought my jewelry was a priority."

She'd already sat on one of the stools in the kitchen, so I did the same. My mother usually had a dignity about her, but now she raised her voice and waved her arms about as she spoke.

"Oh you have such beautiful baby daughters," she mimicked. "Everyone told me that. I did, and I loved you, but all anybody would let me create was more daughters! Gorgeous marketable girls that could be turned into something better than my jewelry. So I did my best to polish you and shape you the way I would my finest necklaces. I wanted each of you to sparkle enough for the best men in Ilari to want you for their own."

"*We* became your jewelry?" This put my mother's fascination with turning every daughter into a perfect specimen into a new light. "Did Dad, did others, prohibit you ..."

"Oh, they hardly had to. Five, six then seven children five years and younger? I was happy to have time to wear a piece of jewelry, much less create one. Your father, he would not listen when I told him how miserable I was. And then, and then ..." Mom's voice rose as her cheeks got redder. "... when it turns out one daughter has an artistic eye, what does he do? He has the nerve to tell her how important it is she pursues her art!"

Her eyes filled with water. "Every time he says it to her, I just want to vomit ..." The tears began running down her cheeks. "When he made, when he made that varmin metallic paint for Olivine," — the sobs started — "when he spent days grinding up rocks, doing the sort of thing he'd once sworn to do for me and never did ..."

She didn't finish the sentence, but collapsed into the crook of her arm, and sobbed with her head on the table.

I didn't know what to say.

Then I looked up and saw Dad standing in the doorway and I really didn't know.

~ 22 ~

Those Moments of Happiness

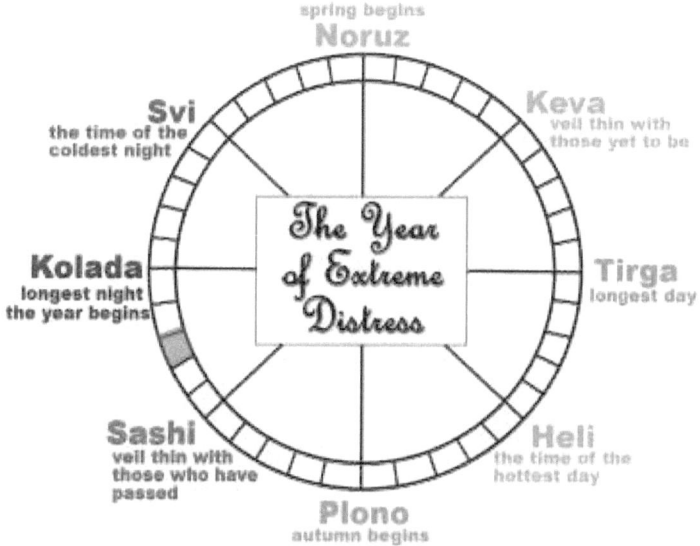

"Markita." He almost whispered her name.

She looked up at him.

"I knew, Markita. I knew. But I had no idea how to make it better. We could only afford local girls to help out, and you never liked the ones we found. And the little ones all wanted you; they clung to your skirts as you walked. What could I do?"

"You *know* what you could have done," she said.

"I couldn't ask my mother to give up her dreams for yours! What kind of choice is that?"

I looked at them both, and for once in my life, they were on stage and I wasn't. I had become the audience, with no speaking part in this scene. I watched, silent, as a decades-old drama played out.

"I wanted you to be happy," he said. "I did. I thought if I kept pretending you were, maybe after a while, you would be."

"That worked well."

She stood up and straightened her shoulders as she blew out a deep breath. She was almost as tall as he when she stood, and she looked him in the eyes. "I leave in six days and may never see you again. I'd rather not part dwelling on this. Can we say no more about it?"

"If I could undo it all, or do it better, you know I would."

"I know."

She turned to me. "Are you hungry? Would you like some sort of snack before dinner? I can make you a little something now."

I suppose I could have done her a favor and said yes, but …

"Um. No. I'm not. I want to gather some things from my room. Things I'd like to have over the next few anks."

"Won't you be staying here at the farm?" she asked.

"No. I need to be … elsewhere. I only rode over to see you before you left."

"Well then, see me. Let's sit on the porch and visit.

Dad glanced at both of us. "I need to get back to …"

"I'll come back to the farm in ank or so," I promised him. He nodded as he left.

"Mom, I'm sorry I set you off. I didn't realize …"

"It's okay." She raised her palm to stop me. "Say no more, please. It's better you know. At least what I have to say to you now will make more sense. Come." She put her arm around me and walked me out onto the porch. Once we sat, she leaned forward, anxious to share.

"I wanted to get married," she said. "To your father. And maybe have a child. But, don't take this wrong. I never had that much interest in motherhood."

"Not every woman does." I didn't hold that against her.

"I don't know where Coral got it from, but it wasn't me. All that girl ever wanted was to have babies. I never understood."

"She is a happy mother," I agreed.

"I was more like Olivine, to be honest," Mom said, ignoring my comment. "But that's not my point. What I'm trying to say is pretending one is happy raising seven children is, well, a lot like pretending to be happy you are married to a man. When you don't want to be. You can pretend all you want but it isn't going to make it true."

Mom really had *wanted to talk to me. Well, if this was going to be an honest conversation ...*

"I'm in love with a woman."

"I realize that. What I only realized recently, however, is that I did not wish the same sort of misery for you that I endured. Misery with many moments of happiness too, mind you, because life will sprinkle those in despite the pretense. And when they do sneak up on you, people will say 'See? She *is* happy.' But those moments don't take away the sorrow of never being the person you wanted to be. No one should live that way."

"Mom? Lots of people do."

She laughed. "My clever daughter. Yes, I think you're right, they do, in many ways. But let's not have you be one of them. Okay?"

"I'm not sure what other options I'll have ...

"Neither am I, but hiding your life from your family won't be part of it. I promise you that."

"Thanks, Mom ... I ..." I don't why, but then I asked her "Am I the prettiest piece of jewelry you made?"

She put her hands over mine and laughed. "Don't tell your sisters, but you've always been that and you always will be."

"Even when I don't marry a prince?"

"Especially when you don't. Any chance this woman is a princess?" she said with a wink.

"Sort of. I mean she was some kind of Royal back in her homeland."

"Really? Well then. We'll call it close enough."

Then Mom listened, as we sat together on the porch in the late afternoon sun and I told her all about Firuza and why I loved her.

I stayed the night at the farm. The next morning the Svadlu had asked us to gather at a nearby farmhouse. so they could speak to everyone involved with the Lions. I'd sent messages to singers who hadn't been able to join a practice yet, begging them to attend this one. Better to have a little preparation than none.

In the early morning breeze, the luskies huddled together on one side, masks on. They each held a wooden cone carved to amplify their voices. The reczavy who would light the fires to halt the horses stayed on our other side. The ten or so herdhands sat on the ground in front of us, scooting forward to be as far from the other two groups as possible. Behind us all stood the hundreds of farmers of Vinx who had trained to capture those thrown from their horses.

"You know what the biggest problem is in battle?" an older man wearing a Mozdol's scarlet cape yelled out into the crowd.

We muttered among ourselves, guessing at the answer.

"It's what I'm seeing now. Confusion. As soon as things don't go according to plan, no one knows what to do. It's a mess."

We nodded. That made sense.

"How often do you think things go according to plan?"

"Never," one of the luskies said.

"She's right, people. Nothing ever goes according to plan. So, does the bigger army always win?"

We shook our heads. We hoped that wasn't true.

"Then who does?"

"Sometimes it's the luckier one," Feene yelled out, surprising us all.

"You're right, young man. Don't underestimate dumb luck. But we can't do anything about it, so if you remove luck, which army wins?"

Coral stood up on the bale of hay she'd been sitting on and yelled "The one that deals best with whatever really happens."

The man shaded his eyes with his hand, the better to see Coral.

"Bonus points to the lady with the red hair. So, today we get ready for the unexpected."

And we did. We talked about rain, snow, wind, and thunder. About a second group of envoys showing up instead of fighters. About half of Vinx coming down with colds the day before. I don't think the scenarios everyone came up with were half as important as the fact that it got us all thinking about "what ifs."

Late in the afternoon, I walked around, thanking every singer and telling them how important their voice would be. I counted as I went. Twelve from Gruen. Seven from Bisu. Fourteen from Scrud. Two singers from Faroo. The drummers hadn't come, presumably because of the long distance and the size of their instruments.

I thought of Zamarran, with his beloved band on pause and little to fill his time other than drumming with relatives he seldom saw. I hoped he cared for himself and stayed well. The Good Fortunes would need him, I would need him, when this was all over.

Then I studied our masked luskies, looking for Ura's unusual mole. I couldn't find her. Had she stayed home today, disappointed that she and her friends hadn't been able to create more problems for my family?

I always left Coral alone at these practices because she preferred it that way, but today I felt sad as I watched her walk off with the other luskies. I could have used a visit with her.

By the time I gathered my things, nearly everyone had left. I thought of asking Feene and Mirva if they wanted to go get a mug of ale before the sun set, but the two of them snuggled together against the cold as they walked to their horses. I knew what they were off to do. So I left alone, with nothing to look forward to other than finding out what the tavern in Vinx was serving for dinner.

The next eight days were the loneliest of my life. I missed my band and I missed playing together. I wanted Firuza in my arms. I wanted my family, whether we got along or not. And yet, the best thing I could do for everyone seemed to be to leave them alone.

At least the hotel had some advantages. It was set near the Vinx market, which served as the pipeline of information going in and out of the forest. I had a lot of communicating to do with the Velka as we finalized the plans for the lookouts. Schools and businesses were supposed to shut down two anks before Kolada, but the many people not going into hiding still needed to be sheltered and fed. So the inn remained open even as the food selections grew more meager. The remaining market stalls provided what little other food could be bought.

Staying at the inn also kept me a short ride from the farm, where I got supplies and checked in on my father. And it wasn't much further of a ride to the lookout house, where I had responsibilities to handle and could see Firuza from a polite distance.

At night, I wrote music to perform someday and I spent an insane amount of time sending letters to singers around the realm. Our next big practice was sixteen days before Kolada. I wanted them as prepared as possible and I wanted Hana to know our strength. Somehow, I hoped that knowledge would nudge her into better behavior.

Sixteen days before Kolada the Lion gathered at my parents' farm. I came early hoping to talk to Coral before others arrived. I found her in the barn with her horse but without her luski mask.

"Davor doesn't care that I'm a luski," she called out to me, with a big grin. "The school doesn't care. Much. And neither does Mom. I am done hiding. I'm going to be Ilari's first public luski!"

Wasn't that a nice surprise!

"I'm so glad. I'm sick of pretending I don't know you!" And I was. It felt so good to walk arm in arm with her over to the rest of the group.

I began my scan of the crowd, counting them in my head. We singers had more than doubled our numbers since the last meeting! Even I couldn't identify some of them but it didn't matter. They were here and I could use them. As the crowd grew, Hana gave me quizzical looks from afar but said nothing to me.

She took charge as we settled into place, leading off by telling us of the various families who had offered to lodge those from other nichnas. Everyone, including *all* of us singers, was to be here and housed in Vinx within seven days.

Then she began to go over the codes and communication plans I'd help develop. No one had bothered to tell me this would be part of the meeting. As Hana explained the elaborate methods of communication Ryalgar, Firuza, and I devised, she did it without ever once mentioning any of our names.

That didn't surprise me. However, I *was* surprised when she moved on to giving us assignments.

"Assignments? I thought we all were working together? What's to assign?" Someone else said it but it mirrored my thoughts.

"I've decided we'll work in five teams to make it easier for us to know where to stand. We'll start with two teams on either side of the line of fires. The clearing in between is only fifty paces wide, so we can move back and forth in safety if the smoke gets too thick on either side. Now. All luskies have been given a number."

Of course they had.

"Singers, you're being assigned by your performing groups. So team one is luskies one through five, anyone from Celestine's performing combo, and the entire choir from Zur. The large gong goes with them. Team two …"

I stopped listening. This was ridiculous. Hana didn't even know about many of the singers who were here today. She'd never bothered to ask me for a list of who was involved. I'd have to find a way to place them within her order later.

"Team four." Hana kept talking. "You're obviously luski numbers sixteen through twenty, all the drummers from Faroo, the three singing duets from Lev, and the kids' choir from Pilk."

Oh, so she had heard about the kids' choir.

"Team five will be a special assignment team, a duo to handle emergencies as they arise. It will consist of me and Coral."

What? Hana intended to keep Coral with her on a short leash? Not if I could help it.

"Your team has no singer," I shouted. "I'll join you two if you like."

A look of surprise crossed Hana's face. She hadn't expected challengers.

"Thank you, Celestine, but I'll manage that part myself. Your considerable singing talents are best used elsewhere."

What could I do?

~ 23 ~

A Fascination for Bugs

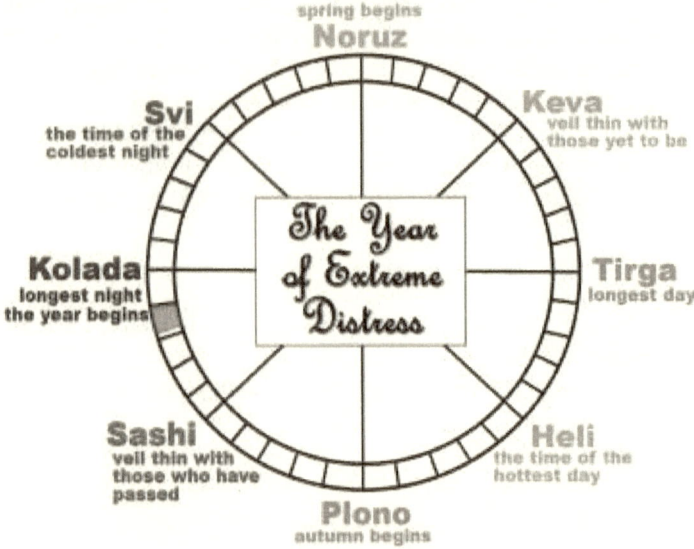

Coral and Hana left the gathering together, their sharp gestures indicating the animosity in their discussion. I couldn't imagine how my joining their conversation would help, so I returned to the inn and my self-imposed isolation.

Alone in my room, I missed Night Sky. I'd considered tucking her into my saddlebags when I left Pilk, but the little cat belonged to no one, not even me, and I didn't feel right taking her from her home. I wished I could have asked her, though. Maybe she'd have come. Maybe she missed me too.

I thought of her as I strummed notes on my psaltery. I seemed to have acquired an unfortunate number of insects in my room. I blamed the colder weather, but perhaps a slow decline in the room's cleanliness contributed, as did Night Sky's absence. She always chased bugs

Bored, I started to sing to the insects. A few of them surprised me when they stopped doing whatever bugs do and looked at me. Well, at least they turned their little bodies so their heads faced me. I kept singing. One by one they took flight and flew towards my face. Straight at my mouth.

I screamed. Yes, there were only three of them, but they came right at me.

When I closed my mouth, they stopped. It seemed to have been an instinctual thing, the way insects fly to candles and lanterns. Once I made no sound, they lost interest.

I didn't want to, but I had to try it again.

"Come to me, little bugs," I sang in my sweetest tones.

Six of them came at my face before I knew it. Those little pruckers were fast. I put my hands up, but again stopping my song diverted them. They flew off as if I'd blown the candle out.

One more time. You can do this.

Someone knocked at my door.

"Madam! Are you okay?"

"Yes. Thank you. It's nothing. An insect frightened me."

I heard his laugh. Fine. Let him think I was a silly woman.

"Come to me, little bugs." I sweetened the melody and prolonged the sound. This time a swarm too large to count took flight towards me.

Don't scream or that buffoon will be back.

I covered my mouth and didn't make another sound for a long while.

Little girls learn that bugs are repulsive. I don't know why. Little boys often find them fascinating. I could speculate on the influence of our assigned roles involving hygiene in the home, but the reasons didn't matter. I needed to develop a little boy's fascination for bugs, and I needed to do it fast.

Why did my solo voice affect these creatures? I recalled them holding still in the past when I sang, but having them fly at me was new. Had all my practice finally enabled me to break through some barrier? I had no other explanation.

Could I control larger creatures? I shuddered. The idea of hordes of rats heeding my summons was far creepier. Maybe I could learn to like bugs, but rats were out of the question.

Yet, the time I'd spent working with my voice left me with an instinctual feel for what I did. The light analogy seemed adequate in that I attracted creatures used to moving with little volition, while luskies could only control creatures with a mind of their own.

Like it or not, rats made active decisions about their actions, as did squirrels, birds, and anything larger. I felt as if I didn't have to worry about a flock of crows diving down upon me. And, my voice had to be heard to be effective, so I needn't fear thousands of mosquitoes from the marshes along Bisu heeding my summons.

Good. I had my limits. That fact brought comfort.

Nonetheless, tomorrow I had to be my bravest self and go outdoors and discover the full extent of this.

It rained during the night, and I woke to muddy ground and cloudy skies. Perfect. Few others would be out for a morning walk. I went as far as the edge of the forest and then I wrapped a thinly woven scarf around the lower half of my face, the way I might on a cold morning. I began to sing a sweet ballad about a young man's love, putting intention into my voice. I already knew anything not human cared about my tones and intent, not my words.

Out in the open air, the results frightened me less. Various flying insects moved in my direction, attracted to the noise but not frantic to reach its source. The scarf made me feel safer. When I had several on the scarf, and a few more on my face, and a couple in my hair, I paused and breathed. Slowly. None were harmful as far as I knew, and none saw me as a threat. I was safe. I was fine. My face itched something horrible at the touch of their tiny legs, but I could stand it a bit longer. I resumed singing.

By the time I finished, I'd amassed quite a collection of insects, including a few too near my eyes. I blinked as I pushed the panic back. Then, softly, I squeaked out an awful version of the same ballad, filled with the message *get out of here*. Some bugs responded faster than others but before I'd finished the song they'd all left except for one ladybug who seemed to like my scarf. I let her be.

Unfortunately, they went off in every direction, driven by whatever whims drive a bug. I could make them go, but I had no clue of how to send them at someone else, which is what I wanted to do. How could the mere act of calling and dismissing a swarm of insects be of any use?

Maybe with a second singer I could at least send swarms of them back and forth and annoy anyone in the middle. It was worth a try. I needed another singer, one not inclined to question my theories. I needed Feene.

Feene and Mirva had gone back to Pilk to locate a cart and bring the rest of their things here. I took it to mean they'd decided they'd be together afterward. They planned to return in an ank, but I needed to figure this new skill out sooner. I hired a messenger to ride over and tell them I needed help with a new idea.

Late the next afternoon, a wagon and three horses arrived at the inn. The wagon contained a lot of clothes and personal possessions, a lot of drums, a small brown dog with a tail that wouldn't stop wagging, and a little black cat. Zamarran rode the only horse that wasn't pulling the cart.

"We all came!" he shouted as I came outside when I heard the commotion. Several other guests took a look but went back inside. Popover ran over and licked my hands. Night Sky came and stood next to me, indicating I would be forgiven for leaving if I petted her now.

"You've got some great new idea?" Feene asked.

"I wouldn't say great. Maybe useful if it works." I turned Zamarran. "I'm glad you're *all* here."

He caught my intonation and gave me a small smile that said *don't worry, we're still the best of friends*.

"Come join me for what passes for supper now," I told them. "Maybe tonight we can play a song in the tavern to thank our hosts. Tomorrow morning will be soon enough for this other thing."

Feene and I spent most of the next day at the forest's edge, falling back into the familiar rhythm of working together. Only instead of trying to please a human audience, we turned our focus to the simplest of creatures. True to my theory, both Popover and

Night Sky found our efforts uninteresting, and after their long hard journey riding in a cart, they spent most of the day napping.

Feene hadn't spent as much time practicing with animals as I had, and the insects ignored him when he sang. But if I sang, and he joined in, many made their way towards him to check out the second source of music. Feene thought that our sound had a synergy, like I was the light source and he was a mirror and we both drew the bugs. Maybe?

Finally, we got them to fly back and forth between us. They could hardly be considered an attack swarm as they moved, but perhaps it would have some purpose.

"What are you planning to use this for?" Zamarran asked when he walked out to check on us.

"She doesn't know." Feene made a face at me. "I can tell." He turned to me. "You don't have any idea, do you?"

"You're right, I don't. I only know that I no longer trust the woman coordinating the Lions, and I'm certain Ura hates us as much as ever and they both will be out there with us. I think we need all the extra ideas we can get."

"Isn't this a stupid time for petty squabbles?" Mirva asked as she walked up.

"A very stupid time," I agreed. "That doesn't stop some people."

We all agreed on that.

Having friends nearby made the time more bearable, and Night Sky's snuggling with me as I slept made my room seem like home. A couple of days later I rode over to the farm to wish Dad luck with his part in this and to say farewell until … after.

When I arrived, Dad worked in the barn, putting together some feeding device for the animals.

"Coral isn't here," he said as I walked in. He and I had spoken little since Mom left, confining what conversation we had to exchanging information about my sisters while I dropped off things I no longer needed and gathered up things I could use.

"I didn't come to see her. She and I will be together when … it happens. I came to see you. To wish you luck in all you are doing for the realm."

"Thank you, Celestine. I wish you the same. I'm proud of all my daughters."

"You're even proud of me, Dad?" I couldn't resist saying it.

He gave me a funny look.

"I've always been proud of you." Then he checked himself. "I don't always understand you but that's a different matter."

I wondered how much he and Mom had talked.

"You don't understand my wish not to marry?"

"I don't understand why you spend so much time on your appearance. I don't understand why you aren't more practical, don't like science, and why you enjoy having crowds of strangers pay attention to you. And yes, I don't understand why you don't like men."

"I do like men. Some men. This has nothing to do with liking any group of people. It has to do with …"

"I understand what it has to do with." He cut me off. "I'm sorry, Celestine. This is a big adjustment."

He surprised me. With all the time he spent in Pilk, over at the schools, he spoke of tolerance for all sorts.

"I thought you accepted …"

"Other people's children being different? Yes, I'm quite tolerant of that. Happy to teach them. Turns out it's more difficult when it's your own."

"Other parents accept …"

"I know they do. And I will too. Someday."

"I see. Do you know who …"

"Yes, your mother told me, and that's part of the problem. Markita didn't understand why it bothered me to learn you slept with a colleague of mine. Your mom never worked outside the home; she doesn't appreciate the undercurrents in a workplace. But, as I said, I'm proud of you and what you're doing. The work you and …" I could sense how he choked on the phrase *you and Firuza*. "The work that was done on the signals and communication is exemplary. It may be what saves us. It is something to be proud of."

"Thanks, Dad." I couldn't resist. "Next time I see Firuza I'll let her know how impressed you are with the work we did."

He winced but he said nothing.

"Be safe, Dad."

"Thank you, Celestine. You go with my love. Remember that."

An ank before Kolada, Hana called a meeting of all the singers. It was basically a roll call to make sure we were there in case the invasion came early. Ura came with her, which was odd given she wasn't a singer, no matter how much she'd once wished she was.

"Where have you been?" I asked Ura, hoping for information.

"I missed some practices because I've been in the forest with the Velka." She said it like she'd received an award.

"Really? They hardly let anyone visit, much less at the time like this."

I thought she was making it up to impress me, but I was wrong.

"*I* took Ura into the forest with me," Hana strode over, interrupting our conversation with a glare at both of us. "I'll be traveling to Eds on some luski business for a few days, and I needed to make sure Ura was informed enough to handle issues for me while I'm gone."

Several things struck me as odd.

One. Why in the Goddess's name would Hana leave town? She coordinated one of the most important things to ever happen in Ilari. You don't go away for a few days in the middle of that. And there was no such thing as luski business.

Two. What in the world qualified Ura to fill in for Hana? I couldn't think of a worse choice.

Three. Why had Hana's glare at Ura reeked of *why did you tell her that?* I didn't care if the little snit went into the forest and wanted to brag about it.

"Did you enjoy your time with the Velka?" I asked the question mostly to annoy Hana.

"Oh yes. I got to go there twice. Both times your sister was too busy for me," she gave a little sniff, "but once I got to spend time with your grandmother, and then I got to be with Ryalgar's friend Joli. They are both very important Velka people."

Hana placed her hand on Ura's arm and gave it a little squeeze.

"I spent lots of time there. With both of them." Ura couldn't help herself.

Hana squeezed harder and pulled Ura slightly towards her.

"Enough talk. We've got things to do."

I made my rounds, counting musicians and noting where each had found lodging, in case I needed to reach anyone. I reminded everyone of the signals we'd see if the horde came early, and I told them all where to find me if they had questions. And just to make sure no one wandered off too far, I scheduled a meeting of my own in six days. I'd take roll call again then. I left knowing my part of this was under control.

As to Hana's proposed trip to Eds and Ura's chummy time with the Velka?

Both events bothered me.

~ 24 ~

Finding an Old Friend

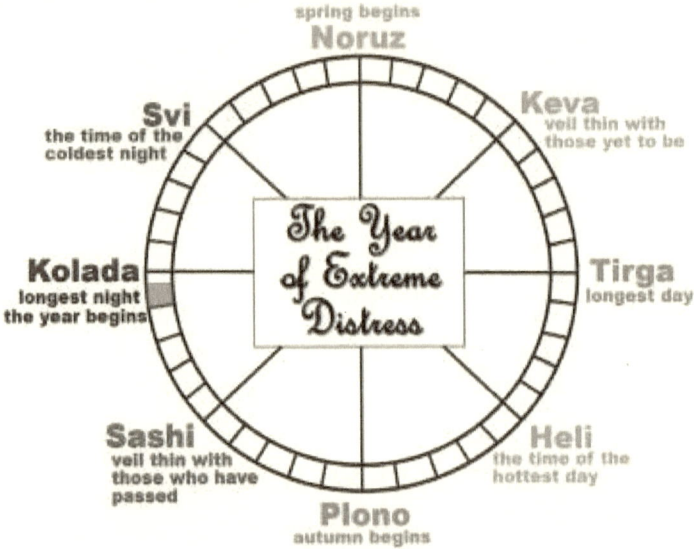

spring begins
Noruz

Svi
the time of the
coldest night

Keva
veil thin with
those yet to be

Kolada
longest night
the year begins

The Year of Extreme Distress

Tirga
longest day

Sashi
veil thin with
those who have
passed

Heli
the time of the
hottest day

Plono
autumn begins

I woke up in the middle of the night wondering how I could have been so stupid. To be accurate, I woke up because Night Sky draped her little body across my neck, and as I pushed her aside I wondered how I could have been so stupid.

I'd worried about Ura using her luski voice on all sorts of people to make trouble and I may have been right in every case. So why hadn't I worried that Ura used her luski voice in the forest to coerce Joli and my grandmother, too?

Why else would Hana take her there?

Hana had ambitions she wanted to further, and she saw the luskies as a weapon to use. Every luski had refused to be bribed or

182

bullied into taking on Hana's special projects, as far as I knew. But Ura was different. She'd more than demonstrated that her only consideration was to get what she wanted or, if not that, to get even for not getting it.

Here, alone in the middle of the night, it seemed obvious. Hana had taken Ura to the Velka to persuade Aliz and Joli to do something Hana wanted done.

When I got to the Velka stall in the market, three women packed up their goods.

"You're leaving for the day?" I asked.

"We've been told to start bringing our wares home," the young one replied. "We'll be back and forth for the next few days and then we'll shelter in the forest until this passes."

"Then I'm glad I found you. I need to get word to my grandmother."

"You'll have a hard time doing that now, Dearie," the oldest one said. "We heard Aliz has headed off to Eds."

"Oh dear. Then I have to get in touch with Ryalgar."

"Can't do that either," the young one added. "She's supposed to go to Eds with your grandmother."

"This makes no sense," I said.

The chubby middle-aged one spoke up. "Joli, she created a ruckus by sending Aliz and Ryalgar to Eds to guard the entrance up there. They didn't want to go but had to do as they were ordered."

I thanked the women and left them to their packing.

Maybe I needn't worry. Eds seemed a safe place to be now, the sort of place you'd send someone you cared about. However, I'd heard Hana couldn't take over the Velka until Aliz stepped down or passed away. And, I'd heard Ryalgar was her main competition for the job. It didn't sound like she'd want to manipulate anyone to protect Aliz or Ryalgar, but more like she'd want to do the exact opposite.

I shared the story with Mirva, Zamarran, and Feene over lunch. Mirva had been to Eds. She said goat herders' homes dotted steep hills where the results of a skirmish might never be discovered. As she described the terrain, a messenger interrupted our growing worry.

"Madam?" He addressed me, awaiting permission to begin. I nodded. He was the one who had attempted to mimic Lady Patela the last time he delivered me a message. As he raised his hand to don the mask, I wondered what to expect this time.

Both of his hands flew into the air in panic and then rested on top of his head in distress.

"Please. I, Lady Patella, have heard you are nearby. You must come to the Vinx castle immediately." He placed the back of his hand on his forehead in a gesture of becoming faint. "It's my daughters. Perhaps they will listen to you. You must try." He reached out both arms to plead with me and held them out for an extra heartbeat for maximum effect.

If we repel these invaders, I'm going to find him a job in a theater and save everyone on the street from his theatrics.

"Tell Her Highness I will come immediately."

"Better go," Zamarran whispered as the messenger left. "She's our biggest fan."

"I like her, but I don't see how I can help. The last time I visited, her daughters couldn't take their eyes off of Sulphur, the amazing woman Mozdol."

I arrived early in the afternoon to find Lady Patela and her youngest son on the porch, their bags packed for the journey into the heart of the Zurian forest where most of the Royals would hide.

"I'm so sorry to hear of your troubles."

"They've run off," she said. "We've searched everywhere. I thought maybe if you played a song they'd come out, and then you could talk some sense into them."

"Are they playing games? Don't they want to be safe?" This puzzled me.

She sighed. "They fancy themselves as women warriors in training. Their father indulged them by letting them practice with the farmers, and now they want to stay for a few more days."

"Could you let them?"

She looked horrified. "Then how would they get to safety?"

There had to be a way. Who could be trusted with two twelve-year-olds?

"My mother is in the forest with my nephew. No place is safer. I'll get the Velka to bring your girls to my mom. I know you'd rather they went with you, but I promise they'll be safe with her."

She hesitated, glancing at her nine-year-old son. She wanted to get on the road.

"I give you my word. Tell your husband to have your daughters ready on the morning of five days before Kolada. I'll bring them to the Velka then."

It seemed so simple. I didn't give the promise a lot of thought.

The next morning I went to the market early, to catch the Velka while they packed up more goods. I explained my need to contact my mother about watching two young princesses.

"You know, that is one of the oddest things Aliz has done in her life," the middle-aged woman remarked.

"What is?"

"Letting your mother, no *begging* your mother, to come be safe with the Velka. Aliz is a good woman, but she had a strong dislike for your mama after the woman made your whole family pretend she was dead."

"Yeah, that is the kind of thing that tends to piss people off," the older Velka agreed. "Never got to see any of you. Hardly got to see her son. We were all amazed when Aliz did an about-face, but I guess having her first great-grandkid brought out the softie in her, huh?"

My insides went cold. My grandmother wasn't mean, but she was strong. She might allow my mother a safe refuge despite their history, but she'd never beg her to accept it.

Unless she'd been nudged. On some deep level, she cared for my dad and her progeny. But Hana wanting my mother safe in the forest made no more sense than Hana wanting Ryalgar and Alize safe in Eds.

That night, I ran my puzzling new information by the Good Fortunes. Mirva thought maybe my grandmother wasn't half as angry as the women in the market thought. Maybe she'd hidden her concern for her family all these years to appear strong.

Maybe. I'd met my grandmother and Mirva hadn't. I wasn't so sure.

Zamarran thought none of this had to do with my mother. "Hana could care less about your mom. It's the other person Hana cares about."

"What other person?"

Zamarran laughed at me. "The baby. He means everything to Coral."

Of course. This *had* to be about little Votto. Okay, why would Hana want to keep Votto safe?

That night, I had to decide. Go to the farm or not.

The only two people who knew more about the situation were at the farm. My fears would alarm Coral despite my complete lack of facts and Coral didn't need that. I didn't particularly want to talk to my dad, not after our awkward goodbye. One of those was enough. But this had taken too serious a turn to do anything else.

I showed up at the farm the next morning.

"Forget something?" Dad said.

"No, but I'll take another hug goodbye." His face softened.

"I can give you that."

"I'd like to run something by you. Coral, too."

"Can't do that. She left yesterday for Eds."

"Eds? Her too?"

He gave me a puzzled look. "That lady she doesn't like ordered her to come along to Eds. Coral thinks the woman is up to no good but didn't think she could refuse."

He looked at me, hoping I'd explain my sudden interest in Eds.

"Ryalgar is there. And so is your mother."

"What are they doing there?"

"That's what I'm trying to figure out."

Dad gestured to the dining table. "Have a seat." This was the sort of problem Dad liked. He got paper and ink from the desk. "Tell me what you know."

I did. Watching him diagram things, drawing arrows between connections, I appreciated how much Ryalgar thought the way he did. But, to my credit, I followed along.

By the time I finished talking, and he finished drawing, we realized little Votto *had* to be in the forest so Hana could get someone there to harm him. And Coral was with Hana in Eds so

Hana could make her do something. And Grandma and Ryalgar were in Eds because whatever Hana wanted to make Coral do would harm Grandma and Ryalgar.

My dad shrugged. "Coral talked to me before she left. I didn't come up with this all by myself."

"So now what?" I asked. "We have to do something."

"You have to do something," he corrected me. "The only people we can contact are the Velka. You can warn them to take extra safety precautions with Votto."

He was right. He couldn't go into the forest, but I could.

The next morning I showed up at the Vinx Palace, as promised, to bring the young princesses to the Velka. I planned to go with them, telling anyone who asked that I had to make sure they didn't scamper off. Once there, I hoped to plead for extra protection for Votto with whomever would listen. It wasn't a great plan, but it beat doing nothing.

But when I arrived at the palace, their father sat in a chair, his head in his hands, moaning. He refused to look at me or answer my questions. His butler Karl had to tell me that the princesses had run off and hidden again, leaving a note that they were determined to fight in the invasion.

I suggested contacting Sulphur. The twins idolized her and if she came to the palace perhaps they'd cooperate. I left while Karl composed the message. I hated to go, but I couldn't afford to miss the Velka.

The same three women packed their final belongings as I arrived. They agreed to take me along, offering to tether my horse in their stall and let me ride with the youngest after she transferred most of her goods to the others.

That was perfect because she was the most talkative of the three. By the time we got to the lodge, I knew that a woman named Natia ran things now, and she was one of Hana's closest friends. I didn't want to ask Natia for help.

I also learned that Aliz had asked another senior member of the conclave named Boyanne to keep an eye on Natia because not everyone trusted her. I needed to speak with Boyanne.

"That's Natia," the young woman whispered in my ear as we rode into the clearing. She pointed to an attractive blonde with perfect posture sitting on the large front porch, possibly waiting for us.

"So, you've removed the last of our things from Vinx?" the woman called out as we rode closer. Then she stopped to stare at me. "What's this?"

"It's Celestine. The famous singer," the young woman with me called back.

"Yes. I can see that. I mean *what* is she doing here?"

I preferred to answer for myself. "I come on family business."

"Pity. Your sister and grandmother aren't here."

"It doesn't matter. I come to speak with my mother."

We dismounted. Several women came out on the porch, curious about the exchange, and one came to take our donkeys.

"I'm sorry but that isn't possible," Natia said in a more pleasant tone. "As part of our safety plan, no outsider can have contact with her."

Many of the observers looked surprised, and I heard their comments.

"We have a safety plan?"

"It's her mother…"

"I can run get her for you," one woman offered.

"No," Natia's tone turned sharp again. "I have strict instructions. Markita is to have no contact with outsiders until this is behind us. I'm sorry."

"That's the first I've heard of that edict. Says who?" A woman stepped forward as if she had the authority to challenge Natia.

"It's not yours to question me, Boyanne."

Boyanne ignored her and turned to me. "I'd be glad to deliver a message to your mother."

"That won't be necessary. I'll take the message," Natia said.

I squinted my eyes at the helpful woman, hoping I'd heard the name right. "Boyanne?"

"Yes."

"It's so good to see you again. Have you been well?"

She hesitated with only a hint of confusion in her voice. "I'm fine thank you. How … how have you been?"

"Oh, it's been quite the year. For you too, I'm sure. Would you, could we ... have lunch perhaps after I give my message to Natia? I'd love to get caught up."

Boyanne smiled. "That would be nice. I'd love to hear more about ... your life."

"I hardly think lunching with outsiders is appropriate now ..." Natia looked around for support but mostly got puzzled looks from the other women. No one told anyone who they could have lunch with here.

"I know you're busy. We'll keep it quick."

I walked over to Natia. "Now about that information for my mother ..."

I strung together some nonsense about my family as Natia pretended to listen. We both knew she'd been thwarted and there wasn't much she could do about it. I smiled when I finished.

"Now if you'll excuse me, I have to get caught up with an old friend."

~ 25 ~

The Howling Winds

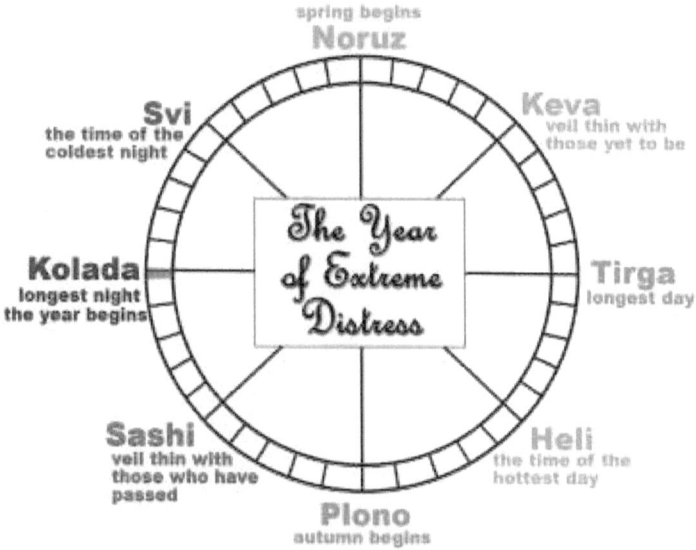

Boyanne arranged for lunch to be brought up to her room so we could talk about old times in private.

"I'm sorry to put you in this position ..."

"Don't be. I thought your claim to know me was hilarious. So did everyone else. Now, what's going on?"

"Can I start at the beginning?"

"Start with your birth if you want. You have until dinner time."

Telling my story took nearly that long. I hadn't realized how complicated things had gotten. Boyanne listened, nodding at much of what I said and asking questions as I spoke.

Dusk comes early around Kolada and even in the dense forest I sensed the day reaching its end as I finished. We'd both been sitting hunched forward talking in low voices for too long. Boyanne stood up to stretch.

"I think your worry is well-founded, but as you admit, it is guesswork. Sensible guessing, but I can't remove Natia from her role as our temporary leader without more justification."

"There's nothing you can do?"

"I didn't say that. I can make sure that good people keep an eye on your family day and night. I'll share your thoughts with others who believe caution about Natia is advised. At the first sign of a problem or even the first hint that your worries are justified, I'll take action. But until then …"

I understood. I'd bought my nephew added vigilance, and I'd put Natia under more suspicion. Hopefully, the two would be enough if my worst fears came to pass.

"I know you left your horse tethered in our market stall, and you're supposed to be in position with the other singers, but it grows dark and cold. Stay the night, and we'll get you back first thing in the morning."

The Velka did offer a fine guest room and a meal well beyond the fare being served in Vinx. I hadn't brought my psaltery with me, but the younger women got me started singing in front of the fire after dinner. Some brought out their instruments, and we let the music make us feel like the danger remained many anks away.

The next morning the young woman who had given me the ride met me with two donkeys.

"Come. I'm to show you the way home. I'll take you as far as the market."

The Velka sent apples and carrots for my horse. She greeted me with a loud whinny, not happy having spent a cold night in a poor shelter but willing to accept my peace offering. I soothed her and considered my options.

I could go back to the Vinx Inn where I was supposed to be. But, I had a Velka guide with me.

"Do you have time to ride over to the Vinx Castle?" I asked her. "It's not far. If Sulphur talked some sense into those twin princesses, I could send them back with you."

"Good idea. Let's go." She hopped up behind me on my horse.

The castle appeared deserted, but we found the girls' father inside, sitting alone in front of the fire with a blanket around him. Sounds came from the kitchen.

"Karl is making lunch," he said as we entered. I found it to be an odd greeting.

"Your daughters? Did Sulphur come? Have they been found?"

He shook his head.

"She came but by the time she got here we'd found another note saying they'd gone off to join the farmers camping on the fields of Vinx. It said ..." He broke into a coughing fit that might have covered a few sobs. "It said they intended to fight with their people."

"I'm so sorry."

"Sulphur promised she'd ask the Svadlu in Vinx to find the girls and move them to the sidelines." He turned to my Velka companion. "Thank you for coming all the way here to get them. The Vinx Royals are now indebted to you forever."

The young woman blushed. She and I knew our arrival was an afterthought but it seemed unwise to tell the man. He had enough grief to deal with.

"Your son Giorgi?" I asked. "Will he fight alongside his people, too?"

"Absolutely not. All the crown princes, and the recently crowned ones like Giorgi, have been sent to a cabin in Zur. We must preserve the royal line."

Several comments came to my lips but none seemed wise.

"When will you go to safety?" I asked. "You and Karl?"

He held his eyes shut for a heartbeat before he answered. "I will stay here so I can ride out to praise my people when they prevail."

I felt one of my eyebrows lift.

"Or I will die outside my castle if I must," he added in a softer voice.

For once, I didn't know what to say.

I spent the night at the Vinx Inn and told my friends of my adventures. The place now overflowed with singers and luskies who lacked the camping equipment to be out in the field with the farmers.

My flags, well, I thought of them as my flags, were in place now and flying the green circle, meaning nothing of interest had been sighted on the horizon. As long as that flag flew, we were free to stay in the relative comfort of the inn.

The next morning, three days before Kolada, I walked around, speaking to the many who had come at my behest. I reminded the musicians we'd meet that afternoon in the abandoned marketplace because it offered plenty of room.

However, a cold wind blew bits of trash around when we arrived and the sight of the deserted market stalls disturbed everyone. I stood upon an old wagon someone had left behind and saw a hundred and twenty-seven faces staring back at me. Yes, I counted them. Most of them had little hope in their eyes.

I'd believed from the beginning that Ilari could prevail. We were clever. We were strong. We had tricks up our sleeves. Everything might be okay in the end. It had to be.

But the faces looking up at me held no such belief. These people expected to lose and many feared they would die. My first instinct was to convince them they were wrong but I knew that even if I succeeded, my spell would soon fade and their fears would come back.

No, I needed to reach them as they were, not try to make them like me. I needed to make them feel the strength within themselves *even* if they were about to die. Especially if they were.

I picked up my psaltery, struck a note, and let out a long, slow yelp. I wanted my wolf's howl to induce terror. I looked at their faces. Some appreciated it. Others looked confused or annoyed.

I turned to Zamarran. He grabbed his sticks and began with a deep, slow beat. Mirva picked up her flute and played an intro. She knew I'd only begun. Then Feene nodded.

I howled again, but this time a little softer as he joined me, his deeper voice producing a yowl in exact harmony with mine.

Everyone became silent.

"We are scared," I said. "Join me, as we became a pack of singers, putting our fears into sound. Join me as we become the howling wind, a shrieking storm, and a wailing wolf. Feel your fear, then use it to make a noise that will terrify others so that in three days we will find the strength to do what we must."

The drumbeat grew. Mirva repeated the intro, louder. This time I screamed out a sound I'd never thought I could make, and Feene somehow did too, and he was in harmony. Many others joined us.

"Again," I said. "We're a pack of singers. Let's howl."

Nearly everyone did.

"Once more."

We made a deafening sound.

"Last time."

Our final yowl went on for many heartbeats. At the end of it, I looked around.

"That's all I have to say," I said. "Go back to your lodging. Stay out of trouble. And in three days, let the world know how frightening the musicians of Ilari can be."

I woke early the next day, still hoarse from yesterday's efforts. My voice needed a break. I decided to ride over to the Vinx Palace while I still had time, to see if the Elder Prince had received further word about his daughters and to let him know I'd made inquiries about them but the girls were uncommonly adept at staying out of sight.

When I left the inn, I saw that the green circle flags had all been replaced with the red squares.

The horde had been seen on the horizon. They would be here tomorrow morning.

I stared at the flag and it felt dreamlike. I struggled to believe it. So much time waiting and now ...

I knew I'd go see Firuza after I left the palace. For a full eighth now I'd done as she asked and treated her as someone I barely knew in front of others. I'd done it because she asked me to, and also because in my heart I believed she and I would have plenty of time to enjoy each other later.

But this morning the flags had changed. This bad dream showed no signs of going away and, as I'd realized yesterday, a hundred and twenty-seven other singers thought it wouldn't end well. They could be right. So, I intended to kiss Firuza today and tell her I loved her. If our encounter with the Mongols ended well, I'd be glad to deal with the consequences of my behavior later.

I didn't know I'd bring the Elder Prince with me.

He sat in front of the fire when I arrived, looking as if he hadn't moved since I last saw him. Once we exchanged our grim lack of news, I said "Are you doing anything special today?'

He blinked, surprised. "Just watching the flags. I see they've been sighted in the distance, right on time."

"They have," I answered. "The Velka will start making fog tonight. Tomorrow, they will be in the grasslands of Bisu."

He nodded.

"Would you like to go for a ride? Out to the lookout house with me?"

He considered it. "I wouldn't mind seeing that place for myself. Perhaps the air would do me good." Then, realizing the oddity of my request. "Why?"

"There is a woman I love out there."

He didn't seem shocked. I guess a ruler learns that countenance early on. "Firuza? The astronomer?"

I nodded. "I hoped, I don't know, that you might somehow bless our love before …"

His laugh had a raspy unused sound to it. "I've blessed a lot of unions over the last eighth. The threat of invasion prompts many a commitment. But none of them between two women."

"Do you object?"

He shrugged. "No, not really. You want a ceremony before the invasion? I see no reason why not."

Now I just had to convince Firuza of the same thing.

When I arrived at the lookout house with Vinx's former ruler, everyone went into a frenzy of curtseys.

"His Highness thought some air would do him good," I explained. "I thought you could show him the horde in the distance through your moon glass." Firuza obliged but continued to give me a puzzled look. Once others had engaged His Highness, I motioned to her to come inside.

"What is this about?"

"I love you, and I want you to know it."

"I do know it," she whispered. "But we agreed …"

"We did. And I have. But now, with them a day away and getting closer, I don't care what anyone thinks, and you don't need to either. You've done your job and done it well. Please. Before they arrive. Will you marry me?"

She looked at me and laughed. "I don't think that's possible."

"Then call it what you will. His Highness has told me he will bless our union, will sanction the joining of our lives, today, right now, if you agree."

"You asked this of him?"

"Under the circumstances, yes. I did. And under the circumstances, he said why the Heli not. Trust me, there will never be a better day for two women to do this. So. Firuza. Will you join your life with mine?"

"Yes. Absolutely yes."

I suppose it was just as well that several of the lookouts had come back inside while Firuza and I spoke and they overheard the end of our conversation. It saved a lot of awkward explaining.

Now that the horde had been sighted and the flags were up, the lookouts had little else to do. So it didn't take them long to get Firuza and me standing out on the cliffs, wearing whatever pretty scarves they could find and holding whatever greenery and fall flowers they could gather up. One lookout poured afternoon wine while His Highness stood looking as regal and happy as I'd seen him since his daughters disappeared.

"I love doing this," he told me. "I don't mind the improvising."

The horde's dust was barely visible on the horizon when the Elder Prince of Vinx did something he'd never done before. He declared us wife and wife.

I spent the night at the lookout house in flagrant violation of my instructions to everyone else. But Heli. It was my wedding night.

Firuza rose while it was still dark. I heard her leave the room to light a candle with embers from the fire, then watched her pull on her cloak. I knew she headed to the cliffs' edge. I dressed and followed her.

The early morning mist thickened already, encouraged by the Velka oomrushers drawing little drops of water up out of the marsh and into the air. A man and woman sat on small stools in the dark near the cliff's edge, bundled in blankets and keeping watch. She used the moon glass; he stared at the horizon. Probably a long eye.

"They are camped in the open marshland between us and the lands to the east," she reported. "We've seen a few fires already this morning. Perhaps their cooks? We think they'll break camp at first light and ride in to see if the tribute awaits."

"Kolada is not for another day," I said. "When they don't find it, do we expect them to give us additional time?"

Everyone shrugged. There was so much we didn't know.

"Even if they want to ask about our intentions, they won't find anyone in this fog to talk to," Firuza said.

She turned to the man and the woman. "Go. Warm yourself inside. I'll take over."

"I need to leave before this fog gets thicker," I told her.

"No. You need light in the sky first. Come sit with me. Let's hold each other while these Mongols wake up. There's little else we can do."

I thought she might have woken angry with me, but her arm around my shoulder said otherwise.

"Thank you," she said when she finally spoke. "For recognizing when we had nothing left to lose. No matter how this day goes, I'm grateful for your courage."

I laughed. "Even if the day goes so poorly that you have to deal with what I've done?"

She understood my humor. "Yes, even under the horrible circumstances that we both live to see the consequences."

We kissed, and when I left a short time later, a part of me thought I'd never been happier.

~ 26 ~

Hundreds of Hoofs

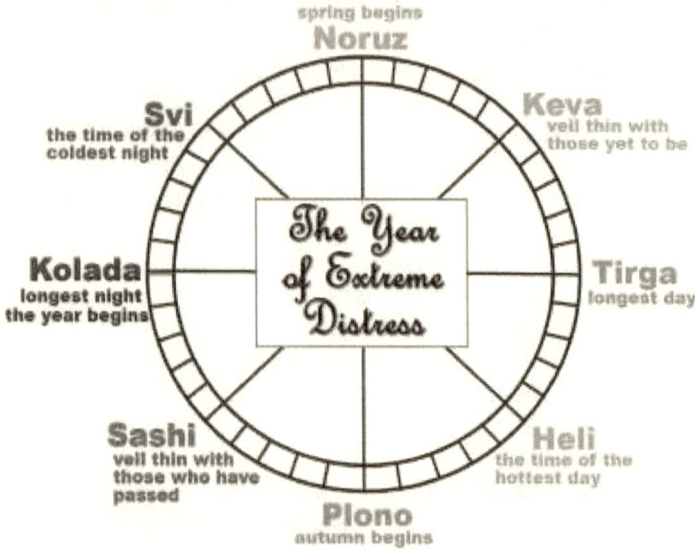

spring begins
Noruz

Svi
the time of the
coldest night

Keva
veil thin with
those yet to be

Kolada
longest night
the year begins

*The Year
of Extreme
Distress*

Tirga
longest day

Sashi
veil thin with
those who have
passed

Heli
the time of the
hottest day

Piono
autumn begins

The fog lessened as I rode west, away from the cliffs and the marsh below them. Those of us who'd taken lodging in homes or at the inn had been asked to camp with the others tonight, so we'd all be together as needed in the morning.

I stopped at the inn to gather my things. Mirva, Feene, and Zamarran had left and taken their instruments and I couldn't find anyone else there either. Those who hadn't gone into hiding before now had a role to play and had moved into position.

The camps were along the forest's edge, not far from the deserted marketplace where Feene and I had howled like wolves two days earlier. When I arrived I saw the fire-wielding reczavy barely visible in the trees. The herdhands camped alongside the farmers who had been there for days. The luskies had mostly stayed elsewhere until now, and they gathered off on another edge.

Messengers rode in behind me to deliver the good news that those out on the cliffs had heard the Mongol hoard riding in the fog this morning and had also heard them stop and set up an early camp near the lush grass the Velka created. Applause broke out everywhere at this news. This initial stop in the fog was crucial to our plans.

I found my band standing near the makeshift tent we'd devised.

"Thought yesterday was a good time for a little vacation?" Zamarran said as I walked up.

"No. Decided it was a great day to go spend the night with the woman I loved. I'm sorry. I should have told you."

Feene shrugged. "You might as well go for what you want."

"We did. We got the father of the ruling prince of Vinx to marry us."

Three sets of eyes widened.

"He can do that?" Mirva asked.

"He thinks he can," I said. "It was kind of spontaneous, or I would have invited you."

"I wasn't going to say anything," Zamarran said, but there was a smile behind his words.

I headed out then to make sure most of us were here, and I'd nearly made my way through half the camp when I heard Feene call my name. He waved at me through the mist, motioning for me to return. I recognized Coral's bright red hair next to him. She'd made it back from Eds. Maybe all my fears had been wrong. I hurried to greet her.

"Coral. I'm so glad you're here! And safe!"

Her face was hard and her eyes held a mix of emotions I couldn't decipher.

"All is well?"

"In some ways."

"How did your trip go? Where is Hana? Everyone is looking for her."

She looked into my eyes, begging for something. Understanding? Cooperation?

"Hana is dead," she said. "She fell off of a cliff."

"What? She fell??" Then I recognized the emotion. Coral's eyes begged me for forgiveness. Perhaps all I'd feared *had* come to pass, except for the part about how defenseless my tenderhearted sister would be against the ruthless Hana. That part appeared to have gone differently.

"I see. Well, she would want us to carry on with the defense of Ilari as best we can, wouldn't she?"

Coral smiled. "Of course she would. Someone needs to step up and continue to lead." The look again, but this time it held more pleading. "Someone good with crowds, able to inspire, and well informed about everyone who is here."

"No, Coral. I can't do that. I'm only a singer and I wouldn't presume …"

"That's why. We have twenty-one luskies; we can't lose one. Yet we know and trust you."

I saw myself as a performer, not a leader, but I could try.

"I'll do my best, but later, when this is over, I want to know what really happened."

"I'll tell you everything. Just not now."

The truth is I don't remember much about the rest of that day. I remember announcing Hana's death to the crowd, speaking into one of the wooden cones. I got everyone to bow their heads in Hana's memory, then I got them to hold their neighbors' hands and raise them high into the air as we swore to do this as best we could.

I admonished them to remain quiet, eat their cold suppers, and maintain harmony.

After that, I returned to the dreamlike state I felt when I first saw the flag with the red square. The this-isn't-real feeling enveloped me as I climbed down off the hay bales and stood there. Mirva told me later that I spent quite a bit of time answering questions and that I answered them coherently. I can't remember one of them.

I do remember it getting dark and having trouble finding the tent Zamarran put up for us. He found me. Then I think Feene gave me some dried meat to chew on and an apple.

I've got to shake this off. I thought it as I crawled under the blankets and fell asleep.

I woke in the middle of the night, needing to get out of the tent and get some air. I grabbed my cloak and an extra blanket and wandered towards the farmers' area, taking my steps in the dark with care. When I reached the edge of it, a man's hand grabbed my arm from the back.

"Stop."

I spun around to see the herdhand who'd teased me as a child and who'd recently told me about bucking horses.

"What are you doing here?" We said it together and both laughed.

"I'm standing guard," he said. "Just in case. We're taking turns."

"It's a good idea," I conceded. "I just had to get out. I don't know why."

He hesitated.

"Celestine? It's normal to be scared and kind of detached at a time like this. You're doing fine. Go get some sleep. You have important work to do in the morning."

I nodded and left. He'd said what I needed to hear.

Zamarran woke me at first light. "Arise, fearless leader."

I pulled the blanket over my face. "Don't call me that."

"Very well. Arise, leader who is scared scumpless."

Mirva giggled. "How can we help you?" she asked.

I sat up, begging my mind to focus. What was supposed to happen first?

"The farmers are walking everybody's horses over to the marketplace," Zamarran said. "When they get back they'll hide first. We need to stay out of their way, but we could start organizing our own."

"You think I should use the four groups Hana set up?"

"Why not? It will cause less confusion."

He was right. The fewer things I changed the better.

"Mirva. Go work with Coral and the luskies. I know they want to be close enough for the horses to hear them but make sure they're back far enough for safety. Feene? Do you mind working with the reczavy?"

Feene still had a blanket over his face, but he laughed underneath it. "I know all of them."

"Good. Make sure they have enough lit torches if this happens quicker than we think."

"Got it."

I turned to Zamarran. "Why don't you work with the new singers and other musicians who've joined us? Get some of the more experienced hands to give them a better idea of what to do."

"What about our magic with the bugs? Are we going to try to use that?" Feene asked, emerging from his pile of blankets.

"Not unless we need to. Let's hope we don't."

The morning was crisp and clear as we grabbed what cheese, bread, and apples we could find for our breakfast. The reczavy had placed twenty-five piles of sticks and logs in a line blocking the narrowest part of the entrance from Bisu. Each little fire was wide enough to scare horses and yet short enough for us to see over.

I positioned Hana's two smaller groups inside the shrubbery the Velka had grown on the constructed hill and directed the other two teams to the forest side, where they could do their work half-hidden by the trees.

I watched Feene walking alongside the piles of brush, listening to the reczavy describe their plan. Our few luskies already knew where to go, but Mirva helped them along as they moved into place.

We heard hooves and a rattling in the brush on the hillside, and everyone tensed. Then we exhaled. It was one of our own, riding in at the last minute. I turned in annoyance. We'd gone to great lengths not to have any of our horses nearby and had told those who couldn't be here on time not to come.

The delinquent could have been one of the many singers recruited at the end, one who hadn't fully understood the instructions, but I knew it wasn't. I'd counted them. Except for Hana, exactly one person, one luski in fact, had been missing when we assembled. Many of us had been glad she wasn't there.

But now, Ura hopped off her horse, walked out into the clearing, and announced "I'm here."

Coral and her mentor Ewalina both came forward to intervene.

"Let's change that," Ewalina said. "We are in place and we don't need you. Or your horse. Both of you get out of here before you become a liability."

Ura looked ready to cry.

"You can't tell me to leave. I'm in charge now."

"In charge?"

"Yes. I've been waiting for Hana. She said she'd come to get me and we'd come here together but …"

A few tears squeezed out of her eyes. "She never came, and I'm worried something happened. Maybe something bad."

Everyone stayed silent. This was not a good time for this conversation.

"But …" she brushed the tear aside, "she told me to take over if she wasn't here so I'm in charge now."

We heard more hooves approaching. A single horse rode into our midst from along the forest's edge, carrying the messenger who'd put on two dramatic performances for me recently.

These people were working today? No, they were fighting for Ilari in their own way, too.

"Coral! Celestine!" The messenger called out. I motioned him closer and held my finger to my lips. He understood and lowered his voice as his hand went up.

"I, Sulphur, send word that the fog cleared this morning and our archers struck. In the first light, they poisoned many horses and our people now hide as they wait for our attackers' to discover what we did. I won't be able to send further word but assume that many Mongols will ride on towards you and will likely arrive on the heels of this message."

He gestured that he now spoke for himself.

"I don't suppose you have a good place for me to hide?"

I pointed to the woods, my fingers to my lips again. I had a reason for quieting him. In the absolute silence, I could make out the sound of hundreds of hoofs in the distance. It sounded nothing like a single horse. The light rumble of the ground added confirmation.

"Everyone in place. Now!" I turned to Ura. "Even you."

Those who'd come forward to hear the message retreated to their positions, and Ura went with them.

We waited in a silence that took forever as the sounds of hooves grew louder.

Until you've seen hundreds of horses ridden by screaming men armed with swords and bows, you cannot comprehend what I'm describing. It was beyond terrifying.

They came around the corner out of Bisu, about fifty horses across and ten to twenty horses deep, and they filled my ears, my vision, my sense of place on the earth with something more monstrous than anything in my memory. I froze, along with every other Ilarian there.

Except for the reczavy. Those five mischief-makers stepped out in the path of that advancing army and, without rushing, without making a sound, they lit all twenty-five of their little bonfires, then vanished back into the trees.

The front fifty or so horses balked at the first smell of smoke. They tried to turn but became hemmed in on both sides by other, less sensitive horses rushing by them. After that, the disarrayed army moved forward in lurches, some horses stopping, others pushing past, as the throng came close enough to the fires for us to see their angry faces on the other side of the flames.

Zamarran hit his drum at the same time one of the Velka hit their gong and the combined sound, the signal to begin, unfroze us all. We knew what to do.

The luskies shouted their pleas in unison. "Rear up! Rear up! The fire will eat you. Rear up!" Though the words meant nothing to the horses, the meaning in their timbre came through as a hundred horses raised their hoofs high into the air and whinnied in fright.

Our voices sang it as well, the beauty of the sound coaxing the animals to pay heed to the luskies urging. Heavy smoke came from both sides as the reczavy crept through the trees, past the line of fires, to light a row of damp torches.

"Throw your riders! Throw your riders!" As planned, the luskies changed over to encouraging the horses to buck, and the singers echoed the idea. "No rider. No rider. You must have no rider."

At first I thought the animals responded only to the fire and smoke, but as we persisted the bucking got wilder. Many horses reared up with no further provocation, then returned to their frantic bucking. Our theories about the tone and intention of the words held and, better yet, the panic spread back through the herd.

Horses ten and fifteen back bucked and reared up with the same energy as those at the front. It was everything we hoped for.

Except for one small problem.

No matter what the horses did, the riders stayed on.

I looked closer.

Through the flames I could see that the horsemen had thick ropes hanging down from both sides of their saddles with what appeared to be a heavy metal ring fastened to the end. The metal rings held each rider's feet and this helped him maintain his seat.

Whatever these things were, they were phenomenally effective for keeping people on a horse. It appeared that no matter how we coerced these animals, no matter how wild they were or for how long, these riders would stay mounted. They couldn't be thrown.

No wonder they had ridden through lands much larger than ours and conquered them by the end of the day.

~ 27 ~

In Charge

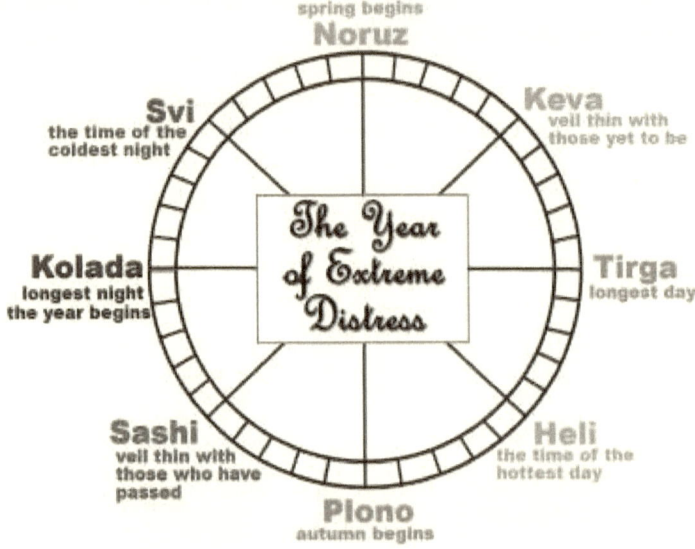

spring begins
Noruz

Svi
the time of the
coldest night

Keva
veil thin with
those yet to be

Kolada
longest night
the year begins

The Year of Extreme Distress

Tirga
longest day

Sashi
veil thin with
those who have
passed

Heli
the time of the
hottest day

Piono
autumn begins

Once I recognized we couldn't succeed no matter what we did, I realized the horses would tire soon. Once the riders didn't have to work so hard to stay mounted, who knew what they'd do? They probably wanted to kill us all just to stop our noise.

Several of the herdhands stood behind me, pointing to the metal foot holders and making wild gestures to each other. I understood why this amazing invention intrigued them. They wanted to duplicate it. I watched them disappear into the shrubbery on the newly constructed hillside, probably so they could talk to each other.

I jumped, startled when someone tapped me on the shoulder.

"Celestine," a young lad yelled in my ear above the noise. "You need to get the fires out now and let their riders move on. The Svadlu want you to know this isn't working and we're not equipped to fight them all."

"I know." I looked closer. The young lad talking to me bore a strong resemblance to a twelve-year-old Vinxite princess I'd met, despite the dirt smeared on her face and a poor attempt to cover her blonde hair with charcoal. I couldn't worry about that now. I knew that all of our fighters, this youngster included, had been told to remain hidden, but I supposed the Svadlu felt justified in sending her out to deliver this vital message.

Once enough of their riders were thrown, we'd intended to use wagons of dirt and carts of water to put out the blazes and let the horses through. If we did that now, it meant accepting complete failure and sending a significantly larger army onward.

But if we didn't do it, we'd end up fighting them all here. There was no doubt who would win.

We needed to give up.

I turned to the youngster.

"You're fast. Run tell them to get the fires out now. We'll do everything we can to make sure these riders charge on through whether they like it or not."

Off she ran.

I thought if we could get most of them out of here, and if the Svadlu and farmers all stayed hidden, then any remaining Mongols might consider us a bunch of misguided amateurs not worth killing. It was our best hope.

A blood-curdling cry ripped my attention back to our attackers. But the noise didn't come from them. Five of our herdhands shrieked as they ran out from the shrubbery on the other side of the fires, brandishing knives.

What in Heli were they doing out there?

Each ran towards a different bucking horse, moving with grace through the fury, unfazed by the wild behavior of animals they worked with all the time. Each reached for a rope holding a metal ring, pulled out his knife, and tried to cut through it.

But the ropes were strong, perhaps treated somehow, because they didn't cut as easily as the men had hoped. One of our attackers managed to keep his seat while running his sword through a herdhand's chest. The herdhand crumpled to the ground, and my breath stopped. It was the young man I'd hated in school, and who had helped me twice now.

The other four herdhands succeeded with their first attempts and moved on to others. Between the flames, those who were putting out the flames, and the horses in the way, it was hard to follow. Each herdhand eventually found a rope too difficult to cut, or a horseman agile enough to counterattack fast. I counted twenty Mongols who lost their metal foot rings and were unseated by their frantic mounts before a rider plunged his sword into the last of the herdhands. I couldn't see their bodies on the ground because of the fires, but I had little hope any of them remained alive.

Five dead. I admired their valor and appreciated their sacrifice but taking only twenty prisoners out of eight hundred attackers was *not* worth their lives. If this was the only way to accomplish our task, the cost was too high.

I saw another group of herdhands, probably the rest of them, gathering at the shrubbery on our side, knives in hand. They looked more scared than the first group.

No. I would not allow another such mission. I ran across the clearing to them.

Then I saw Ura standing behind them urging them on.

"It's the only way," she yelled. "We do this or we fail."

"Then we fail," I yelled back. I'd done the math. We'd need at least forty of the hidden farmers to join the herdhands if we were to unseat two hundred Mongols. Probably more, because many of the farmers were less comfortable around agitated horses and less skilled with knives.

"I will not send another fifty or sixty to their death just to capture more prisoners. It's not that important."

"You would let them *all* ride on? Let everything we did be for nothing? Let us, the Lion, be useless in the end?"

I looked at the scared herdhands, trying to gather up the courage to follow Ura's orders.

"You bet I would."

I turned to the men.

"They need your help putting out the fires. Go. We've got to get them out fast."

Then I turned to Ura. "Get over with the other luskies and help get these horses out of here. Or we'll be worse than failures. We'll be dead failures."

"You're not in charge," she shot back.

I ignored her. I *was* in charge, and everyone knew it.

I stood in the middle of the open area between the constructed hill and the forest, shouting orders to all. The luskies needed to be better hidden for this next part. We couldn't afford to lose one. The musicians needed to quiet down because the horses had to hear the message to keep running more than they needed to be riled up.

I saw the supposed lad who'd delivered my message about putting out the fires. Or maybe it was the lad's twin. Whichever.

"See if anyone, the reczavy or anyone else, can get some sort of flames going behind the horde. It could help make those tired horses keep running. But take no ridiculous risks doing it. Do you understand me?"

"Yes, madam…" Her mouth dropped open in surprise, giving me the only warning I had before an arm encircled my waist and hoisted me up onto a moving horse.

I sat facing one of our attackers, a large bald man. Without thinking I wrapped my legs around his waist to keep from falling off but I needn't have bothered. His arm held me tight as he concentrated on controlling his mount in all the confusion. He glanced at me with mild curiosity as I looked at him, but nothing more.

I thought I recognized him as one of the center front riders when the hoard had first gotten there. In front. In charge. I'd been kidnapped by the man leading their army. Why?

Looking further behind me, I saw that more of the Mongol riders had begun to break through the dying fires on the side towards the constructed hill. As the passable gap grew, more of them came through. As we had hoped, they largely ignored the unarmed Ilarians, seeming more concerned about the welfare of their horses.

The Svadlu and the hundreds of farmers had the wisdom to remain hidden. The sight of so many people, and some in army uniforms, would certainly have turned this back into a battle.

Meanwhile, the luskies and singers, the herdhands and reczavy, looked confused as many of them yelled to others for instructions. They needed me. Somebody had to make sense out of this and figure out what to do next. I had to get off this horse.

Then I knew why I'd been grabbed.

I'd been standing in the middle of the clearing, shouting orders. Because I was in charge. And everyone knew it.

Big and Bald had grabbed me because he knew it too.

I was his best hostage. I'd get the best ransom. My absence would cause the most confusion.

Pruck this being in charge thing. Why hadn't I let Ura boss people around for a while? Maybe he'd have grabbed her instead.

Big and Bald slowed his horse to a saunter, letting his animal regain its strength and its inner calm. The man knew horses. The slow speed also meant I could fall off safely and probably still walk back, except that he continued to hold on to me.

I couldn't overpower this man. If I tried something ineffectual like biting his arm or scratching at his eyes he'd probably hurt me worse and still not let me go. I had to make him *want* to let go of me. Maybe if I howled like a wolf. Given how I felt, howling sounded good and I knew I could produce a sound that would chill his blood.

I opened my mouth. Then I closed it again. I had a better option. Did I dare try it?

The second time I opened my mouth an unexpected sound emerged. Soft, sweet, and melodic. I began to sing one of my favorite songs, a childhood tune Coral had taught me.

He looked at me, his eyes wide, perhaps thinking the shock of being kidnapped had turned me crazy. Then his arm tightened around my waist. This man had seen a trick or two before. He slowed his horse down to barely a walk and watched me. Carefully.

I decided the children's song didn't give me enough of a feel for calling insects. I switched over to a little improvisation.

"Come, little bugs. Come visit me."

I sang the most beautiful bug call imaginable, while my captor reached around inside his clothes, probably searching for a rag with which to gag me. I kept singing, but not a single little winged creature came. Where were they all? The world was full of them. Why couldn't I find a varmin bug when I needed one?

His men had slowed down behind us. Some of the fires had regained a foothold and many of the horses now refused to pass through. Big and Bald moved off to the right, towards the forest, to give his men time to catch up

That was his one mistake. Do you know what's in a forest? Besides trees? That's right. Lots and lots of them, too.

Once the bugs started to come, they came in droves. I feared I'd choke on them if they filled my mouth so I put my fingers over it to keep them out and did my best not to think about what I did.

"Come to me. Come to me." *Keep that voice sweet.*

They covered my hair, and they covered my face. They crawled on my neck, and they crawled on my arms. Yes, they even crawled down the front of my shirt, and I felt their little legs walking on my breasts. But I kept singing.

Big and Bald stopped looking for a gag and watched with fascination. He seemed almost amused until there were so many of them that they started to crawl on his arms too. He swatted them away, but I kept singing and more came.

Once they covered me completely, they went for his face. They preferred the mouth and eyes, but they liked nostrils too. I could barely see by then but his growing discomfort could be felt in his squirming as it got worse.

Finally he shouted at me. I didn't speak a word of Mongolian, but I'd have bet my psaltery that his words translated to "get away from me you monstrous witch!" Or something very close to that.

I'd closed my eyes by then to keep the bugs out of them, so I was surprised when I hit the ground. I screeched out my ugliest get away from me song as I wiped the bugs off my face.

As for Big and Bald? He rode away from me as fast as he could, and I was as happy to see the backside of him as he was to be rid of me.

Once I was nearly bug free, I looked around.

I stood on the plains of Vinx, land of my birth, on a cold clear winter day. The forest was behind me. In one direction, I could see about eight hundred horses heading away from me and across the plain, and they were picking up their pace. Sadly, every horse still had a rider.

As far as those riders knew, they rode on to Pilk to conquer us after having gotten through this little nuisance, whatever it was.

In the other direction, I could see puffs of smoke from fires still not out. I could also see hundreds of people. So, the farmers had come out of hiding, only to discover they had no prisoners to capture. All that training and nobody needed them. They milled around wondering what to do next.

I needed to get back. I rubbed my backside, already sore from my fall, and started to walk.

Then I saw a horse racing towards me. It looked like Ura's horse and my heart skipped a beat. I did not need this nonsense now.

~ 28 ~

A Giddy Royal Decides

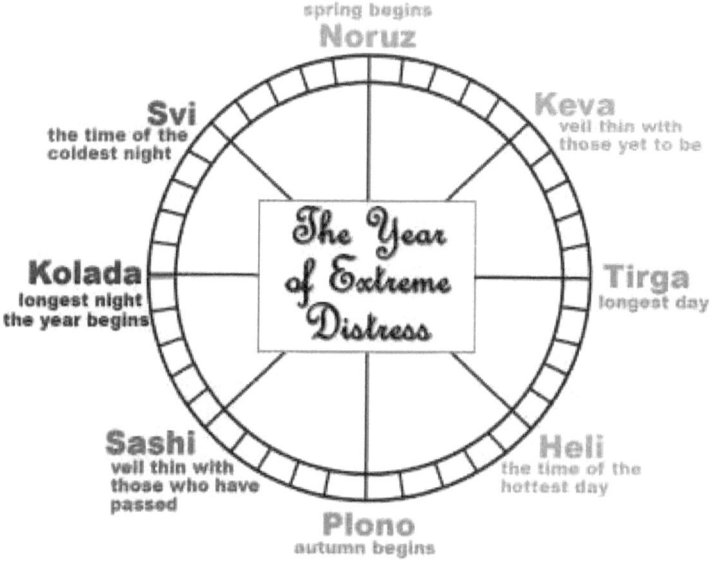

As the horse came closer I recognized the rider. One of the twin princesses had taken off her boy's hat revealing her long blonde hair.

"Where's Ura?" I asked as she rode up.

"She found out Hana died, and she's accusing Coral of murder and demanding the Svadlu take Coral prisoner. The head Svadlu, I think he's a friend of Sulphur's, he's refusing to do it. And one of the farmers named Janx, I think he's in love with Coral because he's standing next to her with a pitchfork ready to defend her. I grabbed her horse and came to get you because you need to get back there."

I couldn't have agreed more.

I hopped up behind her and as we rode I said. "I want you to let me off then ride to the castle and let your father know you're okay. Let him know we're all okay."

"But he's furious with me and my sister," she said.

"Yes, but only because he loves you, and he's scared to death for you. You have to bring him to the battlefield as fast as you can. Tell him that as the ranking royal in Vinx he has to settle a dispute. Our nichna needs him."

She turned around enough to give me a grin. "There's nothing he'd like better. Maybe after he gets to play ruler again he won't be so angry."

"I hope."

The girl barely slowed down enough for me to slide off the horse before she sped off to the castle. I looked around.

Twenty Mongol fighters stood with weapons raised, eying us all with suspicion. The farmers had kept them separated by surrounding each one with about fifty people who kept a healthy distance from their quarry. Another smaller group of observers had formed a circle around Ura. Whether they contained her or protected her wasn't clear, but the group included Feene, the five reczavy, and Zamarran's family drummers so I didn't think Ura would cause any trouble.

The similar circle around Coral included the tall, skinny Svadlu officer Sulphur had told me about. Rooslin. She was close to him. He stood next to a Faroojer holding a pitchfork, who I gathered was Coral's new boyfriend.

Nobody did anything. They all looked at me.

"What's the deal with the Mongols?" I asked Rooslin.

"We planned to get them to surrender when this other, ah, dispute broke out. Now we're keeping these two women apart while we figure this out.

"Okay. I've got the former ruler of Vinx coming to handle the two women. We can contain them until then, so why don't you deal with our attackers?"

"You don't get it," he said. "These women are both *luskies*. Who knows what they might do to this crowd."

"Trust me, neither will cause problems," I said. "Would you *please* get those guys to lay down their weapons? Especially the ones with bows? They really make me nervous."

He scrunched his face, thinking. "What *was* the Mongolian word for surrender? Boo joe goke, I think."

He walked towards the warriors and yelled it. "Boo joe goke!"

They looked at him and several cocked their heads like they were trying to understand him.

Finally one of them shouted out to the others. "Boo joe goke!"

"Ah." Several of them made a sound of recognition. *So that is what the man had said.* "Boo joe goke."

Once they all repeated it, they looked at each other. I suspect they'd have laughed and taken on a crowd of inepts like us at ten to one, maybe even at twenty to one, and they might have prevailed. But fifty to one? These men were too smart. One by one they laid their weapons down and held out their hands, palms up.

"Bit at galza bane," they said.

"Bit at galza bane?" I asked Rooslin. He shrugged back. "It's good enough for me.

The farmers around each fighter moved in cautiously, picking up the bows, swords, and knives they had been offered. The ones with rope, assigned to secure the attackers in the original plan, tied each man's hands and led him away.

Two hundred homes had expected to receive a prisoner. Now, we'd find the twenty closest.

With our small-scale prisoner capture handled, I turned to address my sister and her accuser, to let them know an arbiter of justice was on the way. As I turned, though, I saw several people riding towards us from the east out of the corner of my eye. East? The lookout house was east, but I'd have recognized the woman leading them no matter what direction she came from. I shouted.

"Firuza! Over here!"

The horses headed towards us but the Svadlu decided to ride out and intercept them anyway. I stayed with Coral and Ura, not anxious to listen to a retelling of our failure. Not so soon.

Coral mostly looked at the ground while we waited, her arms crossed tight across her chest. I'd never seen her look so guilty and, frankly, it did nothing to help her cause. Ura stood with her hands on her hips and her chin in the air, managing something halfway between indignant anger and gloating.

I busied the crowd by having various people describe parts of their day, under the pretense that I wanted to chronicle how events had gone. I didn't mind hearing their stories, but mostly I wanted to keep everyone occupied until the Elder Prince arrived. I also think it did people good, for some reason, to describe the events to each other.

Eventually, Firuza walked towards me, her debriefing done. She stopped about thirty paces from me, and held her hands shoulder height, palms up, as though to ask *How do you want to do this?*

I responded with the same gesture. *Want do you want?*

She squinted at me puzzled, then shrugged. She dropped her bag on the ground and ran towards me as fast as she could, arms out.

I could go along with that. I ran towards her and we embraced, first with a long hug and then with a long kiss.

When we stopped, some people looked away and others continued to stare. A few were involved in conversations and either hadn't noticed or hadn't cared. But most had. Some smiled in understanding, some winced and shook their heads. I guessed all around it was pretty representative of how people felt.

The crowd's response occupied me well enough that I didn't notice the Elder Prince ride up with his daughter.

"Ahem," he said from his horse. "It always delights me when one of the marriages I perform gets off to a good start."

Royals tend to get listened to more than common folk, and his comment provoked a lot of muttering from the crowd.

"Yes, yes," he shouted out. "I married these two a few days ago. Had to make up a little policy on the fly what with my advisors being tied up with this invasion. Yup. Guess I set a precedent Ilari will have to accept."

Most people, even those who didn't particularly like what he'd done it, nodded in agreement. Royals tended to get that often. Had he bought us a little more acceptance? Perhaps. I thought he'd likely bought us a lot.

"Now, what's going on over here?" He rode towards Coral and Ura, positioning his horse exactly between them. His jovial outlook didn't slip a notch. I suppose finding his two young daughters alive, his nichna not destroyed, at least not yet, and his own body not at the point of an invader's sword had done wonders to raise his spirits. The question was, who'd be helped more by the arbitration of a Royal giddy with happiness?

He turned to Coral and began to fire his questions at her.

"How did the victim die?"

"She stepped off the edge of a cliff."

"Did you push her?"

"I didn't touch her.

"Did you suggest she jump?"

"No."

"What was she doing along the edge?"

"Showing off."

"I see. Could you have prevented her from falling?"

"Possibly. I could have grabbed her, or begged her to move away."

"Yet you didn't do either."

"I didn't. If I'd grabbed her I might have gone over myself. Begging her to be careful was unlikely to have an effect."

"I see. Did you hold any animosity towards this woman?"

"Some."

"Why?"

"She threatened the life of my child."

"That's not true," Ura yelled. "Hana would never hurt anyone."

"You'll have your turn," the Elder Prince admonished her.

"She also threatened my sister and my grandmother," Coral said.

"Well. That's a lot of people to threaten. Are you referring to your grandmother who runs the Velka?"

"Yes, Your Highness."

His Highness turned to Ura.

"What makes you think this other woman is a murderess?"

"Hana isn't clumsy. She'd never fall like that. And Coral has always hated her, just like her sister Ryalgar, They, they were threatened by how competent Hana was."

"This is the same Ryalgar who masterminded today's attempt to defend our realm?"

Ura sniffed but didn't answer.

"I asked a question."

"Yes. The same defense that went horrible today, because these awful, incompetent sisters were in charge of it. If Hana had lived, I promise you we'd have at least two hundred more Mongol prisoners right now, and we wouldn't be a failure."

"That's not true," the Elder Prince said. "My daughter explained the fancy riding equipment the Mongols had. Sounds like no one could have anticipated that."

"But if Hana had been here, we'd have sent people out there to destroy those gadgets ..."

The Elder Prince held up his hand. "Enough. I've also heard of the lives we lost doing that. Your further comments may serve to make me grateful Hana was not here today."

Ura stopped talking.

"I have one remaining question for both of you ladies. Think carefully before you answer. It seems to me the only way Coral could possibly be blamed for Hana's death was if she used her luski talents to convince Hana to walk dangerously close to the edge."

"That has got to be exactly what she did!" Ura answered without a pause.

"I said *think carefully*. Because of all that's happened, everyone knows Ilaria has twenty, maybe thirty luskies in its midst. Maybe more. Many people are frightened by the idea. Now. I've been assured every one of those luskies adheres to a strict code, so we need not fear them. We need not exile them, or imprison them, or, worst case, execute them. Because ... they can be trusted."

The crowd became silent. The fear the prince spoke of was real, and if Ilari survived, accepting its luskies would be one of the adjustments to be made.

"Ura. You are a luski, correct?" She nodded. "Coral. You are one too?" My sister nodded also.

"Think, Ura. Do you believe Coral broke her oath and killed Hana?"

It had taken Ura a while, but she got his point.

"I spoke in anger. No luski would do such a thing. We *all* adhere to our code."

He smiled and turned to Coral. I wondered if Coral had done exactly what the prince described. If she had, she might not lie to save herself. Or she might. Because if Hana had threatened so many people she loved, it was at least a morally grey area.

But it wasn't only Coral's life and well-being at stake. I knew Coral. She'd say whatever she had to say to protect so many other innocents, and I think the Elder Prince knew it too.

"Coral?" he said.

"You can trust the luskies of the realm," she answered.

"That's not what I asked."

"I did not misuse my powers to kill Hana."

She may have interjected a technicality with the word *misuse*, but the prince let it go.

"Very well, I declare this issue resolved." His two daughters had ridden over to him. "Now if you'll excuse me, I have some family matters to attend to.' He gave his daughters a stern look and gestured in the direction of his castle. "Ladies?"

I felt for the girls, but their behavior couldn't be ignored by any parent. They were lucky no harm had come to them, and that their father was at least as proud of them as he was angry.

I wasn't surprised when soon after four more horses arrived along the path the Mongols had arrived on. Sulphur led the group, pushing her horse and probably hoping to arrive in time to help subdue our captives. Olivine rode behind her with Ryalgar's friend Joli and with a man I'd never seen. He wore Scrudite clothes though, so it wasn't hard to guess this was the unacceptable boyfriend Olivine had spoken of long ago. They brought a Mongol captive with them, too, a young man who carried himself as if he were someone important and who had two short ponytails on top of his head.

After the Elder Prince left, most of the crowd dispersed, either helping out with our few prisoners or preparing to head home. I was grateful. For once I wanted to be without an audience, as I confessed to my sisters how we had failed.

Coral brought Janx over with her, so I gestured to Firuza to join us too. Once Sulphur saw her fighting skills weren't needed, she rushed over to hug her friend Rooslin, and the two of them walked over as well. Somehow the nine of us ended up sitting together on the ground explaining to each other all that had happened.

Once we learned of the successful archery at dawn on the grassland of Bisu, eyes turned to Coral and me.

"It was horrible," I said. "She did amazing," Coral said at the same time. My sisters listened to both versions and rendered their verdicts.

"We knew these Mongols had to have tricks up their sleeves we never imagined," Sulphur said. "It's no failure on your part because it was true. You did what you could."

"I'm glad you didn't send anymore herdhands to their deaths," Coral added.

"I bet you were magnificent leading this crowd," Olivine said.

Firuza thought the longest and said the most. "You have no idea how you affected these warriors. Or their horses. All the bucking, the fire, the agitation. The loss of confidence to them when they couldn't gain control of their steeds. Even the fear you put into their leader as he became covered with bugs. They indeed left Vinx with nearly the same numbers as when they arrived, but they didn't leave as the same people. They rode on exhausted and fearful and ripe for whatever tricks Gypsum and the reczavy have in store."

"Well said." This came from Rooslin, but everyone nodded and I felt better than I had since the first time I saw those metal rings around their feet and knew we were in trouble.

"Speaking of Gypsum..." Sulphur said. "Nobody needs my help here, but things should be winding down soon along the river in Gruen. I think I'll ride down there and see if I can help with the clean-up."

"I'm going with you," Rooslin said.

"You're not leaving me behind," Joli added.

Bohdan, I'd learned his name was Bohdan, turned to Olivine. "Do you mind if I go, dear wife?"

"Wife?" Three sisters said it in unison.

"Uh, yeah. There's more to my story you haven't heard yet," she said. Then she turned to him. "Only if I and my bow come along to protect you, dear husband."

He laughed but didn't argue. Then he pointed to Two Ponytails. "Should we leave him here or bring him?"

"I can keep an eye on him for you," Janx said as he patted Coral's hand. "As I ride with you," he added. "You never know when a hostage will be useful."

"You're not going without a luski," Coral responded.

I turned to Firuza.

"Yes," she told me. "You do need an astronomer with a moon glass. I'm coming too. My dear wife."

Eyebrows went up all around. I shrugged.

"We all have more to share," I said. "Later. For now, let's get our horses and go see how Gypsum is doing. She may need our help."

Thank you for reading my story of
how I saved my entire world
from oblivion
—Celestine Renata Glonti

About These Books

The War Stories of the Seven Troublesome Sisters consists of seven short companion novels. Each tells the personal story and perspective of one of seven radically different sisters in the 1200s as they prepare for an invasion of their realm. While each of these historical fantasy/alternate history books can be enjoyed as stand-alone novels, together they tell the full story of how Ilari survived

Which sister do you think saves Ilari? That will depend on whose story you are reading. How do they save it? Each sister will offer you surprising information on why this didn't go as planned.

Want to make sure you don't miss a release? Go to my landing page at https://mailchi.mp/11db23804c68/tell-me-about-new-books to be notified when each book is ready for purchase. I promise you'll only get notifications about the release of these books.

If you enjoyed this story, please leave a review somewhere. If you enjoyed it a lot, please leave a review in several places.☺

Celestine's Sisters

She's the One Who Thinks Too Much

Ryalgar, a spinster farm girl and the oldest of seven sisters, has always preferred her studies to flirtation. Yet even she finally meets her prince. Or so she thinks. She's devastated to discover he's already betrothed and only wanted a little fun. Embarrassed, she flees her family's farm to join the Velka, the mysterious women of the forest known for their magical powers and for living apart from men.

As a Velka, she develops her special brand of telekinesis and learns she has a talent for analyzing and organizing information. Both are going to come in handy.

When this prince keeps meeting her at the forest's edge for more good times, she wonders if being his mistress isn't such a bad deal after all. Then she learns more about his princely assignment.

He's tasked with training the army of Ilari to repel the feared Mongol horsemen who have been moving westward, killing all in their path. And, her prince is willing to sacrifice the outer farmlands where she grew up to these invaders if he must. Ryalgar isn't about to let that happen.

She's got the Velka behind her, as well as a multitude of university intellectuals, a family of tough farmers, and six sisters each with her unique personality and talents.

Can Ryalgar organize all that into a resistance that will stop the invasion?

She's the One Who Thinks Too Much has been available in eBook and paperback since November 2020.

She's the One Who Cares Too Much

Coral, the second of the sisters, has been hiding her affair with the perfect man until Ryalgar can get her life together. But the perfect man is getting impatient, and now she's gotten pregnant. Coral decides it's time to consider her own happiness.

But what does she want? The perfect husband turns out to be less than ideal. She adores the small children she teaches but the idea of being a mother fills her with joy. Meanwhile, her homeland is gripped by fear of a Mongol invasion, and she can't stop crying about everything now that she's with child.

Then a friend suggests the ever-caring Coral has a power well beyond what she or anyone else imagines. Does she? And why is the idea so appealing?

When Ryalgar loses faith in the army and decides to craft a way to use magic to save Ilari, she decides Coral's formidable talent is what the realm needs. Can Coral raise a baby, placate an absent military husband who thinks he's stopping the invasion, and help her sister save her homeland?

She's the One Who Cares Too Much has been available in eBook and paperback since February 2021.

She's the One Who Gets in Fights

Sulphur, the third of seven sisters, is glad the older two have been slow to wed. It's given her the freedom to train as a fighter, in hopes of fulfilling her lifelong dream of joining Ilari's army. Then, within a matter of days, both sisters announce plans and now Sulphur is expected to find a man to marry.

Is it Sulphur's good fortune her homeland is gripped by fear of a pending Mongol invasion? And the army is going door to door encouraging recruits? Sulphur thinks it is. But once she's forced to kill in a small skirmish, she's ready to rethink her career decision. Too bad it's too late. The invasion is coming, and Ilari needs every good soldier it has.

Once Sulphur learns Ilari's army has made the strategic decision to not defend certain parts of the realm, including the one where her family lives, she has to re-evaluate her loyalty. Is it with the military she's always admired? Or is it with her sisters, who are hatching a plan to defend their homeland with magic?
Everywhere she turns, someone is counting on her to fight for what's right. But what is?

She's the One Who Gets in Fights has been available in eBook and paperback since May 2021.

She's the One Who Doesn't Say Much

Olivine is Celestine's twin and she has been hiding a secret as she travels to K'ba to meet her artist friends. Others assume she has fallen in love with another artist, and it's not a match Mother would consider suitable. But it's much worse. For on the way to K'ba is the dirt poor nichna of Scrud, a place scorned by other Ilarians. And in Scrud is the only man who has ever understood her.

However, Bohdan also recognizes the dangers posed by an impending invasion. When he learns of Olivine's unusual visual powers, he convinces her to pick up her bow and start practicing.

She does, though she'd rather be producing enough art to raise the funds to run away from home and live in K'ba, where she can paint all day and sneak off to see Bohdan as often as she wants. If only her sister Ryalgar hadn't learned of what she can do and decided Olivine and her fellow long eyes held one of the keys to defending the realm.

Then, as if life wasn't complicated enough, Olivine learns the artist community she yearns to be part of has developed a different take on the invasion. They feel certain the only way to survive is to capitulate completely to the Mongols' demands. Artists who feel otherwise are no longer welcome.

Where does her future lie? In Scrud, with the only man she's ever loved? In K'ba, where her talents can shine? Or with her family, who needs her help to stop a threat far worse than anything her people have ever encountered?

The invasion is coming soon and Olivine doesn't have much time to decide.

She's the One Who Doesn't Say Much has been available in eBook and paperback since August 2021.

She's the One Who Won't Behave

Gypsum, the sixth of seven sisters, has always been a rebel. Yet no one thought even she would go so far as to join the reczavy, a group living in tents on the edge of the desert and known for their sexual promiscuity and playful ways.

But as the date of the Mongols' return draws near, Ilarians of all types must work together. And the reczavy, for all of their odd ways, do have plenty of tricks up their sleeves. Well, up their sleeves whenever they are bothering to wear clothes, that is.

Gypsum recognizes that the reczavy have as much to lose as anyone, and as much to contribute. Unfortunately, her playmates don't all feel the same sense of urgency. Many would rather simply enjoy the time they have left. A few claim to be allergic to long term planning. And some are too busy with their own poorly-timed plans to overthrow the government Ilari already has.

Good thing needlepoint is the one traditional skill at which Gypsum has always excelled. She will need to thread a fine needle in order to coax this recalcitrant group into becoming life-saving warriors of a very different kind.

She's the One Who Won't Behave will be released in July 2022 and can be preordered until then.

What About the Youngest Sister?

Look for more information about **Iolite** in the next book.

About the Author

Sherrie Cronin is the author of a collection of six speculative fiction novels known as 46. Ascending and is now publishing a historical fantasy series called The War Stories of the Seven Troublesome Sisters. A quick look at the synopses of her books makes it obvious she is fascinated by people achieving the astonishing by developing abilities they barely knew they had.

She's made a lot of stops along the way to writing these novels. She's lived in seven cities, visited forty-six countries, and worked as a waitress, technical writer, and geophysicist. Now she answers a hot-line. Along the way, she's lost several cats but acquired a husband who still loves her and three kids who've grown up fine, both despite how eccentric she is.

All her life she has wanted to either tell these kinds of stories or be Chief Science Officer on the Starship Enterprise. She now lives and writes in the mountains of Western North Carolina, where she admits to occasionally checking her phone for a message from Captain Picard, just in case.

Find her at:
Facebook: facebook.com/46Ascending
Goodreads: goodreads.com/author/show/5805814.Sherrie_Cronin
Amazon: amazon.com/Sherrie-Cronin/e/B007FRMO9Q
Twitter: twitter.com/cinnabar01
Book Series Blog: troublesome7sisters.xyz/

About Ilari

Words Used by Ilarians

Ank: Nine days. Business is conducted during the first six days while the last three are intended for family life and leisure.

Heli: The hottest time of the year, but sometimes used as a cussword.

Frundle: A person born with a condition that mildly alters their appearance, causes some health problems, and leaves them prone to visions of the future and other psychic experiences.

Luski: A feared, possibly imaginary person who can control others with her voice.

Mozdol: A member of the Svadlu who has been made into an honorary prince due to brave actions defending the realm.

Nichna: One of the twelve principalities of Ilari. Each has its own royal family and is ruled by a prince. All twelve coordinate as regards the Svadlu and other matters of the common good. There is no king, therefore Ilari is not a kingdom.

Oomrush: telekinesis.

Pruck: An extremely rude word sometimes referring to copulation and other times merely expressing disgust or dismay.

Pruska: An extremely rude word referring to a female having any number of undesirable qualities.

Rantallion: A man who is being disagreeable, dishonest, or disgusting.

Reczavy: a group of free-spirited people living in the open forest who choose to continue and extend the sexual freedom allowed to tidzys.

Scump: a rude word referring to excrement.

Svadlu: The Ilarian army and police force. A member of the Svadlu is called a Svadlu.

Tidzy: A young adult who is searching for a mate and is allowed a great deal of sexual freedom around holidays.

Velka: A group of women who live in the open forest, possibly performing magic. A member of the Velka is called a Velka.

The Ilarian Calendar

A year in Ilari is divided into eight parts based on the seasons. Each eighth lasts for 45 days and is named for the holiday at its start.

Each eighth is subdivided into five anks. An ank is nine days long. Businesses and schools are open during the first six days of an ank while the last three, called the ank-break, are intended for family life and relaxation.

Every year astronomers consult the stars to decide which of the holidays will be inside their eighth and which will be treated as extra days. Most years, five or six are ruled to be extra days.

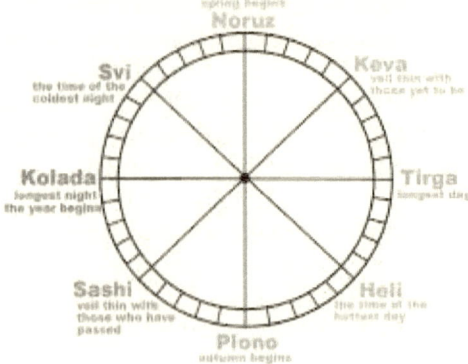

Holidays Marking the Beginning of Each Eighth

Kolada: The winter solstice, the shortest day of the year, and the start of a new year.

Svi: The coldest time of the year, halfway between the winter solstice and the spring equinox.

Noruz: The spring equinox, the start of spring.

Keva: A celebration of those yet to be, held halfway between the spring equinox and the summer solstice. More babies are conceived at Keva than at any other time of the year.

Tirga: The summer solstice, the longest day of the year, the halfway point of a year.

Heli: The hottest time of the year, halfway between the summer solstice and the autumn equinox. Ilarians are not fond of the heat and sometimes use "Heli" as a cussword.

Plono: The autumn equinox, the start of autumn.

Sashi: A celebration of those who have passed, held halfway between the fall equinox and the winter solstice.

The Twelve Nichnas

Ilari is a small hidden land consisting of twelve principalities.

The Entrance
Bisu: These low grasslands at the eastern edge of Ilari supply coveted beef and cows' milk to Ilarians.

The Dry Lands
Scrud: Rain-deprived Scrud is the poorest and least populated of the nichnas and the most lacking in natural resources. Most Scrudites survive by taking menial jobs in adjoining Bisu or K'ba.

K'ba: This drought-stricken nichna has survived by becoming home to artists, entertainers, and those seeking more freedom of choice. It is also a playground for the richest Ilarians and boasts a densely populated area known for its spectacular food and lodging.

Eds: These dry hills leading up to the mountains are sparsely populated with independent-minded goat herders.

The Mountains
Tolo: Home to the highest mountains in Ilari, independent Tolovians mine for ore, produce lumber, and serve as a gateway to the even higher mountains to the north.

The Farmlands
Lev: This nichna is home to the realm's famed vineyards and supplies Ilarians with wine, their most important beverage. It also leads the fashion scene and sparks trends within the realm.

Kir: Ilari's oldest farming region nestles between Pilk and Lev and grows specialty items for the connoisseurs in both of its neighboring nichnas.

Gruen: The fertile soil along the river makes for easy farming of fruits and vegetables and makes Gruen home to one of the two more densely populated areas outside of Pilk.

Vinx: With incredibly flat land sitting above cliffs, the high plains of Vinx provide the wheat, oats, rye, and barley that are the staples of an Ilarian's diet.

The Wet Lands

Faroo: This flood-prone nichna in the rivers bend struggles during heavy rains, but is known for fishing and the boating prowess of its residents.

Pilk: As the informal capital of Ilari, Pilk is home to the Svadlu headquarters, most of the institutes of higher learning, and much of the commerce in the realm. The ruling prince of Pilk coordinates cooperation among the twelve ruling princes. The Pilk Palace outshines any other building in Ilari.

The Forest

Zur: As the only nichna inside of Ilari's large central forest, Zur shares the woods with occupants of the Open Forest including the Velka, the reczavy, and scrounger Scrudites.

Map of Ilari

Meet the Ilarians in this Book

Aliz: Celestine's grandmother
Celestine: Fifth child of Markita and Yasen, a musician
Coral: Celestine's older sister, a luski
Davor: Coral's husband
Ewalina: an older luski who mentors Coral and helps Celestine
Feene: A musician from K'ba, one of the Good Fortunes
Firuza: An astronomer from another land
Gypsum: Celestine's younger sister, part of the reczavy
Hana: an ambitious Velka from Pilk
Iolite: Celestine's youngest sister, a frundle
Ketevan: Davor's girlfriend from Pilk, Hana's friend
Markita: Celestine's mother
Mirva: A piper from Tolo, one of the Good Fortunes
Nevik: a Prince of Pilk, Ryalgar's secret lover
Olivine: Celestine's twin, an artist and a long eye
Patela: Lady Patela, mother of the ruling prince of Vinx
Ryalgar: Celestine's oldest sister, a member of the Velka
Sulphur: Celestine's older sister, a member of the Svadlu
Ura: A young luski who wants to be a singer
Yasen: Celestine's father
Zamarran: A drummer from Faroo, one of the Good Fortunes

www.ingramcontent.com/pod-product-compliance
Lightning Source LLC
Chambersburg PA
CBHW022008170626
46808CB00001B/329